THE TIME WRITER
AND
THE ESCAPE

A HISTORICAL TIME TRAVEL ADVENTURE

THE TIME WRITER
BOOK FOUR

ALEX R CRAWFORD

Copyright © 2023 Spilled Red Ink
All Rights Reserved
Cover design and original illustration by Roland DeLeon.
Cover copyright © 2023 by Spilled Red Ink LLC
Image from James Webb Telescope used with permission from NASA and Space Telescope Science Institute (STScI) under public domain free use webbtelescope.org/copyright

Spilled Red Ink is an imprint of Spilled Red Ink LLC. The Spilled Red Ink name and logo are trademarks of Spilled Red Ink LLC.
Spilled Red Ink
PO Box 731
Garrisonville, VA 22463-0731
spilledredink.com

Names: Crawford, Alex R. | The Time Writer and The Escape.
Title: The Time Writer and The Escape / Alex R Crawford.
Description: Spilled Red Ink trade paperback edition. | Virginia: Spilled Red Ink, 2023.
ISBN: (ebook) 9781953485113
ISBN: (softcover) 9781953485120
Subjects: BISAC: FICTION / Fantasy / Historical. | FICTION / Science Fiction / Time Travel.

INTRODUCTION

Beware of doorways through time... and the Spaniards.

Amelia and Henry thought they were done with time travel. All they wanted to do was settle down, get a cat, and lead a quiet life in modern-day Virginia. If you think that will happen with these time travelers, then you really don't know them or the time travel gods.

Keep up, people! We're going on an adventure.

A walk through a ship's door and a rip in time, launches our duo to the 1690s and on separate journeys of survival and adventure. Henry joins a crew on their way to Spain, hoping it will take him closer to Amelia. What can a group of privateers do when a shady business deal leads to the crew to being sold to Spain? MUTINY! Joining a pirate crew, led by Henry Avery, and sailing around the world in search of fortune only takes him further from his goal of reuniting with Amelia.

Amelia's mission to survive the 1690s and find Henry in Spain, takes her on a journey where she meets old friends and finds new ones. Her plan to make money to survive and help friends escape the clutches of a young Lord, sends her on an unexpected path through France.

Where will Amelia and Henry find each other in the past when pirates and fortune are keeping them apart?

When they can't find another doorway through time, how will they escape the past?

The Time Writer and The Escape is a historical time travel adventure exploring the beginning of the Golden Age of Piracy and the rise of a pirate legend. Oh! And don't forget the trouble with French hats.

DEDICATION AND RAMBLINGS

Have you ever wanted a book dedicated to you?
Congratulations!
This book is dedicated to *you*

Content warnings found on the Copyright page include, but are not limited to: violence, pirates, mild language, slavery, and mild sexual situations. There are a few more listed; however, I'm sure I missed something that someone will find troubling to their good senses.

As a reminder, Amelia is a typical Gen X woman full of piss and vinegar. She's not perfect and neither am I. Life is a learning process, and it is never my intent to offend anyone.

My Spanish is slightly better than my French. Both are terrible. Just know that going into the story. It will make things easier for all involved.

If I missed a warning that someone finds disruptive to

their reading enjoyment, I apologize in advance. I'm not blaming it on the fact that my lucky rabbit's foot is in the shop, but I'm supposed to get it back next week.

Grab a drink, sit back, relax, and enjoy the adventure.

CHAPTER ONE

"*E*lizabeth, we need to leave," Anna hissed as she gently opened the large wooden door to Lady Elizabeth's room. "Now," she added through gritted teeth. Anna kept her movements gentle and her volume low, but the sting in her words gave her impatience with Elizabeth away.

"I'm nearly ready." Elizabeth frantically scuttled about the room shoving a shift, kirtle, and extra stockings into her bag. She fingered through the jewelry on her dressing table, picking a string of Scottish pearls, and shoved it, with the handful of coins she had saved over the past few months, into her small, blue fabric purse, embroidered with silver and gold threads. Securing the purse to her girdle, she then picked through her jewelry box and pulled a few rings, necklaces, her delicately carved comb made from a deer antler, and the small hand-held mirror to round out her bag. A small, folded paper was discreetly left on the table.

"You should've packed earlier." Anna looked over her shoulder and down the darkened hall towards the other occupied rooms in the Scottish manor, then towards the stairs to her right. She pulled the hood to her brown wool cloak, with thistles embroidered along the edging of the hood down the front, over her light auburn hair. "We need to leave before someone alerts your father."

"Aye, I'm coming." Elizabeth threw her satchel across her body and swung her green wool cloak over her shoulders. The embroidery on her cloak matched Anna's, the only difference was the added silver threading mimicking water droplets. She chose her plain gray kirtle to blend in with people she may meet on the road. Two unaccompanied ladies riding through the countryside on their way to Edinburgh would draw much more attention than two unaccompanied maidens on their way to help a friend's birthing or to market. She pulled a small blanket off the bed, rolled it up, and slung it over the bag.

She padded over to the door with her shoes in her hand. She grasped the edge of the opened door, turned, and looked around her bedroom for the last time. One more look at the fireplace that kept her warm during the many cold nights in Scotland. Her bed, covered in wool blankets and soft furs, turned down for the night, remained untouched. How she ached to crawl into it instead of slipping away into the night with Anna, but she refused to meet the upcoming day with Lord Hector Black, third son of the Duke of Ormonde. If the arranged marriage was to be with the young Lord Hector, instead of his father, Elizabeth might have considered the match. Not that she had met either man but decided to choose youth over any other factor. Lord Hector was to arrive that morning to ensure the nineteen-year-old bride-to-be favored the portrait sent to the duke, and the portrait was not a ploy to saddle his father with a homely maiden, regardless of the included dowry. However, marrying a man old enough to be her father was not in her life plans. How could it be her plan? She wanted to experience the freedom beyond her father's land. Not to be taken from one old man's house to another and turned into a broodmare. Escaping from her father's and her future husband's clutches was her only choice. Thankfully, her dearest friend, Anna, agreed to the dangerous plan.

With a gentle pull, Elizabeth closed the door behind her, careful not to allow the lock to click. Hugging the wall, the two women gingerly descended the stairs, careful to avoid the creaky spots on the second and seventh tread. During a lifetime of late-night trips sneaking down to the kitchen for a snack, Elizabeth would haphazardly race down the stairs and wake her mother with the creaks and groans from the stairs. Discipline from her mother would follow early the next morning. She couldn't afford to have her mother come early into her room to find her missing.

In the shadows, they crept down the hall and into the passage to the kitchen. The spotlight of the moon cut through the window onto a side table where trays of food from the night's supper laid. Elizabeth and Anna shoved meat, cheese, candied fruits, small loaves of bread, and a couple bottles of wine into an extra satchel. Elizabeth hoped it would be enough food to last them the trip to Edinburgh. The trip would be a two-day ride, three days tops, by her calculations. She had only been there twice when she was younger, and hoped between the two of them, they could remember the way.

Growing up in the house, Elizabeth and Anna had played in the secret passages that led to safety beyond the walls. Anna left their getaway horses saddled and ready at the other end of the tunnel. They only needed to get to the other side without alerting the sentry. A tapestry on the wall hid the door tucked neatly into a darkened corner under the stairs, lit by a dimmed lamp Anna had left when she snuck into the house like a mouse, to retrieve her friend. Elizabeth felt around for the slight notch in the wall, gulped down her rising nerves, cracked the door open wide enough to squeeze through, and slipped away down the dark passage. With her left hand, Anna held onto Elizabeth's hand, and the other held the lamp. Light reflected off the stones covering the floor, walls, and ceiling of the corridor. Shadows sank deep in the crevices, holding tight to the secrets of those that stole away for an illicit liaison or to escape to safety when there was an attack. When they got to the end of a corridor, they turned left. Taking a right would have sent them back into the maze of the secret passages. They repeated the process of rights and lefts, their feet pounding on the cobbled stone path beneath them. The twists and turns in the corridors were designed to confuse and frustrate an unwanted guest. However, spending their time exploring the passageway throughout their youth, Elizabeth and Anna knew every twist and turn by memory.

The pathway led to one of the hill forts outside of the manor grounds. Hamish was to man the fort that night. With a generous bribe to Janet, Hamish would be distracted for the next half hour while Anna and Elizabeth found their way to the horses secured in the copse. Janet had visited Hamish on more than a couple of occasions, without Anna's bribe. Anna had overheard her gossiping with one of the other maids, and knew that Hamish would neither suspect Janet's appearance, nor reject her proposal for a bit of fooling around at the top of the watchtower. The April night still carried a bite in the air, but nothing that a few blankets and some physical activity couldn't overcome. Nearly out of breath from excitement and exertion, they eased the final door open and stepped into a world of freedom. Or so they hoped.

Moonlight lit the field outside the walls of the manor grounds like a cold blue ocean. The breeze swayed the tall grasses like waves gently lapping the shore. To the east, hidden from sight, their horses rested, unaware of the work they were about to undertake to deliver the women to freedom. Looking over their shoulders towards the manor wall, torches flickered around the perimeter, reminding Elizabeth that the longer they took, the more likely they would be caught by her father's men. Stealth and speed were the answer. Anna took another look to her right towards the wall. She could see the silhouette of one of the men move towards the west wall. They would have but a few moments to run across the remainder of the field to hide in the trees before he would turn around and stroll back towards their direction. The brightness of the moonlight was great for travel, but a hindrance for their escape.

With a slight squeeze to Elizabeth's hand, Anna signaled their sprint. Pulling their skirts high enough for long unobstructed strides, they ran the hundred yards into the tree line and threw their bodies behind the first set of trees they could find. Chests heaved. Their breaths came hard and heavy. Time ticked fast. Horses needed to be packed and mounted. They needed to be on the road headed west towards Stirling, cross the narrow section of the River Forth, head west to Edinburgh, before Janet finished her business with Hamish. Anna wanted to take a boat across the Firth of Forth. However, Elizabeth thought that would have been an obvious route and would've been easily followed. Besides, she wanted to sell the horses in Edinburgh to help fund their trip. There was no time to catch their breath.

With swift strides, they stood at the saddled horses. Elizabeth tied the blanket and satchels behind the saddle. Anna added the additional satchel of food to the bag already attached to the rear of her horse's saddle. With a firm grasp on the saddle and a graceful pull, they were on their horses, headed as far away as they could ride.

"You know, there is still time for you to turn around," Elizabeth said as they made their way down the path, trees on either side. The sound of pounding hooves would signal the men. So, an easy gait to keep the volume down allowed the women to chat at a whispered volume. "If you want to stay here, you should stay. I'm the one being auctioned off to an old man."

"Why would I stay?"

"You're supposed to marry Gareth. At least he's young and good looking."

"Aye. He's good looking, alright." Anna adjusted her cloak over her head. "He would be a good provider, no doubt. He is also my brother's best friend. Do you think I would want Robert always in my business?" She shook her head. "Nay, best that I go with you."

"Do you think we can really do this?"

"Elizabeth," Anna began with a strong voice. If Elizabeth was having doubts, she needed to be the one to be focused enough for the women. "Unless you want to be used for your father's ambitions, then I suggest we find our way to Edinburgh and head on the first ship away from here."

"I don't trust he is doing what's right for me."

"Exactly. Let your mother deal with his fury in the morning when he realizes his prized pawn has gone missing. He is only marrying you off to get in the good graces with the King William and Queen Mary for his support of King James."

"It's false homage to the king and queen. You know he's a Jacobite. Mother will just agree to whatever he says. He'll rant and rave. A few broken plates and bottles of whatever his drink of the day is, and he will send his hounds out for me." Elizabeth cleared her throat. "For us. He'll send them for us. Your father will take a strap to your back for accompanying me." The weight of her decision and the danger she put Anna in, hung heavy on heart.

"Shall we make some distance then?" Anna sat tall in her saddle. "I would prefer to have the flesh on my back and not on my father's belt."

Nudging their horses with their heels, the women picked up speed and rode away from the rising sun.

CHAPTER TWO

*L*ord Hector Black, third son of James Black, 4th Duke of Ormonde rode towards the mid-morning sun towards the gates of Balcarres House, home of Alexander Lindsay, 11th Earl of Crawford, to inspect his father's bride-to-be. Hector happily took the request from his father upon his return from serving a term with the Royal Navy. The fact that it wasn't him taking a bride, didn't bother him as much as the thought of his father marrying a woman three years younger than himself.

This trip was just another excuse to get out of the chaos of his father's house. "Andrew, please ride ahead and announce my arrival," Hector said, glancing at the man riding on his left. "I desire this to be a quick visit, William."

"Aye. Do you have something better to do?" Asked William. Hector brought a small entourage on this mission. It was more so for the lot to spread their wings and enjoy a trip together after Hector's return to Ireland, and away from the responsibilities of a household, collecting rents, and managing businesses. A guy's trip, so to speak, sanctioned by the duke. How could William's wife deny a mission for the duke?

"I didn't say I was eager to get home. My father wanted to ensure my disappearance while King James visited Ireland, something about ensuring obedience, religion, Scots, bishops, and a load of other business that I would rather stay away from. I just have no desire to stay in Scotland longer than required and end up fighting in some war." Hector gave a sly smirk towards William. He had enough military service while he served with His Majesty's Royal Navy.

"Shall we head over to France and frolic around the court? You know how scandalous the French court can get." The rising sun fought through the heavy dark gray clouds, matching Hector's mood to his day's agenda.

"Gracious, no!" Hector huffed out. "You might not have heard, but there seems to be tensions brewing with France. I don't think we will be as welcome there as we were a few years past."

"Again?"

"Of course, again," Hector said flippantly. "When isn't there nearly an act of war between us and them?" They continued towards the house at a slow pace. The small chapel along the way caught Hector's eye and left him wondering how many Earls of Crawford were buried there to watch over their land. When Elizabeth would be taken from there to live in Ireland, who would inherit the title when the cemetery population would expand with the current earl. As she was the only child to the earl and countess, there was no son to inherit. Perhaps the earl's brother or cousin. It mattered not to Hector, he hoped to find his fortune in India and let his father and older brothers concern themselves with titles and inheritance.

"Don't say that loud enough for your father to hear. He'll happily send you off to sea before you could finish unpacking your bags."

"Don't tempt me. If it were not for the wretched captain thinking he is God, I would have stayed longer." Dogs barked from behind the house. The barks blended and formed a chorus of warning to the intruders. A few men working in the gardens ran towards the back to provide assistance to the approaching men.

"You could have requested a reassignment." Silhouettes of the inhabitants were seen stirring around the house through open windows. Four men ran from the stables towards the approaching guests, while another two led Andrew's horse away.

"Think I didn't?" Hector shook his head. "My father doesn't realize or doesn't care what terrible men he keeps as friends."

"One day we will be those terrible men." William snickered in response to their situation.

"We are fortunate our fathers didn't send us to the church."

"We get to come to Scotland to inspect your father's prized cow instead."

"I'm not sure which is worse."

Before William could respond, they had arrived in front of the large home. The building was a large stone home commanded a view of the Firth of Forth. On a clear day, when the fog had lifted and the sun shone, the skyline of Edinburgh could be seen. For Elizabeth growing up in that house, the twenty miles across the estuary might as well have been on the other side of the world.

Two attendants took the reins from the riders, while the other two brought a step to assist the men from their dismount. Hector and William slid off their horses, stepped down the step. Hector held out his hand to stop the attendant from leaving with his horse and rummaged in one of his saddlebags. The men were promptly greeted by their host standing at the top of the stone steps leading to the front door of the house. Andrew waited near the steps for the men's arrival. Hector stood two steps in front of William and Andrew, and the three men gave a synchronized, graceful bow to the earl.

"My lord," Hector said as he raised from his bow. "My father, James Black, the fourth Duke of Ormonde, sends his sincerest regards to your lordship." Hector produced a letter, sealed with thick red wax with his father's signet pressed into the center, from under his black wool cloak.

Alexander Lindsay was a tall and imposing man. At five-ten and hair black as a moonless night in the highlands, he lorded over his lands with an iron fist. Everyone knew he was disappointed in lacking a male heir. Mary had Elizabeth months after the wedding, and that was the last living child they produced. Miscarriages, infant deaths plagued the couple until he avoided Mary's bedchamber altogether. Alexander dabbled about with other women, only to not produce any heirs to claim. He was angry at not only himself, but the women that were obliged to give him children. He wondered how he disappointed God to not have a son. As he watched Elizabeth as she grew up, he often wondered if it was possible that she wasn't his daughter. Her auburn hair, green eyes, and fair skin was replicated from her mother. She didn't get her father's dark hair or fierce brown eyes. He pushed her to the side, showed no affection, and when the opportunity arose to use her as a pawn in his game, he agreed to have her marry the Duke of Ormonde, thirty years her senior. The title wouldn't go to the Irish duke, but to his brother, if he lived long enough.

Alexander invited the men inside the house, leading them to the sitting room on the right. "Lady Elizabeth will be down shortly." Alexander said, shifting in his large chair. The young men found the dark blue chair, with intricate wooden accents, as intimidating in size as much their host.

"Yes, my lord. We look forward to meeting your daughter. My father wanted me to ensure all was well and that the maiden is eager to join him in Ireland." Hector wanted to add that he would've preferred waiting for her to await his arrival, instead of him awaiting her.

A light rap of a gentle hand came from the door before it gently opened. Hector stood, ready to greet his father's bride-to-be. A woman in her forties slipped in through the parted door. She was attractive, but older than Hector had been led to believe. His father was expecting to marry a nineteen-year-old lass, not a forty-year-old woman. Hector shot a look towards William and then towards Andrew. Did they see the same woman as he did? William shrugged his shoulders.

"Lord Hector, might I introduce you to my wife, the countess."

A sigh of relief fell over Hector and his shoulders relaxed from being drawn tight around his ears.

"My lord, might I have a moment of your time?" Mary said meekly.

"Please fetch Lady Elizabeth."

"Aye, my lord, about her..." Mary stitched her brows together and looked towards her husband and then the door. "I believe I need but a moment of your time."

Alexander rushed up the stairs, taking two at a time, ignoring the creaks and groans on the second tread and skipping over the seventh. He reached the top of the stairs and opened the first door on his left, leading into Elizabeth's room. The bed showed no indication of being slept in—the pillows fluffed, the blankets tight and neat.

"That's what I'm trying to tell you, my lord," said Mary. "Our daughter was not in her bed this morning when Janet went to wake her."

Ah, yes. The same Janet that helped the two women escape, played the innocent maid unknowing as to where Lady Elizabeth could have possibly gone, nor with whom. Elizabeth treated Janet kindly, and Janet was well paid for her services. She wouldn't be the one to face the wrath of the earl, and her purse was thankful for the contribution. For all she knew, Lady Elizabeth and Lady Anna were

THE TIME WRITER AND THE ESCAPE

playing a trick on the earl and countess. She had no idea she played a part in what Elizabeth would call, "The Escape" or the lasting repercussions of the women's bold behavior to leave in the middle of the night. Janet stood outside the door; hands linked in front of her. She knew there was no way the earl and countess could link her to Elizabeth's departure. "No, my lord. I know nothing of Lady Elizabeth's departure. I was in my room, sleeping," she lied.

"Where? How?"

"Her maid found this on Elizabeth's dressing table." Mary held the small, folded paper in her right hand between her index and middle finger.

Alexander snatched the missive from his wife. His eyes raked over the words. His anger brewed deep, causing the words to jumble his vision. He rubbed his hand over his eyes to adjust his vision. He reread the note, blood boiling hotter with each word. "Why are you just now bringing this to my attention?"

"My attempts to tell you earlier, husband, went unanswered." She shook her head causing her hastily tied hair to fall loose. "What more could I do when you refused my call upon you." Mary's red, wavy locks tumbled midway down her back as she pulled herself to her full five-foot four-inch height. She read the note and knew she was not to blame for her daughter's flight. Alexander's brusque behavior towards his daughter and her future was to blame. Mary knew Elizabeth would escape from under Alexander's thumb, something she could only dream for herself. A slight satisfied smile pulled at the corner of her mouth. Elizabeth left on her own terms and was not married to a man old enough to be her father. She would miss her daughter, of course, but vowed to send well wishes into the universe in hopes the message would get to her daughter to never return to their home or to Scotland.

Hector grew impatient from the bickering between the couple somewhere up the stairs of the large house. Alexander's voice, bouncing and booming off the stone walls, rattled Hector's teeth. He hadn't planned on spending more time than necessary at Balcarres, and the longer the couple stood on the other side of the door quarreling about—who knows what—the longer he would be in Scotland. The three men stood, awaiting the return of their host with the young Lady Elizabeth, turned to look at one another, unsure if the melodrama was truly happening.

"It is my understanding," William tilted his blond head towards Hector, "that the young maiden was not prepared for our early arrival."

"We were only a half day ahead of schedule," Andrew chimed in. "Surely, she will be better prepared for your father."

The three men chuckled in response to the jibes on the elusive Elizabeth's expense.

A door slammed. Followed by heavy, heated feet bursting through every stair as the beast descended. Two treads groaned under the fury of Alexander Lindsay. The door to the parlor unabashedly flew open. Fury danced in Alexander's eyes as he scanned the room for his victim, causing Hector to take a step or two back. Hector gathered his wits and pulled himself to his full height of five-foot-ten, not to be intimidated by Alexander. He cleared his throat as Alexander continued across the room in four strides. "Shall the lady require a few moments to finish dressing?" Calm, cool, collected. At least, that is how Hector tried to appear. In reality, he stumbled over the word 'shall' more than once. The first time, his voice cracked. The second time, it squeaked. Third time's the charm.

Alexander stood next to the window overlooking the front gardens. He took great pride in the appearance of his home, his family, his earldom, and especially, his ability to control a situation. Elizabeth's actions threw him into a panic, and his fury was the only way he knew to respond. He took a deep breath, held it, and released the flames out through nostrils. "It would appear that the Lady Elizabeth is having doubts about the marriage to your father." He choked on every word trying to maintain his dignity.

"Mayhap, if we could only speak for a moment..." Hector began.

Alexander held his hand up to stop the twenty-one-year-old. "Not possible." He shook his head and hand simultaneously. "It would appear that my daughter would rather live in exile than to be in an arranged marriage."

The three young men's ears perked at the declaration of Elizabeth's disappearance. As much as Hector didn't want his father to marry, more than anything, he couldn't face his own father's wrath at his failure to produce confirmation that the bride-to-be not only existed, but that she was as lovely as the portrait he had been provided not six months prior. "Are you to send men to retrieve Lady Elizabeth?"

Alexander's face turned twelve shades of red. "I have no intention of claiming that child as mine. I should never have allowed my wife to lie to me. No child of mine would disrespect me in such..."

"Yet, she is your child, as recognized and declared. Her standing as your daughter is the reason my father agreed to the marriage."

"Aye, that and her dowry."

"Aye, her dowry is promised to my father, with or without the bride," Hector said matter-of-factually. He could see the barometer of Alexander's temper rise as his ears turned bright red and his cheeks flushed in anger and embarrassment.

"If you want her for your father, you're welcome to find the lass. I'm done with her."

"We will take the dowry, regardless of your daughter's presence. You may send your men to chase after her and possibly bring her back, but I'd wager you'd damage my father's property." Hector tapped his finger to his lips. "I have a proposition for you."

Slowly, Alexander said, "Aye." Not trusting the deal, the young buck was about to make regarding his daughter.

"My men and I will seek your daughter's whereabouts. She will come willing or nay, it matters not. However, tis required she is unharmed for my father, and I don't trust you or your men for that task."

"You would find her?"

"Aye. And she shall not return here." Hector took a

bow to his host. "You will escort her belongings and the dowry to my father, along with the message that I will bring her to him thusly."

With a discussion of possible headings and an interview with servants, the lady maids, stable hands, and guards, Hector, William, and Andrew left the room and bounded down the front steps. "You've got a large pair of bullocks on you," William laughed and slapped Hector on the back. Hector finally let out the timid breath he held.

CHAPTER THREE

"*E*lizabeth," Anna shook her sleeping friend's arm. "We cannot rest for long."

"They're not going to find us," Elizabeth said as she groaned and stretched out of slumber. She sat in the bed they shared at Missus Graham's small home on the other side of Stirling in Linlithgow, close to Linlithgow Loch. Careful to avoid encountering the inhabitants of the castle that sat alongside the loch–who would surely make haste to inform Elizabeth's father of the women's travels–they discreetly found the widow had a spare room to rent. With a small bribe, Missus Graham filled their bellies, the horses' bellies, and gave a safe place for all of them to rest. "All will be well." She snuggled back down into the bed. A light April rain pattered on the roof. "We will leave early in the morn after we break our fast."

Early the next morning as the sun fought the gray clouds, the outlook was grim. The sun would lose the battle for the remainder of the morning. "Aye, stop complaining, it's but a *smirr*," said Anna, as she pulled her brown cloak tighter over her shoulders.

"It's enough of a drizzle to make my hair look like a wet cat."

"Aye, and that is why you have a hood." Anna pointed at Elizabeth's hood that had slipped off the back of her head. "Cover ye head, and let's get on with it."

Elizabeth let out a slight sigh and they were on their way to make the last fifteen-mile ride to Edinburgh. "On to the adventure then, hm?" Elizabeth, excited about the prospect of what the future had in store for them, also needed a bit of reassurance that she was taking the best path for Anna and her.

The green hills dotted with sheep and cows, and fields were being worked for the summer harvest. A farmer lifted his hoe over his head, thrusting and yanking, as he pulled chunks of dark, wet dirt from the ground. The man's hair dripped wet from working outdoors throughout the morning drizzle. His brown shirt clung to his torso, accentuating the hard-earned muscles in his arms and chest. Elizabeth continued to watch as they rode past the man. She twisted around long enough to see him pull out a stone, larger than a man's head, from the garden. He picked it up and hurled it to the side, as if it was nothing but a small gourd. With a smile, she turned around and faced the road ahead. Elizabeth wasn't sure where the ship would take them, but she couldn't imagine that anywhere would be as beautiful as Scotland and her people.

Anna was ready to be on a ship and sailing away with her friend. It didn't matter to her where they ended up.

Anywhere was better than being separated from Elizabeth. They had made a vow to be best friends until their dying breath, and she refused to allow Elizabeth to leave on her own.

The plan was to find their way to the docks to find passage out of Scotland on the next ship out to sea. First, they had to make it to Edinburgh without being caught by Elizabeth's father.

"You can still go back and marry..." Elizabeth broke the silence an hour into their ride.

"I'm not marrying Gareth. Even if his arms are the size of a tree trunk and lips as..."

"Anna!" Elizabeth's eyes were wide in shock and amusement. "You didn't?"

"We were to be married." Her shoulders raised to her ears in an exaggerated shrug. "Why wouldn't I just fool around a bit?" She let out an unladylike snort.

"I don't want you to regret coming with me." Elizabeth's voice was sincere. She meant every word and feeling. She didn't want Anna to hold a sense of regret over leaving Scotland. She wasn't sure if they could ever come back. Could they leave for a week? A month? Would they be scarred as undesirables? They could turn back now, and it would be seen as they were out for a ride. They would soon be at the point of no return. That was more frightening than not knowing where they were headed— being without a home to return to.

"If you go back, I go back, and you're not going back to marry that old man. Besides, there will be other Gareths, and we are not yet twenty. We are young."

"And, hopefully," Elizabeth added, "free."

"Well, eating and finding a place to live will not be free." Money came easily to Elizabeth and Anna. They were ladies of standing and knew nothing of the expense of life outside castle walls. "How are we going to do this with the little coins we brought with us?"

"We will find positions as lady's maids or as a governess."

"Or marry a man of means?"

"The point of our adventure is not to feel like we have to marry." Elizabeth nodded, satisfied with her decision. "We will find a way to eat and have a roof over our head. Mark my words."

The walls of Edinburgh Castle loomed tall on the horizon. As the sun began to break through the clouds, the beam hit the castle like a homing beacon. "Aye, it's a good sign." Anna interrupted Elizabeth's unblinking gaze at the stone castle high atop *Creag a' Chaisteil*. The rock cliff faces on the sides of Castle Rock made the fort appear fierce and impenetrable. Carts filled with merchandise, pulled by people and horses, made their way through throngs of people and animals walking through Netherbow Port into the burgh. Packs on overburden backs filled with wool, potatoes, and carrots passed by the women. Elizabeth wondered if they were fresh, considering it was the beginning of the season, or if it was leftover reserves, and the farmers were getting ready for a new season of fresh produce. Either way, the excitement of commerce and people caused a stirring in her stomach. It could have been nerves, or Missus

Graham's fiber-filled porridge. They passed merchants on the way to the gate, selling wares and services. A man near the gate wove baskets while a little redheaded girl begged and cried nearby. It was almost too much excitement for the women to take. Elizabeth glanced up at the clock on the tower over the gate. It was nearly eleven in the morning. They paid their toll and proceeded inside to find their way through to the docks.

They would blend in with the crowds, purchase additional food items for the trip, and find their way to the docks. "Do you smell that?" Elizabeth covered her nose and held her breath. The stench of feces from people and animals, a corpse or two of rats, dogs, and cats littered alleyways. The close quarters of hundreds of people crammed into the narrow streets assaulted the women's noses. The drizzle earlier in the morning did nothing to rinse away the filth, only to reactivate the stench and amplify it as the sun warmed the ground and dead wet dog. Smoke billowed out of chimneys, heavy and thick. The tall walls of the stone buildings trapped the smoke, along with the stench, grabbed a tight grasp around their throats and lungs.

"Aye, the heavy smoke is a stark reminder why it's called *Auld Reekie*," Anna choked out—half laughing, half fighting the lump of heavy stench caught in her throat.

"Soon we will smell the lavender fields in France or the salty air off the coast of Spain."

"First, let's see if we can find our way through all of these people." Anna looked down from atop her horse.

"Look, there are a few tables with wares, let's see what we can find for our trip."

They pushed and worked their way through the congested streets. A group of young boys no older than seven, covered in a layer of filth, wearing tattered clothes of shirts and breeches, and barefoot, ran past, startling the horses. Before the baker could open his mouth, one of the boys in the middle of the pack snatched a loaf of bread off the table and disappeared into the throng of pedestrians. Elizabeth's horse gave a yank back, raising his front feet up, ready to bolt. She reached out and stroked his neck in reassurance. "We'll get out of here soon, love." Elizabeth looked towards Anna, who was yelling at people to move out of her way. They couldn't hear her above the roar of conversation and commotion. A man yelled back as Anna's horse nudged him to the side, causing him to drop his basket with heads of cabbage. "Should we dismount?" asked Elizabeth.

"Aye, that way I can yell closer to their ears." Anna gave a snarl towards another group of boys cutting close in front of her horse as a granny yelled curses at them. "They might hear me then." Anna shook her head, frustrated with the crowds.

The town near their homes was quiet, reserved. The closest thing to a crowd was when everyone would come out to the market. The streets didn't overfill, there weren't hordes of children running amok. Sure, there was gossip and scandal, but the unbearable amounts of people were saved for the larger cities, a place both women were ready to leave. The looming walls, sea of people, and clenching stench, left both women feeling claustrophobic. Yet, a twitch of excitement stirred in Elizabeth's stomach. This was a new beginning for her, and she needed to go with the current and see where it would lead her.

The strong smell of beef and pastry wrestled with the city stench. An older woman, who reminded Elizabeth of Missus Hughes—stern in her facial expressions which hid the soft, loving demeanor—their family cook, walked by holding a tray filled with hand pies. A cord was attached to the sides of the tray, offering to take the weight of the mound of meat and bread off her arms and allow her to conduct business as she made her way through the crowd. The breakfast of porridge and preserved strawberries felt like an eternity to Anna's stomach. It argued in protest as she walked past the bounty.

Doors and windows to businesses were open inviting shoppers to enter to view more wares. A young man, no older than fifteen, laid out a blanket on the road next to the wall leading down a side street. It was filled with various household goods spread across for better viewing and in piles. Wooden plates stacked four high, small bowls, mugs, a couple of baskets, women's clothing, a child's well-loved rag doll, and two items that caught Elizabeth's eye—a *sgian-dubh* and a *dirk*. The blades looked as though they had passed through a couple generations of Scots and were in search of a new guardian. They were looking for her to take them in her hand, calling out to her at first in a whisper. When she tried to keep walking past with her horse, the call grew louder. She called out to Anna to stop for a moment. She knelt and ran a finger along the sgian-

THE TIME WRITER AND THE ESCAPE

dubh's four-inch blade and up to its antler handle. The dirk was longer, thinner, with a crudely carved antler handle that matched the sgian-dubh's handle. The edge and point seemed sharp enough to cut or poke, although simple, they were well taken care of over the years. Simple sheaths made of leather laid next to the knives. They were tools, family heirlooms being sold for less than the hand pie that tempted them not moments earlier.

"Are you sure you can handle a blade?" Interrupted a man who stood too close for Elizabeth's comfort. Anna took a step towards Elizabeth, ready to put herself between her friend and the goon. Elizabeth held her hand to stop her, in hopes to diffuse the situation and prevent a scene. They were trying to slip in and out of Edinburgh without being noticed. Getting into an argument over the handling of a knife was bound to cause a curious crowd.

"I'm sure my husband appreciates any trinket I bestow upon him."

"Husband? Humph." The man looked slightly disappointed at not being able to get a rise out of Elizabeth and score the knives for his own collection. He complained to a few bystanders of how a woman should let her husband pick his own blade. Elizabeth gave the young man double his asking price and slipped the knives in their sheaths and into her deep pockets. They guided their horses down the side street where it was quiet and fairly empty, except for two men holding up walls on either side. She sighed in relief knowing it would be an easy walk the rest of the way to the docks.

CHAPTER FOUR

"*D*ivide and conquer?" Hector looked towards his right and left toward William and Andrew, giving a mischievous smirk to his friends. "Lady Elizabeth and Lady Anna escaped in the middle of the night Delicate women, as such, couldn't have traveled with haste."

Andrew let out a chuckle, tossing his head back, trying to maintain his delight at the quick mission. As they rode gently to the end of the road leading away from Balcarres House, he started counting the minutes until they were on their way out of Scotland and into warmer weather. Deciding the women would stay on the main roads, William took the route towards Aberdeen, Andrew headed to Glasgow, and Hector decidedly would tackle the chaotic Edinburgh. They would ride hard and meet back in four days. Their horses loped towards the town outside Balcarres, where they would part ways. The wager was simple. Whoever failed to come back with Lady Elizabeth, was paying for passage on the next ship to Port Royal, where the men planned to soak up some sun and find some action amongst the ale houses. It was completely ungentlemanly, they knew it, but didn't care.

They were out to seek their fortunes. They were young and not willing to settle down to what they considered boring lives managing estates. Running estates were for the old and settled men. Undiscovered business opportunities around the world enticed them—to find their fortune away from Ireland and England. Of course, William would make an excuse of one or another to his wife, leaving her to tend to the house and their daughter, whilst he sowed his wild oats. He would pop in long enough to ensure his family line, then off to look for silks from China or spices in India. Andrew was interested in finding new lands and considered entering the slave trade. Hector was in it for the adventure of it all. Whatever their reasons, finding Lady Elizabeth and returning her to Hector's father was the steppingstone to jump on the next ship to Jamaica.

"What's to happen if none of us can find them?" Asked Andrew as they stood at the edge of the village, deciding what provisions they would need for their rides. "They may have sought help and disappeared, never to be seen again."

Hector hissed through his teeth. "You should perform in the theater with that dramatic speech." He hopped off his horse and tied it up outside a tavern. "They're women," his tone matter of fact. "I would say they are likely to fall into a fit of hysteria and come crying back home before the day is through. Then, none of us will be the victors and we will have to drown our sorrows in the bosoms of a bar wench in Port Royal. Besides, war is brewing here, with the Jacobites."

After a meal in the tavern and a gathering of provisions, they each rode off in the direction in search of their prize. Hector followed the road to Stirling, arriving late evening at Linlithgow Castle. After his unexpected arrival to a ruinous palace, he left early in the morning twilight with a few men to help with his search for the runaway maidens in Edinburgh. If the women, in fact, headed to Edinburgh, he would need all the help he could get to find them.

The city was bustling with activity. People moving in and out of the port. Coming in to buy and sell goods. Silas Graham—no relation to Missus Graham, Elizabeth's cook —one of the Linlithgow's farmhands, and his brother, Rob, joined the small group. Curiosity of what was happening with troops being brought in to protect Edinburgh Castle and the rise of religious tensions, helped fuel the men's cooperativeness. That and the potential of a reward. Money speaks the Graham's language, and Silas and Rob were not above looking for an easy payday. They were joined by James and Fergus, one tended to sheep, the other cows, in the land surrounding the palace.

The men yammered on the walk towards Edinburgh. Hector only halfway paid attention to the antics, while the other half was amused by their bawdy conversation. "Aye, Rob, your nose never went straight," teased James. "It bends to the left, like I hear your middle leg does."

"His sister was less agreeable to his advances," added Fergus with a rambunctious laugh. "How is Morag? I missed seeing all her offerings at the gathering." He mimicked breasts with his hands, and with a high-pitched voice, he teased, "Oh, Fergus, slip me a wet kiss."

"Aye, I'll slip you my fist in your face if you keep at it." Rob raised a fist towards Fergus.

Silas laughed at his brother's expense, and tugged at his dirty, slightly too small, wet shirt that clung too tightly on his body. He figured he didn't need a clean shirt to look for a couple astray women, and slipped on the shirt he wore the day prior while working in the fields, along with his plain brown kilt.

The men grew up together. Brothers, Silas, and Rob Graham, along with James, their cousin on their mother's side. Fergus, the annoying younger brother of their friend Robert Cameron, agreed to join the group to assist Lord Hector, if he paid a fee and a reward. Hector knew some light jabbing was all in good fun but grew weary of the men and wondered if their help was worth listening to their raunchy antics. It wasn't as though he hadn't heard language like that, he had served on a ship, and participated in the same type of jests with his friends, perhaps with a little less violence, and not in mixed company. He required their assistance; they knew Edinburgh better than he possibly could imagine.

As the men approached the large Netherbow Gate at the end of High Street, with its commanding turreted towers on either side of the entry, Hector sat tall in the saddle. Stone tenements, wooden makeshift shacks, beggars, and merchants helped funnel pedestrians, carts, horses, tradesmen, residents, and visitors to the main port of entry into the burgh. People begged for money alongside the road. Some begged for the entry fee through the gate, others for food. A redheaded girl—wearing not much more than a dirty shift, a brown ratty shawl, and no older than five—cried for her mother. Hector tried to pay her no mind. However, the small tug at his heart proved to be more powerful than his will to push forward and retrieve Lady Elizabeth. He glanced up at the two-story spired tower, standing proud, above the arched gateway. The elegant clock showed half-past nine. They would have plenty of time to canvas the city for the women and stop for a moment to provide for the child.

Hector halted his horse and the men. Confused at the stop, Fergus shrugged his shoulders to James, Silas, and Rob, and approached Hector's left side. As he dug into his pack, Hector leaned over to Fergus, "Take this coin and bread to the child."

"Are you certain, my lord? One of those boys standing in the corner will take it from her before we make it through the gate." His brows stitched a deep x, as he looked towards his left at the corner of the wall and another street leading to more travelers. Leaning against a wall, stood three teen boys, watching every person approach. Sizing up who they could rob, and which ones would give them more trouble than they were worth. "That is, if she isn't already working for them. Best let her *mam* care for her."

Hector wasn't having it, he hopped off his chestnut horse, landing with a squishy thud on the wet ground. He worked his way through people trying to walk past him, and into the gate, and found himself next to the merchant stand and the girl cowering next to a basket. The little girl's eyes reminded Hector of an injured puppy, showing fear, which caused an ache in his chest. Gently, he knelt to the girl's eye level and extended his hand with the small loaf of bread. Hesitant at first, she gingerly reached towards the loaf. Hector nodded with encouragement, she snatched it and ran behind the stall. Ripping and tearing into the bread, she devoured a quarter of it, and then gently covered the rest in her shawl and hid it behind the merchant stall. He tried to tell himself that it was nothing to offer the food, but deep down he wondered why the merchants that saw her there day-after-day allowed it to continue. Surely, one of them could take her in and give her a job cleaning their stall or home.

When the girl emerged, Hector placed a coin in her small hand. She wrapped her thin fingers around the cold metal and looked at it, unsure what to do with it. Looking over towards the merchant in the stall weaving a basket, Hector pulled himself to his full height and walked over. "Where are her parents? Surely, a girl this young must have parents or a guardian." He motioned to the little girl who moved on to continue her begging to passing travelers.

The man glanced towards the little girl, and then up at Hector, before continuing his weaving. "Aye. I remember her mother, Winnie. She came from inside the walls, dressed in clothes I had never seen before. She said they were French." He pulled a pliable reed from a bucket of water on his left and wove it between support reeds. Back-and-forth around the base and up the sides. He continued weaving as he sat on his stool. "Pretty face, with red hair like the child. Seemed friendly enough. Mentioned she struggled for a couple years and then found her way out here, saying she was looking for the proper door. Made little sense, I tell you. She sold trinkets of sorts and told wild stories. Don't know where she got them, the trinkets nor the stories. I suppose some she made. Others... I canna say." He pulled another reed out and continued his weaving. "She caught the eye of some Presbyterian minister one day on his way inside. Things went sour and her mother was convicted, hanged, and burned a witch, four months past." He shook his head. "I remember the trial. Nothing else exciting going on that day. She started spouting nonsense that she walked through a door in the future and ended up here. Wanted to get back to her time." He paused mid-weave and stared intently at the girl. "Witch if you ask me. We do what we can for the child, Krissy, but we don't wanna bring the devil's child into our home and curse us."

Hector nodded, looked at Krissy once more, joined his impatient traveling companions, and mounted his horse. He spent more time than he should've worried about the child. He didn't believe in witches and devils, only in what he could see as facts. The child seemed pleasant enough. If Krissy was still there when he returned with Lady Elizabeth, he would consider taking her with them so she could serve the household in some manner. However, his men would first need to find Lady Elizabeth in the expanse of Edinburgh, and they only had the next twenty-four hours or so to do it, or he would lose the bet and quite possibly be disowned by his father.

CHAPTER FIVE

"*D*oes it always smell so foul?" Hector coughed out. His hand swiftly found its way under his nose. The men moved down the narrow streets, the smoke from the chimneys billowed out black smoke which choked the people as much as the stench from Nor' Loch, the city's drainage site. The site was filled with waste washed down the streets from chamber pots, animal waste, food scraps, and the sort. Occasionally, they would find a corpse—dog, cats, more rats than they could count, and people. How the people would get into the loch varied as much as they did. Some were tossed in, found on the street by someone, dead from exposure, starvation, or illness. Others were murdered and tossed in to get rid of the evidence. The poor would sometimes slip in while trying to scrounge for items or food scraps, never to make it out of the loch alive. It was a wretched place with a wretched stench that snaked its way through the narrow streets of

Edinburgh, held down low from the heavy smoke from chimneys.

"Aye. Auld Reekie," Silas said with a pretentious flair. "With the smoke so thick you could eat it for supper." Silas took in a deep breath, only to cough up a lung in response. When he finally could speak again, he asked, "Are you sure those lasses would come here? It seems like they would find somewhere a wee bit gentler to their disposition."

"I'm not sure where they would go. You have their descriptions. Spread out and find them." He looked towards the four men, standing around waiting for further instructions. "Make haste."

Everyone looked towards Silas to speak up. "What should we do with them when we find them?"

"Secure them, but no harm shall come to Lady Elizabeth, or it will be your head." And his own, he thought. He started to have second—or was it third?—thoughts about hiring this group of men.

The men spread out, Silas and Rob worked their way down a quiet street to watch people coming and going down the main street. Fergus and James walked further into the city, bickering more than they were looking at the people around them. Hector rode his horse down a narrow side street trying to find his way towards the castle and to any Lords' homes. The women might seek out assistance from local Lords or Ladies, or so he thought that made the most sense of what a lady in Elizabeth's standing would do in this situation.

Silas and Rob stood on either corner of the street,

watching men, women, and children wandering up and down the thoroughfare, shopping, chatting, or trying to get somewhere of great importance. A group of young lads loitered along a set of stairs which led up to a doorway to a tenement. *Up to no good*, thought Silas. He was once a young and carefree lad. Now? Now, at twenty and seven, he is taking a break from his backbreaking farming to chase down Lady Elizabeth in hopes for the small reward. A woman walked by, holding a tray of pasties. A cord draped around her neck helped take the weight of the tray piled with meat-filled hand pies.

A woman walked by, with auburn hair, catching Rob's eye. *Could that be Lady Elizabeth?* She traveled alone, carrying a basket in the crook of her left arm. Perhaps the women split up. It would be easier to capture one woman than it would be to capture two. Besides, there wasn't a reward for Lady Anna. Rob raised an eyebrow toward Silas, then flicked his head in the direction of the woman walking down the street. The men watched her move from stall to stall. Purchasing a loaf of bread, a few vegetables, and a pasty from the woman calling out the song to buy her goods. Silas's stomach grumbled; it had been far too long since he broke his fast before the early morning sun. Silas gave a nod to Rob, and then held up his hand to stop his brother from approaching the woman. "She looks a bit too homely and old to be Lady Elizabeth. Lord Hector said she was nineteen." He looked over towards the woman again. A small child appeared from behind her cloak and grabbed hold of her mother's hand. Definitely not Lady Elizabeth.

They stood there for a while longer, cleaning the dirt from under their nails and wishing they would have brought something to eat. Expectations for what they were, they had expected Lord Hector to pay for a midday meal in a tavern, and perhaps add a few drinks in there to help with the hunt. Instead, it was inching on eleven in the morning and there was no meal—or drinks—in the foreseeable future.

No sooner had the brothers considered moving on to a new position, they saw two women on horseback come through the Netherbow Port and work their way down the congested street. "Do you think it could be them?" asked Rob.

"Aye. I do." Silas pinned his back to the wall leading down the quiet side street and looked around the corner to size up the women. They seemed genteel—easy targets.

"How should we do this? Pull them off their horses and drag them to Lord Hector?" He watched as they dismounted and spoke to a lad selling wares, piled, and laid out along a blanket. The foot traffic was too thick to see what they were purchasing from the lad. No worries, they would find out soon enough and add it to their pockets.

"They won't be able to mount their horses with all the people around. We'll wait until they pass and then we'll relieve them of their freedom and whatever trinkets they purchased."

"Do you think Lord Hector will allow us to keep the horses? They look strong enough to carry you."

Silas glanced down at his shirt, dried and no longer clinging from the bit of rain earlier, but still tight for his round stomach. "Maybe we won't find them with the horses. We deliver the women and take our reward from the lord. We come back and take our prize."

"Ha! They're headed this way," Rob moved down the empty street to give room to capture the women. The *wynd* was a deep cavern with tall buildings looming overhead on either side. Doors pocked the walls, some at the top of a set of stairs three or four high. Others with a single step or at ground level. At the other end of the narrow alleyway, laid another road, busy with people and carts. Rob leaned next to a door in earnest attempt to look nonchalant. Silas followed suit on the opposite side of the narrow, dirt street. The door next to Rob flung open, missing him by a flea's hair. "Either get back inside or make haste, woman." The older woman gasped at not only someone standing directly outside her door, but the forwardness from the man thirty years her junior. She regained her composure, before letting into him. She yelled and swung her basket at him. He dodged and pleaded. Silas stood, watching, laughing, and then remembered the purpose of them waiting down the street.

"I beg my brother's pardon, mistress. We are waiting for guests to conduct business with and would prefer if you either went back inside or leave the other way." He glanced at the corner when the two women turned down the street with their horses. The older woman huffed and went back inside her house. The men took up holding the walls up with their backsides, trying to blend in with the scenery. The quiet and empty street did nothing to conceal the men, but the women paid them no mind.

As they approached, Silas figured he would attempt to confirm their identity and negotiate their surrender, as to ensure no harm came to them. Looking up as they approached, he opened his mouth to call out, "Lady Elizabeth." When suddenly, another woman, wearing a heather green cloak, ran up and drove a shoulder into him. All hell broke loose. There was no opportunity to negotiate when a fight broke out. The women punched and kicked. Scratched and screamed. Silas and Rob hadn't expected the women to fight back, and ended up bruised and winded, and left empty-handed.

The three women took off down the street, captured their horses, and were on their way down another busy street before Silas and Rob could regain their breath and hobble towards them. They were certain that it was Lady Elizabeth and Lady Anna. But who was the other woman?

By the time they trudged to the end of the street, the women were nowhere to be found. The streets were filled with more people selling and transporting goods. A man pulled a cart heavy with fish in front of the men. "The docks," they said in unison. Even though they temporarily lost the women, they were certain Lord Hector would be pleased to know they were in the city and would reward them for the find. They were already counting the money and thinking of at least a half dozen ways to spend it. Silas continued to hope for Hector to feed them and leave his reward to spend on a new Ghillie shirt, one that would fit around his stomach with more ease.

It took over an hour to find Lord Hector, who had just left Fergus and James to head to a pub near the docks.

They mentioned heading to *Cock and Cannon* for a meal, drinks, and to regroup. "We're certain that it was Lady Elizabeth and Lady Anna," Silas began to explain the situation to Lord Hector who sat atop his horse and looked down at the men and through the throngs of people. It gave him the advantage point to view and command. "There was another woman that interfered, and that's where it went wrong."

"Well, don't hold back." Hector's irritation was not only at the fact that the men lost the women, but at the slow pace the story was unfolding. "Who was she? Did she have a name? What did she look like?"

"She wore a long green cloak," said James. "However, her clothes were..."

"Odd," Silas finished James's thought. "She wore an odd pair of breeches. Must be some of those fancy French clothes like the witch wore. You remember the one the merchant was telling you about."

"You're telling me that Lady Elizabeth and Lady Anna are traveling with a French witch?"

Silas panicked. He hadn't planned on his excuse for being abused by three women to head in that direction, but it seemed like a good enough reason for them not to be able to capture them. "Aye. She could have bewitched the ladies." Silas looked over towards Rob who was standing to his left and noticed a woman walking down the busy street towards their location. It was the woman in the green cloak who helped the women escape. He would recognize her anywhere. A few growing bruises on his ribs reminded him of their encounter. His eyes grew the size of saucers at his find. She was oblivious to the men and seemed more interested in the woman selling beef pasties. As she turned to walk up the quiet street where they had their encounter, Silas snatched the woman's arm. She let out an excitable scream, pulled and yanked on her arm, and thrust about like a wild creature. *Witch.*

"What have you done with Lady Elizabeth?" Lord Hector began after a few quick introductions. He knew roughing her up wasn't going to provide him with the answers he required. Polite conversation was in order for as long as he could put up with her insolent tongue.

"You're young enough to be her brother, and you're trying to marry her off to your father?" The witch's auburn hair was pulled back in a tie at the back of her head, the ends flew about from the wind and her erratic movements.

"Shall we get rid of her, my lord?"

"Be gentle with her and keep her out of the way so she cannot warn Lady Elizabeth of my presence."

With that, Silas and Rob carried the kicking, hitting, and screaming witch to Tolbooth Gate to hold her in the jail while they found the ladies.

"Silas, cousin," called out the guard. "Who have you brought me today?"

"Duncan," Silas called out as he threw the witch on the ground, next to a steaming pile of horse manure. "We need you to keep this witch locked up for a bit." Silas dug a coin out of his sporran and tossed it to Duncan.

"Aye." Duncan tossed the coin in the air and looked

down at the witch pulling away from the horse apples. "For how long?"

"She's a witch, keep her locked up until they can move her to the witches' jail."

"Cheese and rice!" The feisty witch called out. "I'm not a witch. I'm American. You can't lock me up. I demand to speak to the embassy."

"You cost me the bounty on Lady Elizabeth," Silas pulled the witch up by her hair and got within inches of her face. Angry at the loss of money and the continued fight from her.

"They held their own against you pathetic men."

"Lock the witch up," Silas said through gritted teeth as he shoved the woman into Duncan's grasp.

With Duncan's vice-like grasp, he hauled the woman into the prison.

"Let's head to the *Cock and Cannon* for food." Rob slapped his brother on the back. "I hear Lord Hector is paying."

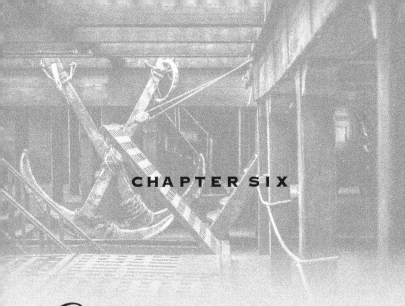

CHAPTER SIX

"*W*e need to sell the horses and find a place to sleep for the night," Elizabeth put her tankard of ale down. "I'll see if they have a room available here."

"Should we be staying in such a..." Anna trailed off as she looked around the room. The tavern was dark and filled with sailors, merchants, and anyone else that found their way into the dockside establishment.

"We'll do well here." Elizabeth's eyes darted around the room. A group of men in the corner played cards, taking bets, and slamming the table. A few times she was concerned they would brawl over a hand. She sat straight in her wooden chair at their small round table in the corner. "'Tis only the night. We meet Mister Campbell early in the morn."

After being attacked in a wynd, Elizabeth and Anna fled with a woman that either helped thwart the attack or made it worse. Anna had her opinions, and they weren't kind. Elizabeth thought Amelia was trying to help, even if she mostly got in the way of the women's defensive maneuvers. When they arrived at the tavern to find a captain who would allow passage on his ship. They met with Captain Murray. Murray's wild crew needed a little convincing that they should take on special cargo for the trip, but remarkably, Amelia helped with that.

Amelia kept the crew entertained while Elizabeth negotiated travel with Captain Murray and his crew on board the *Good Fortune*, his merchant ship. To be fair, Amelia was quite amusing, asking the crew if they were pirates and telling absurd pirate jokes, before bestowing pirate names upon the men. Elizabeth tried to remember their names. One-Eye-Pete, although he had both eyes. Then there was Sea Dog Stede. According to Amelia, he was given the name of Steven at birth, but changed his name to Stede because he thought that was more of a pirate name. Barnacle Bart had some sort of a growth on his cheek, but Amelia said that's where the mermaid kissed him. Gulliver the Traveler, running away from his many wives and children. Gunnar Big Guns, a giant Nordic man. Skinny Bones Jonesy, the young boy of about fifteen. He was a skinny little lad; a stiff breeze could knock him over. There were a few more names that she couldn't recall off the top of her head. The men found it amusing, but it gave the women the opportunity to negotiate with the less-than-agreeable Captain.

An early morning sail to France beginning the next morning would take them a week, maybe two if the weather wasn't agreeable. In April, you couldn't predict the weather off the coast. Heck, you couldn't predict the weather on the coast. Unless your prediction was gloomy, with a side of rain. Then, the sun would fight its way through the clouds only to tease you and arouse the biting midges out of an early slumber.

After their meal, a quick jaunt to the stables and their prized and beloved horses were an easy and quick sale. They didn't get their worth for them and was offered much less than they could've received had they had time to find a proper buyer. It would have to do. Time was not on their side. Elizabeth knew her father would send men to drag her back. She couldn't go back. She refused to marry an old man and live in Ireland. In fact, marriage was the last thing on her mind or in her heart.

Elizabeth and Anna made arrangements with the barkeep's wife. The older woman was rougher around the edges than Amelia, but she was just as protective of the women. As Elba took the women up the wooden flight of stairs, and down a dark hall–lit by the window at the end and a single lantern–Elizabeth wondered if her circumstances would lead her to owning a tavern. A smile cracked in the right corner of her mouth at her wild imagination. She wasn't sure she was rough enough to be in the middle of it, but running her own business could be worth her while. That would show her father. The three women walked single file down the hall. Elba unlocked the third door on the right and handed Elizabeth the key. "Pay mind to keep it always locked. If the men know where you're staying, you never know which one will want to take their liberties with such fine ladies of standing, such as yourself."

Elizabeth nodded in response. The room, the situation, the constantly looking over her shoulder, was a lot to take in. The room was small with a bed wide enough if they both slept on their sides. The linen bedding seemed clean enough. Elizabeth laid her bed roll over the bed. Sunlight poured in from the small window on the other side of the room. Anna unlocked the latch and gently swung the window out. An easy breeze came in from the docks. Birds cawed and yelled, looking for food to steal from an inattentive fishmonger, or a small child carrying a piece of their meal in their grubby little hand.

Fortune fell on them, as they didn't have to share a room with any other travelers. An early morning meal and pack of extra provisions for their journey, and they would leave Scotland behind them.

Hector walked into the bawdy *Cock and Cannon* to meet with his search party for a hearty meal, before continuing the hunt for Lady Elizabeth and Lady Anna. Elba walked down the wooden stairs which led to the second floor of rooms to rent for weary travelers and sailors looking to spend the evening on solid ground. Scanning the room, Hector found James and Fergus engrossed in a card game at a table in the corner. James slammed his hand down and the rest of the table roared in fury. He collected his winnings as a few men left, shaking their heads and with empty pockets. Sensing someone staring at him, James raised his head and found Hector standing next to him, with a look of disapproval.

"I'm not paying you to play cards. Am I? I thought you were to help find Lady Elizabeth." Hector sat down at the empty round table next to the card table. He raised his hand to gain the attention of Elba. "Besides, it looks as though Silas and Rob will be earning the reward. They've already come across the fair maidens once today."

"Aye? They couldn't keep their hands on a couple of wee lasses? Eh?" James swept his winnings into his sporran and moved to the table with Hector. Fergus swiped his tankard half-full of ale off the card table and plopped in a chair across from Hector. Hector raised an eyebrow at Fergus. He must've been on his third or fourth ale.

Elba made her way through the growing crowd. Mid-afternoon was turning into an early evening. Sailors, merchants, men looking for a good time, would all file into the tavern and fill it to the gills. *Cock and Cannon* was not only a favorite amongst the sailors, but a favorite of the local rowdy crowd. By the time the sun went down, and the lanterns lit, there wouldn't be a free chair to sit, or clean air to breathe.

"What can I get for you, my lord?" Elba asked, looking Hector in the eye. She glanced down at Fergus and James. "These two bothering you? Shall I kick them out?"

"Yes, well, no." Hector shook his head. "Yes, they are bothering me. They would bother me less if they would do what I hired them to do. No need to kick them out."

Elba looked at the trio with confusion. What was a man like Lord Hector Black, dressed in fine clothes, doing with a couple of farmhands like Fergus and James? They had come in enough times for her to know their names, and the trouble they usually brought along with them. "Shall I get you and your business partners something, my lord?"

"Food, drinks, and we'll need a couple more plates for two more guests."

She left to take care of their order. Silas and Rob, crept into the tavern, looking for Hector and food.

"We took care of the witch problem," Rob said as he sat next to Fergus, leaving an open chair next to Hector.

"Aye, she's full of piss and vinegar, that one," said Silas, plopping down in the chair. "Put up a bit of a fight." He looked around the room. "I'm hungry. Where's the barmaid?"

"She's coming. You didn't harm the woman? I said not..."

Silas raised his hand. "We didn't harm her. We just took her to my cousin, Duncan, to watch over her for a bit."

James sat straight in his seat, "You took her to Duncan?"

"Why? What's wrong with Duncan?" Hector asked.

"Oh, she'll be fine. Duncan will take good care of her," Silas answered with a smirk.

James and Fergus unsuccessfully tried to contain their laughter.

"I don't believe you." Hector looked around the table at the men laughing at a joke that he wasn't in on. "And if I cannot trust you, then I believe our business has concluded. I'll pay for the food that was ordered, but you are no longer employed."

Following his meal, which he ate quickly and in silence, Hector left the four men sitting at the table as he went to search for Elizabeth and Anna on his own. He traveled up and down the streets, looking for any sign of the women. He stopped at a few pubs and inns to inquire if the women bought a room for the night. After the third false alarm, where he ended up being promptly escorted out of the inn due to the hysteric fit a young woman threw, he gave up. As the sun dipped beyond the city to the west, he headed back to *Cock and Cannon*, to look for a bed for the night. If any search were to continue, it would be in the morning with a fresh outlook.

"We just had a room open up," Elba informed Hector as she led him up the stairs set off to the side of the room. The sun no longer filtered through the window at the end of the hall. Another lit lantern hung from a hook on the wall. Two sparse lanterns were the only light offered down the dark hall. Just enough light so you wouldn't crash into the person in front of you. Two doors down, on the right, Elba unlocked the door and handed the key to Hector. She lit the lantern on the small table on the left side of the room. "You can break your fast downstairs in the morn." She closed the door behind her and left.

Hector looked around the small room and sat his saddle bags on the bed, which lined the right-hand wall in almost its entire length. The bed and the room were narrow but would serve him well enough for the night. He walked to the far end of the room and unlatched the window, swinging it open to bring in the cool evening breeze. The smell of the breeze coming off the water was welcomed over the stuffiness of the room.

Sounds from the docks of people finishing up their day, a dog barking, the lap of waves, and a woman's laughter floated through the air. He stretched out on the bed and wondered what Lady Elizabeth was doing at that moment. Was she laughing with Lady Anna? Was she scared? Would she be relieved when she found out he was there to rescue her? He dozed off listening to the song of the sea and the melody of women's conversation.

CHAPTER SEVEN

*E*lizabeth stretched out in the bed, and smacked Anna in the nose. "Watch it, will ye," Anna cursed out. Cold, thick air coming in through the open window crept from the water and into the room.

"Oh, I forgot that you were in the bed." Elizabeth gingerly adjusted to her side, as there was no room to move without knocking Anna out of bed.

"This is the second night we slept in a bed too small for two." Anna sat up and threw her feet over the edge, landing them firmly on the floor. "The way you toss and flip, I canna forget that we shared a bed." She padded over to the window and peeked outside into the thick fog, before locking it closed. "We should get downstairs and break our fast before meeting with Mister Campbell." Anna began slipping on her layers of clothes from her stays to her mantua. Her wool sage green mantua sported a small train, giving additional volume to her backside. The mantua was opened in the front skirt, to reveal her soft, cream cotton petticoat. Mid-forearm sleeves were completed with a cream lace frill. The collar that was worn close to the neck, provided additional coverage for warmth. It was edged in cream lace, matching the end of the sleeves. Elizabeth wore a similar ensemble, but with a deep blue mantua. Anna pinned the top of her hair back with a bit of tease to give some elevation to the top of her head, leaving curls to hang over a shoulder. Elizabeth went for a simple plait, a thick, auburn rope trailing down mid-back. Their cloaks would top their simple clothes, leaving their finer clothes in their packs to keep pristine until their arrival in France.

In the room next door, Hector stretched out in the small bed. His sleep was terrible. He tossed and turned, feeling every lump and bump. The noise from the tavern paraded up the stairs, through the floor and window, and rattled his door. He was almost asleep when a ruckus of singing turned into a brawl. The early morning quiet lulled him back to sleep for a moment longer.

Elizabeth and Anna galloped down the stairs, eager to grab the food Elba prepared for them and to meet up with Campbell. The sun was splitting the early morning horizon as they turned left outside of the tavern and walked to the docks.

Leaning against the wall, Campbell picked at his fingernails, digging the tip of a sgian-dubh under each nail and prying out the dirt. As the women, approached, he stood straight, looked slightly annoyed, and said, "The *Good Fortune* is this way." He flicked his head to a ship docked at the end of a long-planked dock. "It's best you remember the passage is for cargo."

Anna grabbed Elizabeth's hand and gave it a nervous squeeze. "We can turn back, if you want."

Elizabeth straightened up and pulled the hood of her cloak on top of her head, then wrapped her arm around Anna's waist, "You don't have to join me. It's not too late for you to go home."

Anna took a deep breath, "Mayhem and adventure." With that, she pulled her cloak over her head, feeling prepared to handle what was ahead, a cloak of armor.

"And freedom," Elizabeth's voice quivered. They were wrapped up in their conversation, and a man bumped Elizabeth's shoulder as he passed. She didn't give it much thought, as he kept walking, and it hadn't caused her pain. Their impending journey brought Elizabeth's emotions crashing into her all at once. The fear of the unknown. Sadness for leaving her mother and Scotland behind. Happiness and strength having Anna by her side. Excitement for the adventure and new path laid ahead of them. It was a lot for anyone to take in, especially for two nineteen-year-old women. A deep breath and a giggle of relief later, and the women were at the gangplank, ready to embark on their journey. The man who bumped into Elizabeth, stood at the end of the dock with his brother Silas, and watched the women board the ship.

At the end of the dock, floated the merchant ship, *Good Fortune.*

Campbell held his arm out, blocking them from entry.

ALEX R CRAWFORD

"We might have allowed you on as cargo, but you need to board proper, and all."

"I... I... I don't understand," Elizabeth said, confused. How was she supposed to properly board? Flap her arms and fly on like a bird? Swim around the ship three times and then board?

"Ask the captain's permission and pay mind to pet the dog."

"There's a dog on board?"

Skinny Bones Jonesy—christened that name in the tavern by Elizabeth's guest, Amelia—came up behind the women, pulling two goats behind him.

"You're late," called out Captain Murray, as he stood near the helm looking over a map with Raymond Olson, the man Amelia had named Hawkeye Hank. She was correct, he was able to see land and approaching ships from miles away. He was also the ship's first mate, responsible for navigating and doling out discipline, when needed. Jonesy gulped down, thinking that his tardiness would warrant such discipline.

"The little black one here is a troublemaker." Jonesy tugged on the goats. "I say we eat this one first." The goats put up a fight the entire path from their pen on land to their pen down below deck. The combined weight of the small goats weighed more than Jonesy. They worked in tandem to cause Jonesy to pant and rub his sweaty brow on the chilly morning. The women stood there watching the chaos of the spirited goats outwit Jonesy. Elizabeth covered her mouth to hide the fit of giggles emerging.

Elizabeth and Anna followed Jonesy and his naughty

goats, reaching the top and coming to an abrupt stop. "Permission to come aboard, captain?" Elizabeth called out. She turned her head to look at Campbell, who stood mid-way down the ramp. He gave a quick nod. They passed the first step, and hoped the captain would give his permission so they could finish loading and get on their way.

"Aye, permission granted," Captain Murray called back and gave a wave of his hand as if to say after you. He turned back to Olson to finish their discussion. Near the tall center mast in front of them, stood a brass head of an Irish Wolfhound on a metal stick. The nose on the dog was worn shiny from the constant rubs from people honoring the dog as they boarded the ship or looked for extra luck. Sailors were a superstitious bunch; that much she knew from listening to stories from the merchants and travelers making their way through her village. Whether she believed their superstitions or not, would remain her secret. She needed to just roll with the waves.

Elizabeth reached out and touched the cold metal, still damp from the morning fog. Her fingertips danced over the nose and up the snout. It seemed odd to her, but if petting the statue meant they would be accepted on board, then she was ready to pet the head every time she walked past it. "I know you don't want to but do as he say. Pet the dog," Elizabeth said in a whisper over her shoulder to Anna.

Anna let out a sigh as she gave a rough pat to the top of the head. She was less inclined to follow their superstition, only for the fact that they were a bunch of sailors.

Superstitions ran aplenty amongst the Scots. Some she pretended to believe, if to save face with the rest of her friends. Only a few months ago, one of the young maids gave birth to a little boy. He came sooner than expected, so tiny and fragile. They were sure he wouldn't survive the week, if not the night. Louise took her delicate son and placed him on a fairy mound in the forest. The fairies swapped her child with a changeling, who died before the sun came up. Her child would live happy and strong with the fairies and the changeling would take its place to die in their world. Anna wasn't too quick to believe that story. She thought it was an easier way to deal with the death of the child. However, like she said to Louise, she would say to the sailors, if that's what they need to believe, then she will go along with it.

Who was she to argue with superstitions? She went to church every Sunday, kneeling and praying before the cross. Even religion changes with whoever is sitting on the throne. The push for protestant churches drove her family to support James to claim the throne in Scotland in a revolution. A failed revolution. Now, they were proving their loyalty and praying at their protestant churches, led by their protestant ministers. Fake religion. Fake smiles. Fake prayers. Fake promises. If she could make fake prayers, then she could pet the dog's head.

Campbell led them to an opening in the deck. Elizabeth looked down the steep ladder down, took a deep breath, and followed Campbell down. Anna didn't waste any time on the deck of the ship and followed close to Elizabeth, nearly kicking her in the face. "Slow down.

Aye?" Elizabeth called up to Anna. "I don't want to taste your shoe for supper."

Anna looked around the deck, canvas hammocks hung on either side, attached to posts. There looked to be just enough for the men she eyed scurrying about up top and below deck as they moved crates and barrels. Tying barrels and crates to one another and to anchor points as they moved them from one side to another. They would rush down one ramp and up another ramp. It was an organized chaos, with shouts and grunts. It began to come together.

"Keep moving," Campbell shouted to Anna as he led them towards the aft of the ship and down another passage to the next deck below. Another ladder down, and the room was darker, stacked high with boxes. It was the main cargo hold and their destination was found behind crates stacked nearly as high as the ceiling. They were lashed together and secured to anchor points on the wall, floor, and posts. Behind the crates was a small room with two cots and a couple of smaller crates that could be used as seats and a small table. Campbell walked over to the side of the hull and opened one of the windows, propping it open with a latch. "We set sail as soon as the captain receives the manifest seal. You'll stay here until he comes down to talk to you ladies."

The women could only nod. Thankful they were spared the crew bay; they had hoped for a cabin on the ship—not the cargo hold. Anna dropped her bag on the wooden floor next to the hammock along the side directly across from the small opening. Elizabeth found a hook on one of the posts and hung her bag on that, then rolled out her bedroll in the other hammock. They plopped down on the two smaller crates, which were their makeshift chairs. With her chin in her hands and her elbows planted on the larger crate, which was their table, Elizabeth said, "Well, this is exciting."

"Is it?" Anna looked around their cubicle. "It's a bit dank and small. Seems a bit disrespectful to force us in here with these boxes and rats."

"Rats?" Elizabeth perked up. She swallowed a few exaggerated times. "How would rats get in here?"

"They hitch a ride in our walls," she said as she pointed to the crates and barrels. "They need a dozen cats in here to rid us of our furry little demons." She bucked her teeth, mimicking a rat's face, and stuck out her hands like claws. "They'll eat us alive while we sleep."

"Please, don't say that." Elizabeth's eyes darted around the room, ready to jump at every shadow and scratch. She pulled her cloak tight around her body, hoping it would protect her from the things that crept and skittered in the dark shadows between the walls of her little fortress and in the belly of the ship.

The sound of men's boots and shoes thudded above them. The activity above moved to the other side of the ship, which left the deep timbre of the two men's voices in friendly conversation above them. Their voices were too muffled for her to understand what they were discussing, but it seemed friendly enough, and it seemed to get closer overhead. The men worked their way down to the cargo level, right outside the women's cubicle. Unless the men walked around to the side and noticed the small opening, then the women would remain hidden. Elizabeth threw a finger over her mouth and Anna nodded in response.

"Look at all this, Sean." One man said enthusiastically to the other. "This is fantastic."

"Aye. I've done quite well since our time in the navy." They continued down the length of the ship, moving further away from Elizabeth and Anna.

"Where are you headed now?"

"We've got a shipment to France, then to Spain." Their footsteps were heavy. "Headed to India, eventually, and then..." The men's conversation faded in the distance.

Elizabeth let out the breath she desperately held onto and said, "I thought it was my father's men."

"Or the men from yesterday." Anna stood and peered out the window. The fog crept off the water, leaving pools of sun on the dark water. A bird swooped down, skimmed the surface, and abruptly left clasping tight to a fish. Poor fish, she thought. It was just out for its morning meal and now it's the bird's morning meal. "Do you think we'll make it to France?" She asked, her gaze fixated on the horizon.

Elizabeth nodded. "Why wouldn't we? Only the crew knows we're here." She stood to look out the porthole with Anna. "I suppose Amelia knows we're leaving, but she wouldn't tell anyone."

"Do you trust her?" She searched Elizabeth's face for the answer. "We only just met her."

"Aye. I do." Elizabeth pulled her shoulders back and stood confident. Her hand grazed Anna's shoulder as she walked by and sat down on her seat. "We'll be in France before you know it."

Hector walked down the docks; the sun began to melt the fog. Through a squint, he saw Silas and Rob holding up the side of a tavern. Ugh. "Are you following me?"

Silas picked at the dirt beneath his fingernail. "Nay. Just wondering why you didn't return from that ship with those maidens you were looking for?"

"What do you mean? I was on the *Good Fortune*. There were no maidens on that ship."

"Aye. We saw them board this morning."

"Why didn't you say something?" Hector in a panic looked down the dock and watched the *Good Fortune* leave the harbor.

"Yesterday, you told us we were no longer employed. didn't see it was any of my business to tell you," Rob said as they stood and walked away, leaving Hector with his heart in his stomach and his good fortune sailing away.

CHAPTER EIGHT

"Wakey, wakey, eggs and bakey," I poked Henry in his side. The April sun crept through the curtains, greeting us to another wonderful morning in Fredericksburg, Virginia.

Henry took a deep inhale and pried an eye open. "Mayhap, my dearest, Amelia, if you did prepare eggs and bacon, I would have smelled it and awoken on my own, instead of you jabbing me in the side."

"No eggs and bacon. We ran out yesterday when I made French toast." I threw back the blankets and slid out of bed. "There's cereal. Or! We can head over to Betsy's Biscuits and pick up breakfast."

I stood in front of the rack of clothes in the closet, wearing my white, sleeveless nightdress that hung to just above my knees. debating on my outfit for the day. April weather could be unpredictable in Virginia. I flipped a couple of hangers past me.

A white blouse? No.

A long dress? Heavens no.

Black slacks? Oh! Maybe?

A pair of jeans? Always at the top of my list.

"Nay, my love." Henry slipped his hand around my waist and pulled a plaid skirt off the rack with his left hand and handed it to me. "If you go to Betsy's, then Maggie will meet you over there. Within a blink of an eye, four hours will have passed, and we'll be late for Beth's presentation." He kissed the top of my head and headed to the ensuite.

"Just a quick bite?" I grabbed a pair of brown knee-high leather boots to match the brown in the green and brown plaid of the skirt. Well, it was close enough to match. I pulled a cream blouse and a brown cardigan. Holding them up in front of me as I stood in front of the mirror, I thought I might pass for a sensible adult in that outfit. "Maybe we can pick something up at the drive thru?"

The toilet flushed and Henry raised his voice above the sound of the faucet running, "You know of all of the food of the twenty-first century that you could possibly eat, for the life of me, I cannot understand why you would choose to eat there." He turned off the water and made his way to the closet. My eighteenth-century husband, who somehow time traveled back-and-forth with me through two hundred and sixty years, stood there wearing lightweight blue pajama bottoms without a shirt. Wow! I'm a lucky woman.

I met the dashing Captain Lord Henry James Spencer, after I time traveled through a door at Fort Ashby, was taken hostage by a French military unit, headed by Ensign Jumonville and his lackey Bouchard. Well, I suppose I didn't find him very dashing when I met him. I had left Fort Duquesne, after escaping the French, and warned the colonial soldiers of the impending attack of the fort. Henry met me and Private MacDonald on the road. Everyone was my enemy at that point, it was a matter of who would beat me less, and who I could trust more. Henry never raised a hand to me. He thought I was a spy for the French. We spent most of the first week together with him interrogating me at every turn. Looking for me to slip up my story. I couldn't tell him that I had no clue how I ended up two hundred and sixty years into the past. Well, I suppose I eventually told him. We became great friends and confidants, and, eventually, we married in 1755.

In the 21st century, he isn't supposed to exist. He doesn't appreciate it when I call him an undocumented immigrant. I poke fun at him, it's one of those times he doesn't find me funny. But it's the unfortunate truth. No birth certificate. No passport. No social security card. No identification. According to the United States government, he doesn't exist. He owned a large tract of land and a beautiful home in Williamsburg. He was a captain, had employees, and held influence with Governor Dinwiddie. In my time, he can't hold a job, have a bank account, or use commercial transportation. He is completely reliant on me and the money I earn writing books. We do have a stash of gold and silver to move. Blackbeard's lost treasure that we hid in 1755 in Elizabeth

Wood's cellar in Fredericksburg. The cellar was two floors down from where I stood, as I debated shaving off all my hair or if I should wear my hair in a chignon for the day's event.

He pulled a pair of khaki trousers, a green button-up shirt, and his favorite dark brown sport coat. If I didn't know better, I would've sworn he planned coordinating outfits. "Are we going to look too matchy-matchy?" I said as I carried my clothes to the bathroom for my morning routine.

"It's our team uniform for the day. Team Spencer and all that comes with it." He laughed out loud. We didn't usually coordinate our outfits, it sometimes happened. I would joke it made us look like a sports team and one of us would change a shirt. Apparently, that wasn't going to be one of those outfit-changing days.

A few minutes later, I was dressed and twisting my wild, wavy hair back into a chignon. "Do you think I should get my hair cut?" I studied myself in the mirror, trying to slick down the flyaway hairs. No, no chignon. It made me look like Beth, my friend, and a university professor, with the outfit. I went with a thick braid that hung like a heavy auburn rope over my left shoulder.

"I'm quite fond of your long, wild hair," he said as he joined me in the bathroom. He ran a thoughtful hand on my head, down my braid, giving it a little flick between his fingers. He left his sport coat tossed on the bed. The dark green shirt played well with his blue eyes. He stood in front of his sink and pulled a hair tie out of his drawer. He pulled his brown hair back in a low-hanging ponytail, then pulled it out. It wasn't as much of a ponytail, as it was a little paintbrush of a ponytail. He gave his hair a bit of a ruffle as he added a little pomade through his locks and decided to wear it down. He made any hairstyle look good. Shortly after the last time I asked him to cut it, we slipped back to 1755, and he had to wear a wig when we went to events. That was nearly eight months ago. Wow! It seemed like a lifetime had passed. After that, he refused to cut his hair short again. I argued that we probably weren't going to time travel again. He argued that neither one of us can control when and where we travel, and it had only been four months since we returned to my time. As he saw it, we were due for a slip back to his time. He was correct on all accounts, whether I wanted to admit to it or not. It wasn't that I didn't want him to be correct, it's just that I hated being wrong. I knew I needed a coin and to walk through a door to move through time, but I had no control of when and where that would actually happen.

I stopped and watched him move and place his hair in just the right position—out of his face, but loose around the nape of his neck. A smile cracked in the corner of his mouth. "If you keep looking at me like that, we aren't going to make it to Beth's presentation in Jamestown."

"We could if I could figure out this time travel business. We spend the day in bed, travel to Jamestown, then travel back in time to the beginning of her presentation."

"It doesn't work that way; the time lords decide."

"How many times do I have to tell you, it's not time lords?" I laughed. "It's not the Doctor." I popped my vitamin in my mouth and took a swig of water from my water bottle.

"Doctor who?"

I snorted out a little bit of water from my nose. "Exactly!"

"I don't understand the humor in this. I asked which doctor you were referring to."

"No, you said Time Lord and Doctor Who. Specifically, Doctor Who is a time lord."

"Mayhap," he took a moment, "this Doctor Who, the time lord, can inform us on how to travel back to seventeen fifty-six."

My shoulders dropped. As funny as I found the conversation, it wasn't a game to him. "Oh, my love." I took a breath and his hand. "Doctor Who is a television show." He looked at me with slight confusion. He'd watch television a few times. The first time he traveled to my time he was slightly fascinated with televangelists. They reminded him of some of the ministers of the eighteenth century. This time we watched a few movies. The new Star Wars was one of my favorites, but the action, noise, and flying through space overwhelmed him. For entertainment, we thought it best to stick with books and break into the hidden room in the basement that hid Blackbeard's treasure. We bought the house as soon as we traveled to modern time. It was great luck that the previous owners were selling it. Maggie, my friend, owner of *By the River Bookshop*, and amateur sleuth, said the owners thought someone was trying to break into their house and decided to sell. Well, it wasn't me! I was stuck in the eighteenth century, dealing with war, drought, and Casper Teach trying to kill me. I had enough trouble without breaking into a house.

We walked downstairs and into the living room. I grabbed the remote from the coffee table, flipped the television on to BBC America and found an episode of Doctor Who. "Ah, Matt Smith, the eleventh Doctor. He's one of my favorites. Love his storyline with River Song." Henry looked at me in confusion. "His character regenerates." I went to the first episode for the season. "Each regeneration, you get a new doctor... tenth was David Tennant, eleventh was Matt Smith. Anyway, the Doctor is a time lord and travels through time and space in a T.A.R.D.I.S. that looks like a police box." I sat down next to Henry on the dark brown leather sofa across from the television. "Time is wibbly-wobbly, so he goes forward, back, and across the universes." Matt Smith pulled out his sonic screwdriver. "So, whenever you call the gods of time, or whomever is sending us through time, a time lord, I think of him." I held my hand out towards the television.

"How do you know it isn't real? It looks real. Aye?"

"But it's not. It's just a television show. Someone made it up."

"Your stories about what happened to us in the eighteenth century are real, but people think you made them up." He tilted his head like a curious little kitten. "How do you know there isn't a time lord out there making television shows about what happened to him?"

That left me speechless. My eyebrows stitched together in contemplation. My stories were real, but people thought they were just elements of my overactive imagination. Could a time lord exist and Doctor Who is his memoir? "Good point." I patted his knee and stood. "I'm going to have a quick yogurt and fruit before we go. Wanna a bowl?"

"Aye, please, good wife."

I wandered across the living room towards the back of the house where my large kitchen sat waiting for me to scrounge enough berries, from the mostly empty plastic containers, to make a quick breakfast. I used most of the berries the morning before to top my French toast. I scooped vanilla Skyr—an Icelandic-style yogurt—from a large tub, sliced a few strawberries, divided the last of the blueberries in the bowls, and topped both with toasted slivered almonds. It was like dessert for breakfast.

"We'll need to stop by the grocery store on the way home if we plan on eating tomorrow. This is the last of the berries, yogurt, and everything else." I handed him his bowl and sat on the sofa next to him, digging into my breakfast using caution so I wouldn't wear yogurt and berries down the front of my sweater. "Oh! We're out of coffee, so we'll need to stop by *Starbucks* on our way out. And don't forget I need to go to *By the River* to sign a few books and confirm for the new book signing next weekend." Henry sat with a dumbfounded look on his face. He hadn't touched the yogurt, he sat there holding the bowl. "What? Did I get yogurt all over my chin?" I wiped my hand across my chin and looked at it. Nope! No yogurt. "I thought you wanted yogurt. Can I get you something else? We don't have anything else. Maybe some oatmeal? I might have some Captain Crunch in the pantry, but you said it's too sweet and I only have almond milk, which makes you gag."

He sat back in the seat and stared straight ahead at the blue police box materializing on the screen. His chest rose and fell with a few deep cleansing breaths before he spoke, "Do you realize half of what you said is a lot to process? We need food. Whatever food I want. No need to wait for a harvest or someone to spend hours baking bread. It's just there. Need coffee? We drive next to a building, yell into a sign, pull around and someone hands us hot coffee, or cold coffee in your case. While we sit here and eat yogurt from Iceland and watch time lords on television." He turned and looked at me. "You make it seem so normal. It isn't normal for me. It's... it's..."

"Overwhelming." I finished his thought. I knew that feeling. "I'm sorry. I'll try to slow down. I get a bit wrapped up in the moment and forget this isn't normal for you." I chased a blueberry around my bowl with my spoon. *Ha! Caught it! You're mine! You little sweet berry of deliciousness.* "What if we take a little time after Beth's presentation on colonialism in the seventeenth century and just wander around the Jamestown settlement. It's a bit more primitive than when we were last there. They've gone a bit deep into history, founding settlement, and all that jazz. But it should be fun. They have a few ships there." He raised an adorable eyebrow at me. "Not that we can sail on them, but we can roam around them and kind of reminisce about that nauseating trip we took." I grabbed his hand. "What do you say? You, me, and a puke inducing ship?"

"I say, you have a strange way of looking for entertainment. Why not?" His face relaxed into a smile. "Mayhap, you can keep your breakfast on this ship."

CHAPTER NINE

"Cathy Stevenson!" I slammed the door behind me as I walked into *By the River Bookshop*. "Why are you in *my* shop?"

Her blond hair piled into a beehive on top of her head, could be seen from across three states. She was around my age, maybe a year or two older than my forty-one. But that hairstyle reminded me of my third-grade teacher from the mid-eighties. Missus Jackson was stuck in the fifties from the top of her beehive to her mid-calf length dress, with thick pantyhose, to the bottom of her padded slip-on loafers. It was outdated in the eighties; it was even more outdated forty years later.

"Oh, Amelia Murray." She pursed her obnoxiously red lips and tsked and shook her head. "Didn't you know? You're not the only author in Fredericksburg. There's quite a few of us. And this isn't *your* shop. It's Maggie's shop. If you would look around, maybe you would find a friend or two somewhere in the crowd instead of making enemies."

"The only enemy I have is you." I pointed a finger in her direction. I wondered if I could pierce her heart with it. "You're the Lex Luther to my Superman. The Doctor Evil to my Austin Powers. The Master to my Doctor Who. The sea to my old man. The Moby to my Dick. Wait a minute. I think I got that last one wrong."

Henry pulled my angrily pointed finger down and took a firm grip to my hand and gave it a squeeze. It pulled me out of my ferocious trance.

"Listen, Amelia," Cathy knew how to poke the bear. "I know you blame me for all your failings, but it really must stop. I've heard you tell everyone who will listen that I stole your publishing deal from the conference. Let's face it. A book about how to efficiently pack a suitcase wasn't going to make anyone rich. I know you were a travel blogger, and a post on packing should have stayed on the blog. That wasn't big five publisher material. No agent or publisher in their right mind was going to touch that book."

"You've written engaging books, have an agent, and are a best-seller," Henry interrupted the pot that was about to boil over again. He stood between me and the beast. I'm not sure if it was to protect her or me. "I think it's best we finish what we've come to do and get to the presentation. Aye?"

"Well, now. Who's your new friend? And how can we get to know each other better? You see how temperamental she is. Wouldn't you prefer me? I hear, gentlemen prefer blonds." She patted her beehive head.

Henry turned to Cathy. "I'd prefer it if you stepped out of our way. You want her and everyone else to believe it is she that is the problem. I saw the look you gave her when we walked through the door. Your horns are showing through the nest atop your head, Mistress Stevenson. With that, have a glorious day." He gave a small bow, wrapped his arm around my waist and led me out the door. Books would be signed another day. I was too upset to think straight, let alone see through the red that burned in me. We walked up the street back to the house to pick up the car. I needed that walk. The cool air helped cool my head.

"Your temperament had calmed since we had been back. Well, until today. What happened back there? You can't blame time travel on that scene you caused."

"I know, I know." My eyes burned with the threat of tears. "She just gets me so riled up. I don't know what it is about her or me, for that matter."

"Mayhap, it's time to think about moving if the threat of running into her in the bookshop is going to cause this to happen. It's unbecoming of you. You're better than that." He took my hand and placed it in the crook of his arm. "Would a cat calm your fire? We haven't picked one out. We can go look at the animal store or the dog and cat jail again."

I placed a death grip on his arm to steady my emotions. "No, it's against the universe's cat disbursement law."

"The... *what*?" His head snapped in my direction; eyebrows knitted in confusion.

"When the universe is ready for you to have a cat, one appears in your path." My eyes darted from side to side as I looked around the sidewalk as we walked up the street to our big white house on the corner. Small shops and homes, both new and from many years past, lined the roads. Some were standalone, many were connected in long rows. There was the occasional break between buildings, with a space leading to a courtyard in the back. A gate blocked off the path, keeping the contents out of reach for the passerby. A private oasis for the residents.

"No cats are crossing my path. Maybe the universe isn't ready for me to settle down." I sighed a heavy breath. "I'm uneasy, but it must be time to settle down. Perhaps, I would feel less agitated and ready to pounce all the time." I wanted to fall over from embarrassment, anger, and exhaustion from the scene I made at *By the River*. Ugh. I needed coffee.

Drive-thru *Starbucks* for an iced coffee for me, a Caffè Americano for Henry, a clear mind, and maybe a blueberry muffin sneaked in there, and we were on our way to the Jamestown Settlement. My good friend, Beth Bennedet, history professor at College of William and Mary, and the foremost expert on Colonial America, was giving a presentation that morning on life during the settling of Jamestown and how it impacted further colonization. We had helped fill in a few minor details about the period afterwards, having lived through some of it, and wanted to listen in.

We piled in with the rest of the group into the auditorium and spent the next hour listening to her, looking at slides and the reenactment on the screen. She paced a little on the stage, making sure she gave attention to both sides of the packed room. People queued up to microphones set up in the aisles. She fielded questions left and right. It was as though she had lived through it herself and was reliving it for the audience. I never sat in one of her classes. Sure, we sat across from each other, usually at *Betsy's Biscuits*, and discussed history over a pile of buttery biscuits and apple butter, but watching her work was fascinating. She was like the prima ballerina, and no one's questions were beneath her expertise.

A roar of applause filled the room, and the audience crowded the stage. I caught her eye and waved towards the rebuilt settlement. She nodded and would catch up to us later. I slipped my hand in Henry's, and we strolled out the auditorium and into the museum.

"Cheese and rice," I stood staring at the display in front of me. In a glass box was a wooden chair. There were metal clasps on the arms and near the feet, to clasp down someone's wrists and ankles. The sign at the base said, "Ducking chair." "Women shall be punished by... *ducking*? Are you kidding me? Why would any woman agree to come here if men treated them like that? That is barbaric!"

"Aye, it is," Henry brought the volume of his voice down, hoping I would follow suit. "You know from the eighteenth-century things were rough for women. You lived through that. These women had it worse, but they survived. You survived. And thankfully, it is better for you today than it was then."

"I suppose. But did you know that it was only within

the last one hundred years that women could vote? When I was born in the nineteen seventies, women still had to gain permission from their husbands to get credit cards." We strolled through the exhibit and headed down the hall towards the outdoor settlement. "And..."

"And if it wasn't for women like you to push and fight for freedoms, then you would still be considered secondary citizens. You might have made this argument before." Henry gave a small laugh. "What shall you do? Travel through time to make it happen sooner? Have a ducking chair for men instead?"

"No, nothing like that." We emerged from the darkened displays into the hall that led us to the settlement. The floor was tiled, and the wall to our right was made of windows looking out to a courtyard. I looked down and two shiny pennies sat in the middle of one of the dark brown tiles. "Find a penny, pick it up. And all the days, you'll have good luck." A smile crept across my face. I hadn't found a penny in what felt like forever. The only times recently that I found coins on the ground was when I was about to walk through a door and be thrust back in time. Not this time. The only doors around me were glass. I could see what was on the other side, and there weren't smoke or bright lights to whisk me away to two hundred and sixty years into the past. Near the two sets of automatic double glass doors was a smashed penny machine. "Oh, I used to love getting these as a kid."

"What is it?"

"You put a penny in the machine," I held up one of the pennies. "And it flattens it and imprints a design on it."

"Aye?" Henry stood in front of the five-foot-tall machine, looking at the mechanisms of wheels and gears.

"And does the design on it bring it more value?"

"You can't spend it, if that's what you mean."

"It says it costs one dollar." He pointed to the sign on the machine. "Let me try to understand this. You pay a dollar and insert your penny, only to receive a flat penny that no longer holds value?"

"Well, kinda. Sorta. It's a souvenir penny, just a cheap little way to remember a visit." I pulled out my debit card from the small purse which was slung across my chest.

"You're using your plastic money to purchase a penny that will no longer have the value of a penny?"

I shoved the card in the slot and slipped the penny into the coin slot. "Yup! And not only am I going to get a worthless, flat penny, but I'm getting you one as well."

"What am I going to do with a flat penny?" Henry said as I handed him the flattened penny with the imprint of Jamestown Settlement on it.

I smiled as I grabbed the second flattened penny out of the machine. "You're going to look at it in the days and years to come and remember the grand time we had together. That's what you're going to do with it. Now, stop your moaning, stick it in your pocket, and let's go explore the settlement."

The settlement was divided into separate sections. Down the dirt path to our right would take us through the Native American settlement of Paspahegh Town. To our left, the path would take us to the colonists' settlement of James Fort. We chose to take the Native American settlement path on our way to the place where we would see replicas of the *Susan Constant*, *Godspeed*, and *Discovery*, the ships which brought the settlers to the new world. The longhouses smelled of fire long extinguished, which reminded me of our visit to Tanaghrisson and his people. Henry and I had found a small child, Tomhas, and his murdered parents. I ended up handing the child over to a woman to raise. In turn, Tanaghrisson helped return my confiscated notebook, with dates and locations of George Washington's battles, away from Ensign Jumonville. Well, he returned my notebook after he took an ax to Jumonville's skull. It was something I never wanted to see again, but I was grateful for the return of my notebook. That was the last time I saw the half-king. He died later that year, and I never had the opportunity to properly thank him.

Over to the left side of the town, a man was carving a canoe out of a large log. He was burning part of it to hollow out the middle. We stood and watched him work for a few moments and wandered down towards the docks. Approaching the docks, we could see the three 1600s replica ships. "Let's go explore the ships," I said enthusiastically to Henry.

"Aye? I thought you didn't like ships."

"Well, these aren't going anywhere," I looked down at the sign to read about their voyage across the ocean. "They're docked and here for tourists, like us, to crawl around." We went down to the very end of the dock and walked up the plank to board the *Susan Constant*, the largest of the three ships. "See, we're not going anywhere. I can handle this. It's the rough waters from our trip on the *Alpheus* which caused me problems. That, and, I'd never been on a ship, or schooner. My equilibrium didn't know how to handle it."

Henry remained silent and followed me aboard the ship. We walked around the top deck, and he leaned his elbows on the rail, looking out into the water. "Do you miss it?"

"Aye. Can you smell it? Her scent is intoxicating." He inhaled deeply. "Can you feel the breeze wrap around you like a lonely mistress, aching for your return?"

"I thought I was the one with the flowery language." I smiled and nudged him with my hip as I leaned on the rail next to him. "I couldn't imagine what you went through, spending so much time, having the ocean rock you to sleep, night after night. Sailing with merchants turned pirates. I mean, you're such a mild-mannered Clark Kent kind of guy. Are you going to remove your glasses and fly off to sail the seas?"

"That is in my past. Over two hundred and sixty years in my past." He turned and pulled me in his arms and planted a warm kiss on my forehead. "You are my future, and it doesn't involve sailing ships and taking prizes."

We wandered to the front of the ship and down to the hold below. There was a door left ajar and curiosity got the better of me. "Is this the captain's quarters, do you think?" Henry was looking at a display of a cannon and cannonball, sizing it up for experience, I supposed. He looked over as I opened the door and popped inside to explore. The door shut behind me. The sweet smell of smoke filled the air. A bright light swirled in front of me, beckoning me to enter. A cold breeze embraced me. I knew what was happening, and for the first time I panicked. Really panicked. This couldn't happen to me. Not with Henry on the other side of the door. As I fell into the light, the door opened behind me. It was Henry, there to come with me or rescue me. He disappeared—or I disappeared, whichever it was—before he could reach me. It all went quiet and black.

CHAPTER TEN

"*A*melia," Henry grumbled out. His mind swam in circles, looking for answers to questions he'd yet to form. Running his hands across his face, he tried to make sense of his thoughts, he again realized he was with Amelia only moments ago when the tell-tale signs of traveling through time appeared before him and she disappeared into the bright light. He followed only seconds behind, the swirling bright light, smell of smoke, the cold breeze. He knew he traveled through time, that was the only answer that made sense. If one could call traveling through time sensible.

The wood planked floor rolled under him. No, not just the floor. It was the entire room which moved in rolling waves. He bolted into a seated position. The movement was all too familiar. He was aboard a ship. How? And where was Amelia? She traveled; he saw her disappear in the light. He ground his hands into his eyes to rub out the sleep. As his eyes went back into focus, he noticed the cabin he found himself in was of modest size, with walls painted white, the trim black, and a small bunk modestly outfitted. Nothing in the room gave indication to where—other than being aboard a ship—or when he ended up whenever he traveled.

He fought the exhaustion and the urge to crawl on the bunk and rest his eyes. He had three tasks on the forefront of his mind: find Amelia, food, and figure out where in the hell he was. First, assess his situation. He must be traveling with people; he could hear the footsteps thump on the ceiling. The ceiling would be the deck above. He scurried to the window on the outside wall, which was the back of the ship. Not a large ship, he thought to himself. The view out the window was nothing but ocean and blue open sky dotted with a white fluffy cloud here and there. Padding over to the set of doors to his right, he cracked one open then the other. Closets filled men and women's clothes from different eras. Jeans, dresses, kirtles, slacks, mantua, breeches, shirts of various colors and trends, and petticoats were all hung with care. A collection, of sorts. Nothing had been consistent, other than the constant confusion on what was happening.

He pulled in a lung full of salty ocean air and let it out slowly. There was no use in hiding in the cabin, at some point, he would be discovered, and would have to explain how he found himself on a ship, in the middle of the ocean. Where was Amelia? If she slipped through time on that ship, or another one, after managing her seasickness, she would barrel out of the cabin without thinking. Henry tried to get her to slow down and assess situations before jumping in without taking a second look. On board a ship, that would be a new set of challenges for her that he wasn't sure she would be able to handle. His stomach twisted in knots for Amelia and the situation ahead. He never worried about himself–or anyone else–until he met her, and not knowing if she was safe, weighed heavy on his soul. "She can handle herself," he muttered halfway under his breath, thinking that if he said it out loud, he would believe it to be true. He nodded vigorously and cleared his throat from the lump of emotion lingering behind his Adam's apple. "She survived Ensign Jumonville, General Braddock, nearly being killed on more than one occasion," said Henry, counting off the incidents on his fingers, "and traveled through time. She can handle a little ship."

Henry grasped the black doorknob staring at him, took a deep breath, let it out slowly, and turned the handle. When the door gently opened, he found a crew deck absent of the crew. It was a small deck, with four bunks on either side. Not a large crew. The size was reminiscent of the three masted schooners he had previously sailed on. There wouldn't be any hiding aboard the small vessel. A small galley stood at the opposite end of the ship, at the head. An oven stood in the center of the galley with counters lining the walls on the other side. Total width of the kitchen looked to be about 12 feet. Definitely a small crew. As he stood in front of the door of the cabin, a wooden ladder which led to the top deck, stood to his right. Another ladder and square port led to the top deck. It was closer to the head of the ship, near the galley, with a cover placed over it. There was only one way up or out, and that would take him to the heart of the ship in front of a manned tiller. He rolled his shoulders back, stood to his full six-foot height, ran his fingers through his brown hair, and climbed up the stairs one rung at a time, trying to delay the inevitable.

A salty breeze tickled his nose as he popped his head out of the square port. Henry held his hand over his eyes from the glare from the bright sun as it bounced off the white canvas sails and across the wooden deck. He ran his fingers through his breeze blown hair. Oh, how he had missed being onboard a ship. He glanced around to assess his environment. A schooner! He was on a schooner. The crew was as small as he had expected from seeing the crew quarters. A few men and the one that caught his attention, a woman dressed in all black from head to toe, with the only indication of being a woman was the curve of her breasts on her petite frame. The light brown skin surrounding her brown eyes and her hands were the only bits of skin showing.

He suffocated from his nervousness caught in his throat. He cleared his throat and came up with the best opening line he could think of, "Ahoy, lads." He turned to the woman at the helm. "And, my lady," he added with a tip of his head.

"Good to see you again, Henry," said the man with an Eastern European accent through his thick graying beard. He glanced away from a three-foot square crate on the deck, long enough to size up Henry. His focus went straight back to his task in the depths of the crate. His beard was trimmed and neat, and hung an inch or so past his jawline, matching the wisps of gray at the temples of his dark brown hair. He was dressed much like he had seen men during Amelia's time. Those infernal cargo pants which Amelia insisted he wear. There were too many unused pockets creating bulk. Henry wore them once and decided he would wear a simpler pair of shorts. She complained there were not enough decent pockets in women's clothing, so she tried to overcompensate by insisting he have cargo shorts, cargo pants, jackets with pockets on the breast sides, and insides. It was all too much. Considering he didn't have anything to carry in them, it seemed a waste. Amelia used a card—which he still didn't understand how the little piece of plastic communicated between the shops and the bank to purchase all their goods. She didn't trust coins and doors together. Yet, her little souvenir she bought out of the machine at Jamestown was a coin, Which, by the way, she insisted didn't count as a coin by the time it was smashed. It was enough to transport Henry to this ship. *Where did it transport Amelia?*

Wait! Did he just call him by his name? *See you again?* Henry was certain that was the first time they met. He pondered on trying to play off the familiarity or if he should admit if they had met. He didn't remember them. "Mayhap," he began and took a pause. "Mayhap, could you remind me where we've met?"

Cargo Shorts stopped mid-rifling, gulped down, and eased himself into a standing position. "You're named Henry? Huh, what do you know?" A panicked look was exchanged between him, and a Spaniard man dressed in black breeches and a white flowy shirt. The Spaniard dropped the rope he was securing, and the sail slipped down the mast. Henry reached out to grab the thick rope but missed it all together. Wooden mast hoops slapped down one on top of the other. Henry's eyes squeezed tight, and his shoulders went to his ears with every thwack. A man dressed in all white with a very large cat, sat on a crate near the head of the ship. He uncrossed his legs, calmly stood with his bare feet on the deck, and walked towards the group, with the cat close to his heels.

The people on the ship appeared to come from all corners of the world. Henry opened his mouth to comment on the sudden dismissal of familiarity, when a parrot swooped down from the top of the mast and called out, "Back to the circus. Back to the circus." The vibrant red and green specimen landed on Henry's left shoulder. "Back to the circus."

"Ahoy, bird." Henry reached up to run a finger over its head.

"Sam," called the woman at the tiller. "Her name is Sam."

"Ahoy, Sam." A smile cracked across Henry's face. As many times he had been at sea, he had never met such a beautiful and, seemingly, smart bird.

The man dressed in white approached with his tan and black cat. Henry recognized the characteristics of him being from the Far East. He met many men from all over the world when he traveled around with merchant ships and maybe a pirate ship or two before landing in Virginia. It was a difficult time in his life when he fled England to get away from his brother. He hoped to never set foot on the island again.

"Welcome aboard the schooner *Gretchen*," he said as he placed a hand over his heart and gave a slight bow of his head. "I'm Richard and this is Starboard." He presented the cat with a wave of his hand. She sauntered over to Henry. Starting with her cheek, she rubbed down the length of her body to her hind quarters on Henry's leg. Tan hairs left behind from Starboard nearly disappeared on his khaki trousers.

"She's a very large cat." Henry reached down to pet her. She shot a disapproving look then came back for another pass along his leg.

"You didn't ask permission. Cats are good at teaching boundaries." Richard crossed his arms across his chest as he watched Starboard leave another coat of hair on Henry's khakis. "There. Now, ask her for permission."

Henry's eyebrows stitched together, as he relaxed them, he said, "With your permission, Miss Starboard." He put his hand near her. With an approving purr-meow, she allowed him to stroke her back and give a good scratch behind her ear before she bounded back to the head of the ship. She stretched out in the warm sun and slowly closed her eyes.

CHAPTER ELEVEN

"*A* week!" Henry exclaimed. "I've spent more than my share on ships. I shan't..." Henry caught himself mid-outburst and took in a deep cleansing breath. "Apologies," he said, tipping his head to the crew of the *Gretchen*. "It seems as though time travel has left my mood less than desirable." He rubbed his tortured brow. When he traveled through time before it was abrupt. No time to think about moving through hundreds of years to the past and future. It just happened. Being told he was to travel a week with the crew, not knowing where and when he was going to be left, it all was difficult to grasp.

Richard, dressed in white linen pants and shirt, walked over from his seat at the head of the ship. "We will work on finding your balance during your stay with us."

"Why a week?" Henry's voice continued to drip with agitation. "I need to find Amelia."

Richard put a gentle hand on Henry's shoulder and led

him to the side of the ship. The ocean's expanse laid before them–deep blue water met the blue sky, pricked with fluffy white clouds. "We escort many people to their destinations. For most it is the first time traveling through time. The beings or gods, which control time travel, choose to give the person a week to come to grips with their situation."

"What about the times Amelia was thrown through time? They just threw her into a new time. There was no coddling." He was angry. Previous travels through time seemed to have a purpose. As he stood there next to Richard, his thoughts bounced around. Why here? Why now? What was he supposed to do? And most of all... where was Amelia? It didn't make any sense to travel without her.

"Yes," Richard said with a slow nod. "There are times when people go through rips in time without the privilege of our transportation and guidance. And from what you've told us, Amelia experienced it without a guide and survived. Some don't."

A smile crept across Henry's face, full of pride and appreciation of his wife's struggles and her fortitude to overcome the spears thrown at her. "She is made of tough material—tougher than most, I would say." He reflected on the obstacles she overcame over the years. Beginning from her time growing up with half-absent parents and their disappearance, Todd's murder, raising a daughter on her own, and through trials of time travel. He worried for her wellbeing and safety but knew she would find a way to get through it. Most of all, he wanted to be with his dearest friend and experience the wonders and adventures that lay ahead together.

"Henry," Richard put his hand on Henry's shoulder, pulling him out of his deep thoughts of Amelia. They continued to stare into the blue expanse. "Time travel is never without a cost."

With a furrowed brow, Henry said, "Exhaustion, hunger, confusion, and not knowing why we're sent there. Isn't that payment enough? We didn't ask for this." The fire in him stoked.

"The quick anger you experienced earlier can become worse—much worse. To the point where it can be irreversible or unconstrained. The same will go for your wife, Amelia."

"Aye." Henry stood silent for a moment, racing through his memories of recent events. "That wasn't the first time I struggled with my patience. Cathy Stevenson's comments to my wife... well, I must say my patience waned."

Richard responded with thoughtful elegance, "Patience can bring peace to us and prevent our destruction." He slowly turned towards Henry. "And, sometimes, people need a firmer hand. From what I know of you, I suspect this woman, Cathy Stevenson, knows how to nudge, even the most patient of people, to the point of outburst."

"Have you given instruction to Amelia? She's crossed back-and-forth through time, more than I have."

"Although I cannot say much, as your friend, I will tell you that her path hasn't crossed mine."

"How well do you know me?" Henry lifted a curious eyebrow at Richard. "Rick slipped up when I came aboard, and you've mentioned we are friends. So, I figure that this isn't the first time we've met."

"As Rick said, this is the first time you met us. Which, by and large, is more than he or I should have said to you." He patted Henry on the shoulder and walked towards the port to the decks below. "You will learn, with practice. One week." He looked towards the bow of the ship. Starboard stretched her body out. One rear leg, then the next, and strutted to Richard, adding a couple long stretches along the way. "Let's get you something to eat. Fish?"

"Back to the circus," called out Sam, as she flew a circle around the ship over the water and swooped down landing on Richard's shoulder. Her vibrant green and red feathers glowed in the noonday sun.

"And you as well."

With lunch being made and Jasmine at the helm, Henry headed down to assess the goods from the crate Rick was head-deep in when he arrived. Apparently, the crate was found floating in the ocean at the same time Henry woke up in the cabin. The crates didn't always arrive at the same time as the traveler. Sometimes before, sometimes after, sometimes it came from a shipwreck, and other times the travel through time was only months or a few years that the traveler received nothing. Always, supplies to feed the crew, including Sam and Starboard. There was never time to fish, as they were always on the move. Even when they got near land, unless it was their time to leave the crew, they couldn't step foot on the sandy shores or touch the warm docks leading to the town. If they encountered another ship, they couldn't cross over the gangway unless they were meant to leave with that crew. Richard was the only one to have seen other members of the crew leave. Time isn't linear for the crew of the Gretchen. They travel back and forth through time, without a seemingly rhyme or reason, as they await their end of the service to the gods. The entire crew had a tragic story of the moment they were pulled from their time, as they were about to be killed. Their gods took mercy and allowed them to earn an extended lifetime by serving the ship, and then when their time was up, they would be released. Henry tried to understand how they would know when it was their time to move on, but the only response was Jasmine's quippy, "Oh, we'll just know."

"Back to the circus. Back to the circus." Sam flew frantically around the ship. Circling and calling out, drawing the crew's attention. "Back to the circus."

Henry ran to the starboard rail, white knuckling his grip. In the distance a speck of a ship appeared, raising its flag. He snapped his head back towards Rick. "No worries, Spencer," Rick said, looking at Henry from around his spyglass, and promptly returning to gauge the ship on the horizon.

A boom let out as the ship changed course in a direct line to meet with the *Gretchen*.

"Can we outrun her?" Henry asked. He ran his hand over the cold sweat across his brow.

"Schooners are fast, but we're a small crew. They may

have consorts close by." Rick shook his head. His mouth narrowed. "Flag's French. Ship of the line. She's got more firepower than we can handle."

"Is that a good thing or..." Henry searched Rick's face for an indication of the verdict.

Rick shrugged. "I don't know, man. You haven't been with us a week. It's always a week."

"Mayhap," Henry paused to sort and file alternative solutions. His time with a merchant ship, and later aboard a pirate ship, afforded him the knowledge that this situation screamed danger. "Mayhap, they will pass information or look for information. Clearly, we are but a small vessel and crew."

"They cannot board," Richard joined the men at the rail.

The large ship continued to close the distance between the ships. A rolling thunder clapped behind them, sending Jasmine a mile high off the deck. When she planted her feet back on the deck and her heart returned to a somewhat regular beat, she locked the tiller into place using a rope and pulley system. A loop of rope was slid over the tip from one side of the system, and another loop from the other. She then secured another loop over a peg attached to the side of the ship, locking the entire system into place. She scurried over to the men. Sam finished another rotation around the ship and landed on top of Jasmine's zukin, the black hood she wore when she dressed as a ninja. Ominous, black billowing clouds rolled and collided before nearly swallowing the Gretchen whole. Winds whipped the sails and sent a vicious snap through the air. The ship continued its interception.

"Wind is picking up," said Jasmine. Henry couldn't ignore the tinge of worry hanging off her words. "We need to prepare the ship."

Rick nodded. "Within the hour, is my guess."

"They'll be within range sooner than that."

The crew of the *Gretchen* began to quickly move about the ship.

"I thought you said we'd be protected." There was no hiding the concern in Henry's voice. "Gods and all that."

"We need to reef the sails," Cristobal shouted to Henry.

Richard raced past Cristobal and Henry, and nearly flew down the hatch to secure Sam and Starboard in the crew quarters below.

With a nod, Henry ran to the main sail and began releasing the halyard. Jasmine ran back to the tiller, her delicate hands held steady, using the pulley system to help her maintain balance and heading.

Swells of the angry ocean made the ships lean to port, starboard, bow, and aft. There was no time to feel nauseous from the movement of the ocean. The crew fought to stay aboard the schooner, as they slid along the deck with the swells. Jasmine roped her body. One rope stretched from the port side and looped around her waist, the other from the starboard side, keeping her centered at the tiller. When a wave hit and she lost footing, a rope kept her in place. Her only duty was to keep the ship moving towards their destination.

Henry fought the pelts of rain and smacks from waves while helping to secure the rigging. As he released a sail from its taut position on the center mast, he glanced over to the ship on the horizon. They were caught in the raging storm, halting their advance and ability to fire the cannons. *Survive the storm. Survive the storm.* Another wave crashed into the side of the *Gretchen*. It leaned hard to the port side. Henry's feet gave from under him. Falling to his knees, he reached out for any post, rope, or barrel to keep him from sliding down the deck and joining the crew of Davy Jones. He continued to slide down the tilted deck with nothing to grab ahold of in his path. The dark gray waves licked frantically towards him, ready to devour him for eternity.

This wasn't the first time he had been caught in a storm at sea, and truth be told, he was never afraid of the outcome. Until now. He didn't want this to be the end, without ever seeing Amelia again. He knew their story had only begun. As the rail got closer, he readied his body to grab the rail. He reached up his arms, his feet about to either hit the rail or slip over into the next wave. A sudden jerk at his wrist radiating to his shoulder caused him to look away from the storm raging below him and towards his salvation. The tip of his toes searched for sure footing on the rail only inches below his dangling feet. At the end of his hand, he found Richard. The rain made their grasp slick and desperate.

"Hold tight," Richard yelled to Henry. "Give me your other hand."

Henry brought his right hand to Richard's, but it was

no use. Pain shot through his shoulder just below his right clavicle from his bullet wound he received during Braddock's march to Fort Duquesne. The bullet tried to kill him and left him in the hospital for a week was of no use. Pain and frustration left him weak.

Another wave shoved and pushed the ship in the opposite direction. Henry whipped and bucked as he slid toward the starboard side. Hands were too slick from sweat, salt water, and the rain that continued to pelt down. That was it. He was about to be thrown overboard. There was only one thing left for him to do, he closed his eyes to picture... "Amelia," he said softly, and he conjured her image from his memory. It brought him peace, love, and sadness from not being able to hold her one last time. She lost one husband and survived. She will survive without Henry as well. As he sucked in the last bit of air before hitting the cold water, the thrashing of the *Gretchen* stopped. With a smack of his hands on the deck, he closed his eyes and thanked the gods and universe that he may survive long enough to see Amelia again.

Battered and broken, the other ship sat still with broken masts and a tattered crew. Jasmine took a deep breath and a wide berth around the debris field. No time to stop and even with a crew left in shambles, they were too dangerous and not part of their mission.

Henry watched the crew of the French vessel scramble about the deck. Even if they were to lob a cannonball in their direction, they wouldn't be able to chase them down. They were dead in the water, and Henry felt no obligation to change course to help. Amelia wasn't on that ship, and she was his only focus.

"Back to the circus," Sam squawked out as she emerged from the crew quarters and flew around the *Gretchen* assessing the state of her domain. The schooner suffered no damage, except to Henry's nerves. "Back to the circus."

CHAPTER TWELVE

The large 46-gun frigate dwarfed the schooner. It's three nearby consorts didn't do the *Gretchen* any favors either. They could easily take the schooner within a blink of the eye. Henry's stomach tightened. He knew being pressed into service was highly likely. As he was no longer in his own time, nor a captain in the army, he feared the worst was upon him. Rick mentioned it made no difference where the traveler wanted to go, only that when they got to their intended location, it would be clear. Pressed into service or return to England? Neither one whetted his appetite.

"Ahoy," Henry called out with a wave. Better make this the best possible situation for himself. Jasmine edged the faster and nimble *Gretchen* closer to the large ship. The ship's hulls creaked and groaned as they closed in together. Henry looked to Rick as he stood shoulder-to-shoulder with him, offering support. Rick dressed in clothes to match Henry's, with the addition of a more flamboyant coat. The coat was a dark blue with trim of white and gold. His cocked hat sported more gold trim. "Pulling out the dignified ensemble over your cargo shorts?" Henry elbowed Rick in jest. He was making light of the situation, while he felt Rick's heavy demeanor. Rick transported many people over his time in service, if he reeked of concern, Henry worried about what lay ahead.

"Remember, we're supposed to meet again. Don't go and get yourself killed or do anything stupid." Rick tugged at the edging of his coat, pulling it taut. "Besides, if this is who you're supposed to go with, maybe they'll know where to find Amelia."

"You're sure about this?" Henry glanced over at Rick, who cut his focus on the scurrying about the ship in front of him and looked at Henry. He opened his mouth to speak with the thud of a plank landing on the rail startled the men.

"Something doesn't feel right about this, but neither one of us can change your mission."

"It would be nice if I knew what that mission was." Henry straightened his satchel, heavy with clothes and supplies.

"Maybe you're just supposed to find your way to Amelia?"

"Mayhap. And you're positive you've not transported her?"

"Not yet, my friend. You know there is no guarantee that we ever will." Rick gave Henry a hearty clasp on his shoulder. Henry pursed his lips and gave a couple quick nods. "Until the next trip."

Henry walked to the long slab of wood with roped rails straddling the ships. He wiped his hands on his breeches, pulled himself up to the gangway, and began his ascent up to the ship. He racked his thoughts of how he was going to convince this crew to provide him transport to wherever they were headed.

He stood at the end and looked back towards the mighty crew of Gretchen, raised his hand in farewell, and swallowed the lump of fear caught in his throat. "Lord Captain Henry James Spencer, nephew to the Duke of Marlborough." He found it best to keep his connections to his family obscure. He couldn't be certain, but he thought his grandfather could be the current duke, by the looks of the dress of the men. Although not much had changed in sailor wear since he was onboard ships, his last being the *Constance* with Captain Woods. The odds of direct relations on the ship were low. "Where are you bound?"

"Spain, my lord," answered the man. He was close to Henry's age of seven and thirty, and three or four inches shorter than Henry. He was thick in the middle and dressed easy for his position, not the refined dressing Henry expected of a captain of a warship.

Henry turned towards Rick standing at the rail of the *Gretchen*. "Spain, Captain," he called over to Rick. The men gave a knowing nod. He raised a hand of farewell to the crew of the *Gretchen* before turning back towards the man. "Are you the captain of this fine vessel?"

The jolly man whose face had seen many years at sea, replied with a chortle, "Nay, my lord. Henry Avery, first mate on the *Charles the second*. Captain Gibson has taken to his quarters."

Henry wracked his brain trying to place the year with an English King Charles II, to no avail. The first mate's name was familiar, although Henry couldn't place it. The conversation lingered longer than Henry would have liked. A nagging concern for his friends onboard *Gretchen* grew as more men onboard the *Charles II* amassed around the chatting duo. "The ship is named after an old Scots King?"

"No, the Spanish King, my lord," Avery's laugh was joined by the laughter of others milling about close to the second mate.

Henry's eyes shifted around to the crowd as he continued to stand at the end of the gangway, swaying back-and-forth between the ships, with every wave and breeze. He didn't see the humor in not knowing the ship filled with Englishmen was named after a Spanish king but didn't think standing around arguing over the reasoning made sense either. "Permission to come aboard and travel with you to Spain, Mister Avery?" Henry Spencer glanced over the edge of the gangplank at the frigid, choppy waves smacking the hulls of the ships. "Make haste before a swift wind has me swimming with Davy Jones."

Avery nodded, put out a welcoming hand, and said "I'm sure we can find a spot for a lord among the crew."

"Aye?" Henry raised an eyebrow as he hopped down from the gangway. Men scurried over and began unhooking the end that was secured on the railing. Henry took a step over to the side as men focused on their tasks and nudged Henry out of the way. "I am to meet with

Captain Gibson at the earliest opportunity. And what is the purpose of the voyage to Spain?"

"Make sail!" Avery shouted to the crew. He flicked his head to the side, indicating Spencer to follow. "We are to contract with the Spanish as privateers against the French in the Caribbean." Henry Spencer clasped his hands behind his back, giving him an air of importance and dignity. Spencer and Henry Avery continued to walk towards the helm.

If Amelia was there, the only proper response would be... *cheese and rice*. "I'll never hear the end of this from my wife," Henry said as he placed his disapproving hands on his disapproving hips. Amelia might find it amusing that Henry ended up on a privateer ship, but he had lived that life before. She mentioned settling down, cats, and growing old together. There was no mention of pirating. Privateering was government sanctioned pirating. Letters of marque were dependent on the country issuing against the country to have its ships plundered. He turned his head back towards the *Gretchen*, already on her way out to pick up another time traveler. "Do we have a letter of marque?"

"Ah, you're familiar with privateering."

"Aye, I've sailed from here to there and around a bit." Henry scanned the group, looking for any familiar faces. None stood out. He still didn't know what year he was in and if he would've recognized anyone, or if they recognized him. "My transport ship, the *Gretchen*, was bringing me back to England from Virginia. I've lost track of the date."

Men scurried about the deck. Henry watched a man

dressed in mid-calf breeches, a dirty white shirt, and barefooted, run by with a bucket of water.

"We left London in August. It's now February. We should've been in Spain months ago," said Avery. "Will you not be missed in England? Spain is in the opposite direction, my lord."

"Aye. When I saw your squadron in the distance, I knew we were destined to meet. One of the issues of being an unsettled lord. Always looking for the next titillation." Avery nodded in knowingly response. "It's only a two-week journey from London, you've gone on five months now. Why wouldn't you have turned around and waited for better weather?"

Avery looked over the rail they had leaned against, looking for a mermaid or a way out of the conversation. "The men are paid for their duties on ship, not sitting in a tavern in London." Avery stood tall and looked at the crew. "You tell me, Lord Henry, do you believe any of these fine men sail around looking for their next titillation?" That comment sucker punched Spencer in the gut. "Nay, they look for the pay to support themselves and their families. No sailing. No pay. Families will be looking to receive their six months' pay by the time we get to Spain."

Desperate men desperate for pay. Spencer understood their plight. However, his concern over their terrible luck lingered. Was the sea trying to foretell their future? Five months to travel a distance that should've been two weeks. He glanced over his shoulder in the direction of the *Gretchen*. It was only a speck on the horizon. Not even cannon fire could get its attention. As the ship sailed towards the setting sun, it disappeared in a flash of green light. Spencer looked around to the quizzical faces of the crew wondering, no doubt, why he would want to join them. Did they see the green flash? They all seemed too interested in Spencer to notice the flash.

"Rethinking your decision to join us?" laughed Avery.

Henry thought through his answer before letting out a peep. "I believe your luck has turned fortuitous with my joining of the crew." Spencer scanned the men working around the deck. "Swift winds will carry us to Spain." He nodded. "Now, when may we find proper accommodations for me?" He adjusted the strap on his satchel. "At least a place to secure my belongings."

"Aye, we'll see if we can get a bunk with the officers." Avery slapped Spencer on the shoulder.

CHAPTER THIRTEEN

"*A*very," Spencer called out to the first mate of the *Charles*, standing near the helm, watching the men laze about the deck, the sun cresting over the noonday.

Avery looked over his shoulder.

"Aye, Spencer," he replied. His energy from dealing with the complaints of the sailors took its toll. "If you're here to make a formal complaint, I'm well aware."

"Aye and nay," Henry said, stepping over to Avery, standing shoulder to shoulder, as they both looked over the pathetic lot of men, including themselves in the pathetic lot. "You and I know restless men can bring on trouble. Mayhap, we should discuss the situation with a few trusted individuals that you mentioned the other night."

"Mutiny could get you killed and then you'll never see that little wife of yours."

"Mayhap yay or nay, but you heard them. The

company sold the crew to the Spanish for all the days of our lives. We were to be privateers, not enslaved to the Spanish."

"You were to be transported on your own accord, and somehow you've ended up standing next to me discussing such treasonous acts in the open."

"You could feign innocence. If you hadn't strongly considered mutiny, I don't think you would've told me." Henry's eyes shifted, looking for big ears amongst the group. "You understand, if we're to act, the men will need a leader, a captain."

"Aye, they will." Avery stroked his beard. The course threads tickled his palms. "We still have Captain Gibson aboard. Deep in the drink, as he may be. Are you suggesting you want the position? The men like you well enough, but do you want to take on the responsibility."

"Heavens above, no," Henry said in a surprised shout. Much louder than he intended. "I'll leave the leading of a pirate crew to you. I just want to make a house with my wife and raise kittens." Avery gave Spencer a quizzical look at the raising kittens remark.

"When you find the slippery minx," Avery laughed out.

Spencer joined the laugh. Avery had no idea how quickly Amelia could slip through time. It reminded Spencer of their night of the ball at Governor Dinwiddie's palace in Williamsburg, after their defeat at Fort Necessity. Amelia had accepted his proposal, and they sneaked out the back garden drunk on wine and lust. The festivities had them back at Spencer's house, and she was to go to her bed chambers to prepare for the night. Spencer waited and closed his eyes to rest, for what he thought would've been a rambunctious event. When the sun crept through his bedroom windows and welcomed him to a hangover and a new day, he realized Amelia hadn't come back or she couldn't wake him. He searched her room, the grounds, Williamsburg, and all of Virginia for her. No one had seen or heard of her whereabouts. A gripping crush destroyed Henry's heart for a time. He found only sickening disappointment and sorrow at the bottom of every bottle of wine and spirits. It was only months later when he found her running from Bouchard in the streets of Alexandria, when he discovered she hadn't wanted to leave him, but had been swallowed by the rip in time.

He had to keep that to himself. He also kept the fact that he knew Avery was to become the famed pirate king. Was this the triggering event? He finally understood the weight Amelia carried on her shoulders when she slipped through time. If only he could find her. She had to be somewhere in Spain. Why else would he be sitting with the crew in A Coruña's harbor, waiting on a letter of marque from Madrid that never appeared. If they didn't act soon, they would be slaves on Spanish ships, instead of gaining wealth as privateers in the Caribbean.

"We should act soon, captain," Henry said with a knowing tilt of his head.

Avery chuckled. "I'm not a captain."

"Yet."

"Aye, we'll see. I would rather be on our way, than the captain."

"We need to send a message to the other men. We need to coordinate if we are to be met with the least resistance."

"I have men I trust."

Henry Spencer pointed towards the shore, as if he were giving commentary on which taverns served the finest food and the finest brothels. "We only need a couple from each ship to spread the news."

"Aye," Avery answered. He pointed to the other side of the harbor, pointing out the taverns with the food and the brothels to avoid. Spencer nodded in response. "I'll get a message to my trusted men on the other ships, then we'll sail into town and gather men for our redistribution of freedom."

"Captain Gibson is laid up in bed again."

"You mean, he's drunk in his cabin again," replied Avery, his voice heavy in disappointment with the captain. He spent more days laid up in his cabin than he did commanding the ship.

"Aye, tis true." Spencer ran a hand over his scruffy jawline. He wondered what Amelia would think if he grew out a beard. Amelia. He had to believe she was safe. "We'll be well on our way before he realizes what occurred under his nose."

Avery nodded a silent response. Spencer sensed Avery had been thinking about this since the first letters from home arrived stating Mister Houblon refused to pay the half-year pay to the families back in London. Mayhap, he thought about the contingency before they set sail. When he began to hatch the plan, it made no difference. They were about to be eyeballs deep in it.

Avery, Spencer, Stock, and Gunn lowered a pinnace and rowed towards A Coruña. It was common enough for the men to row ashore for supplies and a night drinking, although they were running low on money.

"I heard from Lewis, Admiral O'Byrne is due to sleep ashore tomorrow night," grunted Stock between the deep rows.

Henry looked back at the *Charles II*, *James*, *Dove*, and the *Seventh Son*. No sign of suspicion. No warning shouts. He needed to grab hold of the nerves twisting his guts. "We need to make sure we have a crew first." Henry spun back around looking ahead at the city quickly approaching. "The four of us could disappear through the winding streets but wouldn't get far trying to crew even the *Seventh Son*." He thought about the tiny crew of the *Gretchen*, navigating the ocean with a crew of four. They had gods on their side. With the way the trip had been for O'Byrne's crew, they didn't have fortune on their side. The gods tried to prevent the travel, but the need for a paycheck drove the men forward. Four months later, and at last they were about to take control of their future and fortune. At least, that is what Henry hoped would happen. He wasn't sure if this was the triggering event for Avery and his journey to become a legend. Spencer's push for Avery to lead the campaign, could have been a push in the wrong direction. What if it was to happen later? No. The time was upon them. Spencer had to believe that to be true.

Before we land and spread out, we know not everyone will want to join us."

"Aye," Avery nodded. "Don't go running your mouths without knowing if they will join us." He looked over towards Stock, who was slowing his row as they were entering deeper into the harbor. Castillo de San Anton stood watch to their right. Cannons stood by the ready atop of the stoned structure. Avery noticed Spencer's eyes shifting from the fort to the shore, and another glance back to the ships. "We will come up with a code to let the ones that will join us know it is time. Stop your worry; it will bring us the luck of the devil."

"Right," Spencer nodded. "Right. Mayhap?" He paused for a moment and looked at the patience level of the men beginning to falter. "Well, we can't say, 'hey we're having a party over on the *Charles*, send over your party animals,'" he huffed out.

"Nay. You're correct." The scratch of Avery's firm hand running across his scruffy face was louder than the breeze and the squawk of the seagulls.

"Why not?" Gunn asked in his baritone voice. The Nordic giant was sincere in his question. His voice could intimidate a miser to hand over his coins, and Spencer was pleased to have him on their side and the mission to recruit a crew. "What if we tell them to send over their drunkest sailor. If they are part of the plan, they will know it's time."

"And if not?" asked Stock. "They'll know something is amiss."

"They will believe we are asking in jest and send us on our way." Gunn dug deep into the row, launching them swiftly across the water. Stock pulled out of his faraway daze where he played the scenarios through his head and joined the work of rowing to shore.

Spencer tilted his head back-and-forth contemplating Gunn's suggestion. "Aye, that could work." He nodded agreeing with himself. "What say you, Mister Avery?" He looked over Gunn's shoulder at the dock quickly approaching.

"Aye. This better work, or I fear O'Byrne will have us hang from the gallows."

"If it does work and we are caught, O'Byrne will have us killed before we reach the gallows," Gunn added. The men took in the conversation and the remainder of the journey in somber silence.

Gunn and Stock pulled in the oars as they eased next to the dock and tied up the small boat. Spencer caught the worry that crept in the corner of Avery's mouth. The slight twitch was his tell-tale sign. "It will work," Henry said as he pulled himself out of the boat and landed his boot on the wooden dock. They found a spot close enough to shore to tie up so they would be in town within a few strides.

"We meet back here at seven. That will give us enough time to be back aboard ship." Spencer looked at the men. "Avery, you're with me. Gunn, Stock, best to stay in a pair. You know how the Spaniards feel about us in town."

"Aye, unless we're spending the money we don't have, they will run us out," said Avery, climbing out of the boat and reaching a hand back to Spencer. "Pay mind that we are gathering our crew, not spreading word to big ears." Avery tapped his right ear with his index finger.

The men gave a nod and scurried off down the dock and to the left. Spencer and Avery strolled down the docks as if they were out for a stroll, wanting to feel the steady land off the *Charles*. Spencer felt the weight of his sword along his left leg and fought the urge to touch the handle. When he strolled through the twisted streets of A Coruña, he ground down on his teeth, waiting for someone to tire of the English on the shores. His money which was sent with him from the crew of the *Gretchen* was quickly diminishing, which added to the tension held from the top of his head down to his toes. He fought against the Spanish after he sailed from England, now he walked through enemy territory. Could they sense his unease? A gray-haired man, carrying a large basket on his twisted shoulder, knocked into Spencer's arm, as if he was a ghost. Spencer held his feet firm and his shoulders back, not wanting to back down from the aggressive stance the old man took towards him. He was a lord, after all, born and raised to be better than the old fisherman. Spencer shook his head. He reminded himself of Richard's teachings during his trip on the *Gretchen*. Time travel can change thoughts and emotions. No one goes through time again and again unscathed. A deep breath to calm the flick of a flame that began to burn. He turned around to help pick up the basket, only to be met with a firm hand on his elbow.

Avery looked at the old man and back at Spencer, and said, "Leave him. He'll pay mind where he walks next time."

Spencer hesitated, while looking at the man

surrendering to the task of picking up the few fish that flopped out during the collision. The mess wasn't as bad as he had expected. He fought the urge to help, turned around, and continued to walk down the stone path to one of the taverns where Englishmen from the ships congregated.

The buildings were a mixture of stone and wood. Tall and squat. Churches and taverns. Priests and prostitutes. Families and the lonely beggars. The elements came together to form the town that held the Englishmen hostage on their ships. Stuck in purgatory, between three hells—the business owners, the Spaniards taking them as slaves on their ships, and the life of piracy. Only one of those choices was the lessor of the hells, and Spencer hoped he would survive it.

Down the windy street, loud conversation, laughter, and music poured out *of La Estrella Blanca -The White Star*. Spencer's hand found its way to the hilt of his sword. The reassurance that he knew how to use it was overpowered with the thought that he might have to put his skills to the test. From the corner of his eye, he noticed Avery had the same thought cross his mind.

"We're here to count our numbers," Avery said over his shoulder to Spencer.

Spencer took a deep, controlled breath, "Aye. Let's make a crew."

Avery nodded and pushed the door open.

CHAPTER FOURTEEN

$\mathscr{T}$he stench of smoke from lard candles and tobacco pipes swirled and mixed with the stench of stale ale, smacked the men in their face as they stepped into the chaos of the tavern. Men sat around tables as though they had no worries in the world. Women dressed in white shifts low on their cleavage and skirts pinned up to expose the curve of their calves. Tendrils of hair fell loose and tempted the men to tuck the wayward locks behind their ears. One of the women looked over to Spencer and Avery as they walked in, cutting a sly smile in their direction. Spencer took a step in and stopped. He cleared his throat and leaned close to Avery's ear. "Recruit and move on. No time to dawdle with the señorita."

"You are reminding me or yourself?"

"Both."

The men scanned the room, looking for friendly faces in the growing crowd of men. They would need to return to the ship soon before it got too dark. In the corner Locke slammed down his hand of cards. "You're a cheat," Locked gritted out. He shoved a pointed finger in the direction of the man sitting across from him.

The man's chair shot back behind him as he darted into a stance. "You've had a cup of ale too many."

Locke sprung up to meet the man's eyes. "A cup too many or no, you're a cheat."

A crowd began to take notice of the two men close to a brawl. Locke clenched his fits at his side. Avery and Spencer, pushed and moved between the growing crowd. A man pushed back, trying to maintain his space for the promising entertainment.

"Move man," Spencer growled out.

With saucer-sized eyes, the man stepped to the side, "Beg your pardon, Mister Spencer."

Spencer nodded and continued his pursuit of Avery towards Locke.

Avery stood at the edge of the table and picked up a card. With a studious eye, he tossed it back down. "Looks like the hand was fair, it's just not your night for a game of *Costly*, Locke."

Locke clenched his fist again.

Spencer could feel the vein pulse in Locke's neck through the thick crowd. One more push aside, and he stood next to Avery. "Costly isn't my game either. Too many cards on the table. I prefer to play *My Sow's Pigg'd*. There's four of us, shall we play?"

Locke's opponent scooped up the coins on the table and shouldered Spencer as he left.

"Looks as though the game is over, shall we have a

moment?" asked Avery, gesturing to Locke's discarded chair.

Locke nodded and sat down in his retrieved chair. The disappointed crowd dispersed into the jovial chaos. Back to tables full of drink and food and harassing the young barmaids.

"I don't want another lecture. He cheated." Locke pointed in the direction of his Spanish opponent as he sauntered away, playing with the coins in his hand. He walked over to a group of Spaniards; they cheered him on with pats on the back and roars of laughter and adulation. Apparently, Locke paid for their next round of drinks.

"We're not here to lecture," Spencer said, his voice even and without a sign of anger. Not to say that he wasn't slightly frustrated at the time wasted in calming the situation. They had a lot of ground to cover that evening, and playing nursemaid to the crew was not helpful to their mission.

Locke scooped up his empty mug of ale, looking to savor the last drop. As he started to raise his hand to gather the attention of the short brunette barmaid, Avery gently pulled his arm back down.

"Listen here, Locke," Avery began. "Stay off the drink tonight. We need you to keep your wits about you for the next couple of days."

That got Locke's attention. He raised a curious eyebrow to the men and leaned in closer to Avery. "As long as it doesn't require money, I lost the last bit of my pay. Unless you're here to tell me, the admiral was able to pull out our pay from the company's arse and set us free from being indentured to the Spanish."

"Not quite, but we have a way to get the company to pay and get us on our way, so to speak." Avery leaned in closer to Locke. He fixed his deep blue eyes into Locke's eyes and slowly parted his lips. "Mutiny."

Locke, still a little tipsy, leaned in closer. "When?"

"Tomorrow night."

"I heard the admiral is staying on shore tomorrow night," Locke said, shifting his eyes around the room to catch anyone dropping in on their conversation. He didn't trust anyone, not even the mice that would come through the tavern after hours, cleaning up any crumbs of food left behind.

"Aye," replied Avery. "Seems everyone knows where he plans to spend tomorrow night. Which means the captain will be in command."

"Captain will be drunk in his quarters," said Locke as he leaned back in his chair. "Which means..."

"I will command in his stead." Avery straightened in his chair and looked towards Spencer before turning his attention back to Locke. "I need you to spread the word to the crew members you can trust. We leave behind those we don't."

"Aye, Mister Avery."

"Go with haste and acquire whatever supplies you can transport from the good people of A Coruña and meet us back at the ship."

Spencer and Avery continued their way through the taverns and brothels, recruiting until long past the setting sun. As they walked back towards the docks to meet with Gunn and Stock, the sound of the call to return to ship was being called throughout the streets. The boats to take the men back to the ships would fill with those that couldn't or didn't want to pay for a room in a brothel or tavern. It wasn't only Locke that was nearly out of money, it was the entire crew.

Men loaded up boats with acquired goods. Avery didn't ask how they came to find the bits of food, drink, and what appeared to be someone's laundry snatched off the line. The boats were weighed down with men and goods. Lighted by a few lanterns and the moon above, the men rowed back to their ships.

Out into the harbor they rowed, passing other ships harbored, and under the watchful eye of Castillo de San Anton to their left. With Captain Gibson likely passed out in his quarters, Avery had his men unload the supplies onto the ship's cargo hold.

No one spoke of the plans and went down to the crew bay, crawled into their hammocks, and had a restless night. Spencer lay on his bed in his cabin, unable to sleep. His mind raced from his past, to Amelia, to what was promised to be an eventful day. By that time tomorrow night, they would be on their way to freedom, or his body on display on the gibbet as a warning to others that may try to mutiny.

CHAPTER FIFTEEN

"*Y*ou know there is nothing I can do about the pay, Henry," Captain Gibson pulled his linen cloth off the table next to his plate and swiped it across his chin. Madeira wine stained the flax-colored cloth. In the privacy of the captain's quarters, Captain Gibson didn't use Henry Spencer's title or call him by his last name. They were equals in private. The rest of the time, in front of the crew, he was addressed like the others, by either last name or position.

"Captain, you are aware I ask not for myself, but for the men and their families who are depending on it."

"Aye, and to answer the next question, they cannot leave the ship." Captain Gibson let out a disapproving growl before he swirled his glass of caramel colored liquid and finished off the remaining half-glass in two gulps.

The answers were the same as they were every night they dined together since the crew discovered they wouldn't be paid and were sold to Spain. Spencer hoped that would be the night he would convince Gibson to side with the crew. Alas, he remained on the side of the company, even if his own future remained in limbo.

Spencer reached into the middle of the table and picked up the green bottle filled with the amber wine. He poured what little remained in the bottle into Gibson's glass, not even filling it halfway. More bottles sat on a shelf nearby. Spencer moved to the shelf, picked another bottle of Madeira wine, and replaced it with the empty bottle. He filled Gibson's glass to just under halfway. Gibson raised his hand motioning for more. Spencer filled the glass with enough headspace to prevent the liquid from pouring down Gibson's chin when he raised it with his unsteady hand to his lips.

"Tall pour," Spencer said under his breath.

Gibson looked up, "What's that you say?"

Spencer cleared his throat, "I was making note that my wife would appreciate this wine as much as we do." Spencer tilted the bottle and poured a little more into his glass. The only one getting drunk in that room would be Captain Gibson, Spencer would remain as sober as possible. He didn't want anything to hinder his mind with that evening's event. Mutiny. *Dear gods, was it really going to happen?* Spencer's job was to either get Captain Gibson on their side or to get him drunk enough for the captain to not care. He topped off the captain's glass before setting the bottle on the table.

A light rap at the door caught both men's attention. "Enter," Gibson boomed. Jonathan Gravet, the second mate, entered.

Well, shit. That's another one I must worry about. Spencer rose and offered Gravet a glass of wine and a spot at the table. He refused both. Spencer sat down in his chair and raised an eyebrow towards Gibson.

"Captain, I wanted to report a rumbling about the ship," Gravet cut his eyes towards Spencer.

Spencer nonchalantly held his glass of wine, as if whatever Gravet had to say was none of his concern. *How much did Gravet know?* Spencer topped off the captain's glass, as he struggled to keep his hand from shaking and giving himself away.

"Aye." Spencer threw his arm over the back of the chair, shifting his body to look at Gravet. The look on Spencer's face was a forced look of irritation to cover up the real thoughts racing through his mind, wondering if they had been caught. "What have you heard, Mister Gravet?"

"There are more men on deck than usual for this late in the evening. And..." Gravet was interrupted by Spencer raising his hand.

"Mister Gravet," Spencer said as he splashed the rest of the bottle into Gibson's glass. "Have you not noticed? It's May off the coast of Spain. It's hot and humid. And, quite frankly, completely miserable during the day. These men have found respite in the cool evening."

"I wouldn't call it cool." Gibson took another swig from his glass. His tongue stumbled over his words as he continued, "It's still quite miserable."

He lost his coat and cravat earlier in the evening. If

Spencer stayed much longer, he was afraid the captain's breeches would be next.

Spencer nodded in response to Gibson. When Amelia complained of the hot and humid summer of Virginia, begging for air conditioning, he couldn't understand what she really meant. That was, until he was pulled 260 years into the future. It was only then he truly began to understand the draw and pleasure of climate control and central heating and air. How he missed air conditioning.

Spencer needed to find a distraction to keep Gravet squirreled away while the plan was in motion. He couldn't get him off the ship, but he had another idea up his sleeve. "Mister Gravet," Spencer stood, filled the rest of the bottle into Gibson's glass, and returned to the cabinet. He pulled another bottle out and replaced it with the empty. "It seems as though the men are enjoying the evening." Spencer ran his finger along the spines of books lining the shelf. He pulled a black leather-bound book and tossed it to Gravet. "There. Now, enjoy your evening and let the men be."

Gravet stared at the book and then back to Spencer. His eyes pleaded with Gibson. The captain sat back in his chair, wine glass in his left hand, he flicked his right hand to Gravet, shooing him out of the room.

One man contained. Spencer glanced over to Gibson. *One more bottle?* Gibson's head dipped. *Ah, we're about there.*

"Captain, allow me to clean up the mess."

Gibson looked at the spread before him with half-opened eyes and flicked his hand towards the table. Scraps of food remained on the plates. Crumbs scattered about the linen tablecloth. He slumped more as Spencer stacked plates. The interruption with Gravet was unfortunate, but containable. If more men saw the captain in his current position, one might assume Spencer killed the old man. No. It was best for Spencer to clean up the mess rather than have someone else in the room. Gathering up the last bits of dinner, Spencer left the room. Before closing the door, he looked back at Gibson passing out at the table with an opened wine bottle and a refilled glass sitting in front of him.

After disposing of the dishes in the galley, Spencer returned for one last look at Gibson. He had moved to the bed, the bottle of wine on the floor next to him. A bare leg hung off the side of the bed as he laid face first into his pillow. He did lose the breeches and Spencer was pleased that he didn't have to witness it. He shut the door and turned the pilfered key to lock the door.

Second man was contained.

Spencer rested his forehead against the wooden door leading to the captain's quarters. "This better work," he said under his breath. A hand slapped his shoulder, jerking him out of his moment of gathering his thoughts and emotions.

"Spencer," Avery's voice called from behind him, close to his ear. "Locke and Gunn are waiting for you."

The men walked towards the port side of the ship, where a boat awaited to take them to the *James*. Stock and Chester were to head to the *Seventh Son*. Another boat with two more men were to head to the *Dove*.

Coordinated gathering of men. Coordinated mutiny. Hopefully, not a coordinated hanging to follow.

Spencer threw his leg over the rail and climbed down the rope ladder to the awaiting boat. It flopped back and forth with the waves. A deep breath and a quick step, Spencer was in the boat. He plopped down on an empty seat and nodded to Gunn. A lantern hung from a hook at the bow, leading the way. They're out for a friendly row, collecting men from ships. No reason to hide. Gunn continued to row towards the ship.

As they approached the *James*, a man called out from above. Spencer wasn't sure of the man's name, but hoped it was one of the men in on the plan. "Ahoy," called out Spencer. "Send us your drunkest sailor."

"What?" the man called out.

"We're having a little gamble going on and we want you to," Spencer paused and cleared his throat. Enunciating each word, he raised his voice and continued, "Send us your drunkest sailor."

"Send you my what?"

Spencer eyebrows knitted as he looked at Locke. "Didn't you say you spoke to men on the *James*?"

"Aye," Locke looked around the small boat as if the answer to the man's question could be found sitting near their feet.

"Send us your drunkest sailor," Spencer repeated, frustration hanging on every word.

"Why would you want..." he didn't finish before Locke interrupted.

"We're having a mutiny! Get the men and let's go."

As dark as it was, there was one thing Spencer, Locke, and Gunn could see. And that was the white of the man's eyes springing open to the size of saucers.

They. Were. Screwed.

They knew they were doubly screwed when he disappeared onto the deck, and they could hear him shouting for the captain. Another man's face appeared over the rail for a split second, followed by scrambling on deck.

Shouts flew through the air. Commands given. A small boat was dropped from the side and splashed in the water near the small boat containing the men from the *Charles*. Spencer looked at Gunn, "Row! To the Charles! Now!"

The captain of the James called out to Avery, who was standing on the deck of the Charles. "Mutiny!" He called to Avery.

Avery cupped his hand to his ear. "What was that? I couldn't hear you."

The captain called out, "They are having a mutiny."

Avery laughed and replied, "I know!"

Men flung themselves over the side. Splashes of water landed in the small boat. "Hold," Spencer shouted to Gunn. Three men made it to the edge of their boat. Spencer and Locke pulled them in, while Gunn held the boat steady. "Go." And with that, Gunn dug the oars into the water and headed back to the *Charles*. Spencer could see the small boat from the *James* following them. Shouts continued to pour on the deck. A light appeared from an opening of a gun port.

"Aw, sh.." before Spencer could finish his word, a

boom from the ship, followed by a cannonball splashing close by was enough for Gunn to double his speed.

When they approached the *Charles*, men were climbing from their boats up the side ladders.

"Move! Move!" Shouts came from the boats, encouraging their fellow mutineers to climb faster.

Locke climbed up first, taking the rope to secure the boat to the ship with him. The wet occupants followed next. Then Spencer, and finally, Gunn. Spencer poured himself over the rail and flopped onto the deck. His heart hammered against his ribs. Men ran around the deck, raising the sails and preparing to leave.

Castillo de San Anton came alive. The cannon shot from the *James* warned the Spaniards that something was amiss. They couldn't have known *Charles's* anchor was being pulled in as they prepared their cannons, and took aim into the waiting darkness, pocked with lights from the harbored ships. No one knew what was going on except the men on that blasted ship.

"The *James*," Spencer panted in heavy, adrenaline-fueled breaths to Avery. "She will follow."

One of the drenched men from the *James* scurried past to help raise the anchor. "We cut the sails. It won't stop 'em, but it will slow 'em."

"Weigh anchor!" shouted Avery.

The raising of the anchor was slow. Anchors are heavy, even with a group of men pulling the rope in. And when you're talking manpower to raise it, it can take some time. Time, they didn't have.

"Cut the line!" shouted Spencer.

Men pulled out knives and blades attached to their belts and began hacking and sawing at the thick rope which held a large anchor at the end. With much effort, the last bit of rope was hacked, and the anchor laid at the bottom of A Coruña harbor. The *Charles II* was on its way out of the harbor and into the open ocean, as cannon fire from the fort exploded into the night sky.

CHAPTER SIXTEEN

*D*awn broke in the early morning. The sky was painted in grays and blues. No one aboard the *Charles* was able to sleep throughout the night. Not even Captain Gibson, who awoke from his drunken slumber to find commotion ripping around him and the door to his cabin locked.

Gravet didn't fare any better. His door was locked from the outside and heavily guarded as soon as the commotion hit his ears.

Not all men on the ship were willing participants to the escape. The ones that complained too much were locked in one of the storage rooms. The crew couldn't risk someone sabotaging the ship.

Avery and Spencer approached the captain's cabin door. Spencer produced the key he held in his pocket since the night prior when he locked the door. With a click, the door was unlocked, and the men cautiously opened the door. One standing to one side of the doorframe, the other on the other side. They couldn't risk Gibson came charging out or a hidden gun awaiting his captors. Avery and Spencer were taking no chances with their lives–not after the events from the night before.

"Captain Gibson," Avery said with a firm voice. Gibson offered no resistance. No more clawing and scratching at the door. He was defeated and outnumbered. Avery and Spencer entered and stood in front of Gibson sprawled out on his bed. "We need to discuss the events of last night."

"As I see it, you," he pointed towards Spencer as he sat up, throwing his feet over the side of the bed, "poured wine down my throat until I couldn't see which way was up." He turned his head towards Avery. "And you stole my crew and ship."

Spencer crossed his arms across his chest. "Aye, I poured the wine into your glass, which you would have drunk with or without me. Makes no difference."

It was true. Most nights, Gibson stumbled his way into bed, drunk on wine. The next day, too ill to crawl out of his bed and take the duties of the captain. Avery ran the ship in Gibson's stead on a daily basis.

"I didn't want to take your ship and crew." Avery's voice rang of agitation. "Being sold to Spain was not part of our deal. We had to make a new deal." He stroked his beard. "Our deal was to leave."

Gibson huffed. "There was naught I could do. The contract..."

"Is no longer," said Avery, taking a breath. "Captain Gibson, you found yourself at the bottom of the barrel more days than I can count. You were a good captain in your day. It's one of the reasons why I sailed with you."

Avery pulled a chair in front of Gibson and sat down. Spencer continued to stand, his back near the door–an observer to the negotiations that were about to take place.

"What say you stop getting drunk every night and you continue to serve on this fine ship." Avery half-glanced back towards Spencer. "You can earn a spot as one of my lieutenants."

Gibson's eyes narrowed. "No."

A chuckle escaped Avery's lips. "Are you telling me that you would rather we toss you over the side than to clean yourself up?" Avery stood up. "You were a captain, start acting like one."

"No." Gibson grabbed his wig, wedged between his pillow and mattress, affixing it on his balding head. "I'm done playing your games, Avery. If I'm still the captain, then I do as I please and we go back to Spain and beg for their forgiveness. Mayhap, they'll let us keep our heads." He swiped the empty bottle next to his bed and turned it over, looking for the last drop.

"You're no longer captain and we're not going back. That's final." Avery growled out; his brown eyes lit with rage. He stormed to the door faster than Spencer could open it. Regardless of his overindulgence with the bottle, Avery was close to Gibson and hoped that he would join forces.

"Gravet," is all he sputtered out as he stomped through the finally opened door. Spencer locked the door behind them, and chased after Avery to Gravet's room on the middle deck where the officer's cabins were located. It was a few doors down from the narrow passage from Spencer's cabin.

Spencer fumbled with the key as he unlocked the door. If Gravet didn't agree to stay, he wasn't sure how Avery would take another hostile rejection. With a twist and a click of the lock, Spencer opened the door and stood out of Avery's way. The room wasn't much larger than the small bed. It was an officer's quarters, which allowed privacy and solace when the chaos of a ship became too much. Instead of the open bay with hammocks hanging from posts. Spencer had been offered an open room when one of the other officers became ill during the trip from London. The rooms were small, but with Avery taking up the remaining space, it seemed miniscule. Spencer remained in the hall with the guard.

"You know I can't." Gravet's voice pleaded with Avery. "I need the money for my wife and kids..."

"We all needed the money, Jon." Avery took another step in and pulled the small wooden chair in front of Gravet, who was sitting on the bed. "You weren't going to get paid. Your wife and kids would end up on the street."

Spencer moved towards the door and leaned against the jamb, half in, half out of the room.

"I'll find another way." Gravet shook his head. "I asked Gibson to let me go home. Even told him I would take a reduction in pay. He told me if I tried, he would have me tied to the mast and have me flogged."

"He wouldn't."

"You know he would. Told me he would make an

example out of me if I asked again." Gravet wrung his hands together, his head hung low. "My wife was pregnant when I left. If I leave with you, I don't know if I will see her again." He looked into Avery's eyes. "I can't take that chance."

Gravet turned his attention to Spencer, standing behind Avery, still holding up the side of the door. "Did you know this was happening when you were in with the captain?"

"Aye, that I did, Gravet. I hope you realize it was nothing personal when I sent you away."

"It was. You could have said something. I could've found a way to shore."

"And you could've let the captain or admiral know what was afoot. No. It was best for us to have you in your room."

"You're a good man, Jon." Avery stood up and put the chair back next to the wall where he found it. "You'll have to stay here for now." Spencer moved out of the doorway to give room for Avery's departure. Avery stood in the doorway and looked back at Gravet. His lips went into a thin smile that didn't reach his eyes. He was disappointed but understood Gravet's concerns for family.

Spencer locked the door behind them, and Young Jonesy, a young man no more than nineteen, reclaimed his position as guard.

"How many others?" Avery looked to Spencer as they made their way to the quarterdeck. They sailed through the night and needed to decide what to do with Gibson, Gravet, and any other men who refused to join the crew, before they sailed too far. They didn't need the extra mouths to feed or the responsibility of taking men hostage. The escape hadn't gone to plan. However, Avery was beginning to question what the actual plan entailed. Other than leaving the grasps of the Spaniards, there was no plan. They couldn't return to England. They would've been hung as mutineers. There was no turning back.

"A handful complained last night. Might've changed their minds by now." Spencer secured his hat on his head, blocking out the morning sun. The waters and sky were clear and blue. The morning was already warming up for what would be another scorching day off the coast of Spain. They would soon be beyond Spain and headed to Africa. They needed to make plans for their guests sooner than later.

"Call all hands to the deck." Spencer nodded to Avery in response. "Include Gibson, Gravet, and any of the others. Make sure they're guarded."

"Aye, Mister Avery." Spencer took his leave, spoke to a few men, and returned to stand next to Avery at the quarterdeck, overlooking the deck.

Men gathered about the deck. A group came up from the sleeping quarters–groggy and rubbing the sleep out of their eyes. They were already taking shifts to crew the ship. It was the first time since they left the harbor of A Coruña that Avery could grasp the number of men that joined the crew.

Spencer leaned closer to Avery and said, "I'm counting around one hundred. Give or take."

"Aye, give or take."

"If Gibson doesn't change his mind, we're going to need a new captain."

"You would do quite nicely, Henry."

"Henry, you know I'm only here long enough to find my wife."

"You'd be so quick to leave?"

"When you meet her, you'll understand." A stupid she-is-a-spitfire-and-will-eat-you-alive smile spread across Spencer's face as he placed a friendly hand on Avery's shoulder. With both men named Henry, they rarely called each other by their first names. They gave a small laugh when they did, out of pure awkwardness and amusement. "However, I'm here with you until then."

"I don't know how you'll find her. You don't even know where she is right now."

"We always find our way to each other." He wanted to add *through all of time and space* but kept those thoughts to himself.

"Spencer, if I didn't know better, I would say you're a romantic."

Spencer felt his cheeks flush, not necessarily of embarrassment for the love of his wife, but from being called a romantic, when he felt he could do more to show her how much he loved her. *Note to self: read those romance novels she likes and get some ideas.* "Time to address the crew." *Smooth transition, Spencer.*

Avery cleared his throat before he began. "Now that we are out of reach of the Castillo, I want to congratulate you on taking the step to your freedom from the repressive hand of the Spaniards and the injustice of the company. It made for a great show."

"Huzzah!" men shouted. Cheers, applause, and hearty pats on shoulders drowned Avery's speech.

He paused, taking in the celebration, before he continued. "You need to understand that we cannot return to England, not now anyways. We will have England and Spain after us." A low grumble and conversation spread through the crowd. Avery raised his hand to signal silence. "It won't be easy, but those who choose to stay will seek our fortune by doing what we had planned. Take what we want and never look back. The world is ours for the taking."

The crew quickly agreed to the settlement of treasure. Every member of the crew will receive one portion of the treasure, and the captain to receive two portions.

"I understand there may be some among us that aren't willing to partake on this adventure to fame and fortune. We shan't hold a grudge against them. Any men aboard that choose to go back to the Spaniards, you can leave now."

"Right over the side of the ship!" yelled a man in the back. Laughter of agreement spread around him.

"Nay, sir. We will ensure their safe return." Avery scanned the men's faces. "If you want to return to Spain, with your tail between your legs and your pride with it, step forward."

Apprehension hung in the crowd. Men were unsure if they would truly be allowed to return or if it was a ploy to out the nonconformists and cause them harm. Avery hoped Gibson and Gravet had changed their mind. However, they were the first two to step forward. Followed by another man. And another. Then, another. A few of the crew shoved a couple men joining those who wanted to leave. A total of fifteen men joined Gibson and Gravet. Standing tall in front of Avery and Spencer, Gibson's face was marked of defiance. As if he was ready to have a pissing match in front of the crew over the outcome of last night's events.

Avery shook his head in disappointment, and then realized all eyes were on him. He needed to set the example of how to treat the men.

Spencer leaned over and said in a near whisper, "Lead by fear or lead by respect. You see where fear has led us. Either one you decide, you need to do it quickly before this gets out of hand. Aye?"

"Aye." Avery rolled his shoulders back, pulling his body to his full height. "Very well. They can row back to Spain in one of the launches."

Gibson flicked his head in the direction of land and looked back at Avery with a streak of fear in his eyes. His overconfidence of Avery backing down crushed in one sentence. "It's at least five miles, maybe more. I'm captain of this ship! You can't do this."

"You can be captain of that boat." Avery looked towards the small wooden rowboat tied to the port side of the ship. "I suggest you learn how to row, Gibson."

Gibson scowled at Avery.

Avery rolled his shoulders back and stood tall. "Charles, like you told me when you trapped us on the ship without pay and knew we were sold to the Spaniards, it's only business."

With seventeen men ready to leave, they would be squeezed into the small boat, but they would have their wish, leaving the *Charles*. The ship's doctor begged to join the leaving crew but was prevented from taking his leave with the others. Ship's doctors were difficult to come by, and Avery had no intention on losing his.

The crew began stripping the departing members of their extra clothing, knives, and shoes. They left with very little to cover their bodies. Avery met the group and stood in front of Gravet. He took back Gravet's coat from one of the crew that had stripped him and handed it back to Gravet. He pulled the pocket watch out of another man's hands. He placed the pocket watch firmly in Gravet's hand. "Take care of that new babe and give your wife a kiss."

Gravet nodded and crammed in with the rest of the men on the boat as they began the long row to shore. Men shouted and heckled the departing crew. Some spat. Others pulled out their peckers and pissed over the side, aiming for the boat. Gravet looked up at Avery watching their departure, lifted a hand, and swallowed his concerns of staying with Avery or returning home to his wife. He chose the sanctuary of home.

CHAPTER SEVENTEEN

"I say Avery should be captain," Spencer called out to the rambunctious crew. "Without his planning we would be sitting in the harbor."

Men nodded and turned to the men standing next to the shoulder. Avery cut a knowing glance to Spencer and crossed his arms across his chest. They stood at the quarterdeck, Locke at the tiller, keeping a steady aim south skirting the coast of Spain and past Portugal.

No one dared to run against him. He had the experience and the backing of most of the crew. With that, Henry Avery became captain of the ship.

"Huzzah!" shouted the crew, lifting hands and pumping fists into the air.

"Do you have anything to say to the crew, Captain Avery?" Spencer egged on Avery to make the crew gain confidence and respect in their new captain.

Avery planted his hands firmly on his hips. "I am captain of this fine ship. We are headed to Madagascar, where I plan to make my fortune. I invite all you brave fellows to join me in this adventure."

"Captain," Spencer leaned close to his ear, "I believe you should give your fancy new ship a new name."

"Aye," Avery said to Spencer, "'tis a fancy ship. And she's mine." Avery turned to the crew. "Men, welcome aboard the *Fancy*" He threw his hands in the air.

The men called out, "Huzzah!" They patted each other on the back, pumped fists in the air, and continued to mill about the deck.

"We'll need duties assigned, shifts, someone to paint her new name, and..." Avery raised an eyebrow to Spencer, "a quartermaster."

"Only until I find my wife, or I decide I've had enough of this." Spencer wasn't entirely sure how time travel worked for him and there was no guarantee that he wouldn't walk through a door and end up back in his or Amelia's time. The deeper he found himself in the business of time travel, the more he understood Amelia's apprehension to the situations she was thrown in and her sometimes short fuse from being constantly on the edge of a cliff, teetering with one foot. The deeper he got, the closer to the edge he found himself.

A satisfied smile stretched across Avery's face. When he was hired by Sir James Houblon, he thought they would sail to the Caribbean, plunder a few French ships, and head home. He wanted to be able to go home one day. "'Til we've had enough," he said in a despondent voice.

⌇

"RESUPPLY IN CABO VERDE?" Spencer asked as he looked over a map with Avery. Spencer tapped his finger on the map to a group of islands off the west coast of Africa. Barrels of fresh water onboard ran low. With a crew of nearly 85, food, water, and supplies were always in demand.

"Slaver?" Avery lifted an eyebrow to Spencer.

Spencer slowly looked up from the map until his eyes met Avery's. "Absolutely not," he growled. His eyebrows knitted together, and he fisted his hand in disgust. "Salt merchant." If Avery hadn't been a friend, that question would have brought them to blows.

A few days later, Spencer woke up agitated. Thoughts of being accused as a slave trader hung heavy on his heart. He laid in his bed and stared at the ceiling as the morning light peeked through his window and slowly made its way across the room. *Amelia's crazy hair in the morning. Home. Air conditioning. Mornings in the garden drinking coffee, while Amelia had an overly sweetened caramel swirl mocha loco latte. Evenings with Amelia snuggled on the sofa with a book. Think calming thoughts. Find your peace.*

"Land, ahoy," called out the watchman from the deck above. The bell clanked repeatedly, sounding all men to the deck.

Spencer let a small, snorted laugh. There was nothing funny about land, but that didn't stop the humorous thought of Sam, the parrot aboard the *Gretchen*. He imagined her flying around the ship, calling out, "Back to the circus," as if everyone understood what she meant. It could've been land, a ship, or she wanted an afternoon snack. Amelia would love that bird.

"Cheese and rice!" Spencer sprung out of bed, his feet landing firmly on the wooden planked floor. He pulled his breeches off the chair and shoved a foot in, getting his toe caught as he haphazardly yanked them on. Stockings. Shoes. Yank. Pull. Tuck. Belt. Blades. He snatched his hat off the hook as he bolted out the door.

Men scurried up from the crew deck, taking every available space in the corridor. Some were in a state of undress. Others were wiping the sleep out of their eyes. Young Jonesy's brown hair stuck out in every direction like a porcupine, as he stumbled behind the men. Spencer put a hand on his shoulder and gave a bit of encouragement.

"Apologies, Mister Spencer," Young Jonesy mumbled. "Night shift." The young man couldn't have been in bed for more than two hours.

"Aye, you'll get some sleep soon enough."

The morning sun poked Spencer in the eyes, and he threw a hand over his brow. The cocked hat did nothing to protect his eyes from the inferno. He scanned the deck and found Avery on the poop deck of the ship with a spyglass pointed in the direction of Cabo Verde off the starboard side.

"We'll go to Moia." He handed the spyglass to Spencer.

CHAPTER EIGHTEEN

"*T*hree ships." Spencer confirmed. "Mayhap, they have not heard about our sudden departure from Spain." They arrived at the small Moia harbor on Santiago Island by the end of May.

"We're going to have a little discussion about trade. Nothing more." Avery stroked his dark beard.

Spencer doubted his friend's words but kept his thoughts to himself.

Fancy slinked closer to the harbor. The ships showed no indication of concern, their flags flapping in the wind. The same wind that carried *Fancy* closer to the shore.

Bright turquoise waters surrounded the treeless spit of land, roasting under a tropical sun. When Spencer suggested this location, he knew they could trade with the locals for salt and gather fresh water. He wasn't sure if there would have been a ship, let alone three to contend with.

"Hoist the colors," Avery called to the crew.

Stock sprinted to the ensign, knocking men out of his way. In his arms, he carried a bundle of black fabric. Spencer watched as Stock raised a black flag.

Where did he get that?

"Show 'em our broad side," Avery called out. "Ready the cannons."

"Captain," Spencer's voice panicked as he went toe-to-toe with Avery. Within inches of his face, Spencer ground through gritted teeth, and said, "You said we were only to have a discussion. Cannons aren't a discussion. Cannons are... well... cannons. And when did we get a black flag?"

"Out of my face before I have you escorted to your quarters, Mister Spencer."

"Captain..." Spencer clamped his mouth shut when the fire in Avery's eyes told him that he would do exactly as he pleased. "Aye, Captain." Henry turned to the crew; heart ready to burst through his chest. "Ready the cannons."

Men scrambled to their positions on the gun decks. Gun ports opened, exposing the massive fire power of *Fancy*. The ship was outfitted for warfare when they left London. And now, it was outfitted for the crew of the *Fancy* to take what they wanted from the three merchant ships.

"Single warning shot on my mark," Avery said to Spencer.

Spencer sucked in a breath. "Single warning shot on the captain's mark," Spencer shouted to the crew.

If these weren't merchant ships, as they had hoped, they would be going to battle for the first time as a crew.

They weren't prepared. *Why hadn't they trained? Note to self: If we make it through this, lessons on tactical operations and skill drills.* Spencer let out a silent prayer to the universe that he would find his way back to Amelia.

Locke was on the tiller, keeping *Fancy* on track to expose the weight of their firepower to the crews of the ships. "Steady on the broadside," Locke called out.

"Light the cannon," Avery ordered Spencer.

Turning his head towards the crew, Spencer called out, "Light the cannon."

From the gun deck, a voice called back, "Cannon lit."

He knew it was coming. He heard hundreds of times before, but this time... this time he flinched. Spencer flinched at the sound of cannon fire. He didn't flinch when *James* shot their cannon, and he was in the small boat not too far. He didn't flinch when he was in battle with Washington or Braddock. He didn't flinch when he sailed on *Constance*, which may or may not have been a pirate ship disguised as a merchant vessel. But this cannon fire, this single boom, hit him in the stomach. They would take what they want and need from the ships. There was no turning back. That single shot announced their entry into the life of piracy. That was the day Henry Spencer turned pirate. Not a I-have-no-direction-and-need-to-find-myself type pirate. But a pirate-pirate. Mayhap, a gentleman-pirate. Amelia was going to kill him if he didn't get himself killed first.

There was no movement from the three ships harbored in Moia.

"Take her in, Mister Locke."

"Captain, we're going in?"

Avery let out a laugh. "You worry too much, Spencer. They're merchant ships, they don't have the firepower to match *Fancy*." He confidently crossed his arms. "Nay, we will take her in, and they'll surrender. That shot was but a warning. Look, they've lowered their flags. Secure the cannons, will you?"

Spencer stood dumbfounded. It couldn't be that simple. Could it? "Secure the cannons," called Spencer to the gun deck.

He turned to Avery, "Next time, why don't we use the swivel cannon? It's smaller and easier to make a signal charge for it instead of securing more cannonballs."

"I wasn't making a signal; I was making a statement. Crushing fear into them." He presented the ships to Spencer with a flick of his hand. "See, lowered flags and we didn't need to shoot twice. All hands, on deck."

"All hands, on deck," called out Spencer. Someone rang the bell, signaling the crew to join the captain on deck.

Avery turned to the amassed crew and took a firm stance. "We will take supplies to get us on our way. I'm not interested in bloodshed. Aye?"

"Aye," called out the men.

"Only move what your captain or your quartermaster authorizes. Aye?"

"Aye," they responded.

Avery turned to Spencer, "Get your men ready."

Men? Which men? Spencer gathered a few men he trusted; sleepyhead Young Jonesy was the first on his list.

Avery took Gunn and Stock. Locke was needed to man the tiller and keep *Fancy* from sailing away while half the crew was transporting goods from the merchant ships.

Locke took them in as close as he could, and men reefed the sails. Without an anchor, lowering the sails and tying others up was their best bet to slow it down and keep the ship from sailing away while the captain, the quartermaster, and their teams, were procuring supplies from the merchant vessels.

When they reached the first ship, Locke pulled in a little too close. The ships jostled on impact, throwing those without a steady foot into each other. A fight almost broke out between two of the crew. Tensions were high and a stumble almost led to a brawl. Spencer shot a don't-make-me-stop-this-ship dad look towards them. Creaks and groans filled the space between the hulls of the two ships.

Long poles with hooks on the end were used to line the ships up. The same gangway Henry used to join the crew, slid across the space between the ships, giving the men easy access. Men from Avery's team swarmed to the merchant ship.

Another team of crew members released two launches and rowed to shore to collect clean water.

Shouts erupted across the deck amongst the crews.

"Get over there!"

"Drop your knife!"

And a few more chaotic words of... eh-hem... encouragement to round up the crew of the ship in the middle of the deck. When the men were contained,

Captain Avery, followed by Mister Spencer, walked over to the ship. Their boots were heavy on the wood. The captain couldn't hide his flinches with every step Avery made in his direction. Spencer's team followed and headed below the main deck to begin raiding the stores.

"I'm Captain Avery of the *Fancy*. Cooperate and we'll be on our way." Avery turned to the captain. "We're here to restock our supplies."

"We don't have much," pleaded the captain.

"More than we do." Avery turned to Spencer. "This is Mister Spencer, quartermaster. Logbooks, captain."

The captain's hands shook while he handed over a large black leather-bound book. Spencer dropped it on a nearby crate, using it as a table. His fingers ran down the pages, tracing line-by-line. Roll calls. Ports. Routes. Illnesses. Two deaths–one fell from the top of the mizzen mast while making a repair, the other from an infectious cut. Traded a couple of axes, rice, and two goats for casks of salt. Left Barbados. Headed for London.

A flash of movement caught the corner of Spencer's eye. On the deck, one of the men belonging to the ship thought he would play the hero and lunged for the blade Smythe held in his hand. With a fierce and quick snap, Smythe hit the man on the back of the head with the butt. The man fell to the ground. Blood oozed from his scalp. "'Tis but a scratch, captain," Smythe called out to Avery, shrugging his shoulders and letting out a boisterous laugh.

Avery shot daggers to Captain Taylor. "Mind your crew, captain. I said, I didn't want to molest your crew. I didn't say we wouldn't."

Captain Taylor raised a weary hand to his crew. "Stand down men. All is well. Aye?"

"Aye, captain," a few despondent men replied.

"Mister Spencer, please have your men relieve this ship of the goods we require."

"Aye, captain." Spencer led his crew below decks to gain an assessment of goods on hand versus goods listed. He pointed to casks, crates, and bundles. His crew began moving the items to the deck.

Spencer entered the captain's quarters on the stern of the quarterdeck, pulling Young Jonesy in with him. "Take this, and this, and ready it for me near the gangplank."

Young Jonesy grabbed a folding writing desk and a chair from the corner of the captain's quarters. Spencer pilfered a couple bottles of wine, along with a few books. Handing Avery a bottle of wine, Spencer sat down at the writing desk to record the items being shifted to the cargo hold into *Fancy's* ledger.

Two hours later, when the final crate was moved over to *Fancy*, Spencer began his next task of copying the list to a sheet in the ledger for the *Pink Rose*.

The crew of *Fancy* repeated the routine with the two remaining ships. Avery insisted on leaving a receipt for the items they confiscated. He mentioned something about not wanting to loot from the English. Was it guilt or an attempt to prevent being a target? At the end of the day, they picked up nine crew members. *Fancy's* roll totaled 94 when they left the harbor. As Spencer recorded the final entry into the ledger, he looked over to Avery.

"Captain, there is one more item I think we should add to the list."

"And what would that be?"

"Their anchor."

Avery raised an eyebrow and let out a hearty and approving laugh. "Weigh anchor."

CHAPTER NINETEEN

Spencer stretched out in his bed and reached to the side to pull Amelia close. Early mornings when the sun would creep through the bedroom window and the air was cool enough to snuggle under the blankets, Henry and Amelia would talk and laugh until it was time to get ready for work.

That morning, the space next to him was empty. The bed was too small to get a full stretch in. The air was warm, and the blanket kicked to the side. He didn't want to open his eyes; he knew what he would see: his cabin on the *Fancy*. After nearly five months in the past, he longed to hold his wife. Thoughts of their bedroom frolicking brought a smile to his face. He missed their intimacy. Henry spent too many years with men unable to fill the level of intimacy he experienced with Amelia. He dreaded spending another day stuck on a ship without her to complain that she was nauseous or hot or cold or bored. There was no way to know where Amelia ended up when they traveled through time, he only hoped that this adventure with Avery would lead him to her. He missed his dearest friend. Certain that one of the days would lead to finding her, he threw his legs over the side and started his day.

Spencer stood on the quarterdeck looking through the spyglass at the land of western Africa. The crew was getting restless and a stop to refresh any supplies or make a trade would be beneficial. Heavy footsteps approached Spencer from behind. He recognized the gait. While continuing to scan the shoreline for a place to anchor, he said, "Morning, captain. Men are restless and need to stretch their legs."

Avery grumbled an incoherent response. Spencer handed him a mug of coffee.

"A few rumblings about the fortune you promised. Nothing extreme. However, after we port for trade and supplies, we need to be on the lookout for a prize."

Avery stood next to Spencer with his arms crossed. One hand stroked his growing dark beard. Spencer kept his brown beard more trimmed than Avery's and thought about shaving it off a few times, before gray hairs began to weave their way through.

"A little further down the coast and we'll find an acceptable group to trade."

Spencer cocked his head towards Avery. Running his finger across the map, Henry noted they were north of Slave Coast. There should be animal skins, gold, ivory, and pepper.

By the next morning, they dropped their anchor off

the coast and took a couple of longboats in to find the tribe Avery had mentioned the day before.

Avery insisted Spencer lead the team while he stayed on board. He was more than happy to leave the ship for a couple of hours. The group of ten men rowed to the white sandy shore through crystal blue waters. Spencer jumped out, splashing ankle deep, to assess the terrain. Mid-morning the mild temperatures began to rise, and the slight breeze rustled the green leaves in the trees that lined the coast beyond the sand. He stood with one hand on his blade, and the other ready to pull his pistol out of his bandolier. Smythe stood next to him awaiting orders while the others brought the boats out of reach of the water.

"Captain wants us to bring the group to the ship to conduct trade negotiations." He looked towards Smythe to ensure he paid attention to his next words. "We're here for peaceful trade negotiations. No attacking them."

"Aye, I only gave the guy a little scratch when he tried to run."

"Humph." Spencer shook his head. "Well, you said you know the way to their village. Mister Smythe, lead the way."

From the sandy beach, the group of men walked up the berm and down a tree lined path.

"You've been here before?" Spencer asked, his stomach heavy. Something felt off but he couldn't place it. Were they being followed? Surely, they must have scouts hidden in the trees, keeping a steady eye on the intruders. He grasped his pistol in the bandolier strapped across his chest.

"Traded here once or twice before I signed on with Houblon."

A group of men emerged from the tree line. Spencer snatched his pistol strapped on his chest and aimed it at the group. He calculated his odds and figured he would be able to get off one shot before it would come to swords and knives against their blades and spears. *Next time, more pistols. Definitely, more pistols.*

A few shouts back-and-forth felt like an eternity. He was there to negotiate trade, not bloodshed. The men followed the short distance to the village. Their bodies were sleek, and their lower half covered with not much more than a cloth. It allowed for easy movement in the jungles and the fabric would help keep the men cool in the heat of the day. It reminded Spencer of Rick and his cargo shorts.

The village was a flurry of activity. A group of four women sat in the shade of a thatched building nestled between a couple of mud and stone buildings, weaving baskets, enjoying each other's company. Laughter and conversation filled the air, competing with the bleats of the goats in a nearby pen. Children ran around playing between the buildings made of mud walls with thatched roofs. A little boy no more than three-years-old, naked as the day he was born, chased after a dog. The dog didn't look interested in whatever games the boy had in mind. A smile twisted in the corner of Henry's mouth. He'd never been to a village in Africa and wondered how many more villages looked like that one. He decided that must be the reason for him to time travel and join Avery. He needed to experience more of the world.

Spencer and the crew were offered seats in an area of what he would consider a meeting circle. Rudimentary places to sit formed around a central circle. Celebrations, meetings, and fellowship happened in this area. In the middle of the ring, were the ghosted remains of fires lighting up the night sky and warming the village occupants. The day was too warm for a fire, but Spencer looked forward to celebrating successful trade negotiations.

Smythe sat to Spencer's left, stretching out his bare legs. The tribe's chieftain sat to Spencer's right. He wore a bright yellow fabric draped over his shoulder. A necklace made of carved wooden beads hung around his neck.

Spencer handed the chieftain a small bag of rice. "We have more supplies on our ship," he said addressing the group. The chieftain was joined by four men and two women. "If you would do us the honor, our captain and the rest of our crew await your visit to browse our inventory."

The chieftain studied Spencer and the rest of the crew. The man to his right leaned in to speak in a hushed tone. Spencer read their faces and could tell they were trying to decide if they could trust the group.

"We have boats at the shore to take you out and after negotiations, we'll bring you back. You have my word as a gentleman." Spencer placed a solemn hand across his heart.

Back on the ship, the crew helped the eleven tribesmen, including the chieftain, bring aboard the ivory, pelts, gold, and spices. Spencer looked around and realized they hadn't brought up the inventory they were considering for trade.

"While you start negotiations, I'll take a few men and we'll bring up the bags of rice, salt, and I believe we have a few axes that we can trade."

Avery didn't say anything, just gave a nod. Spencer took Young Jonesy, Stock, and Ear-less Bern with him to the hold five decks down. Don't let Ear-less Bern's name confuse you. He had two ears. However, his left ear never fully developed. Hats or a cloth wrapped around his head usually covered the little nub of an ear.

Spencer slung a large bag of rice over his shoulder. Jonesy grabbed another bag. The bag must have weighed as much as he did. The lad was lean, no matter how much he ate. Stock and Bern found a large sack of salt and shared the carry of the heavy bag. As the men made their way up the planks and stairs to the deck, they heard screaming and cheers. If it were only the cheers, that wouldn't have concerned Spencer. It was the screams that caused him to drop his bag of rice. The impact caused a small split in a seam, allowing a handful of rice to spill out. He took off into a sprint to the deck, pushing and shoving everyone out of his way. When he reached the quarterdeck, he found the tribesmen clapped in irons.

He stood there, trying to understand what he was witnessing. The tribesmen tried to escape, only to be shoved to the ground. Spencer's blood ran cold. He ran into the middle of the melee and shouted, "Stop this! Stop this now!"

Smythe got another kick into the side of one of the men.

Spencer spun to look at Avery, standing on the quarterdeck with his arms crossed with a darkened snarl across his face. "Captain, they were brought here to trade. Not... not... this!"

"Mister Spencer, stand down," Avery shouted. "Stand down or I will have you join them."

Spencer opened his mouth to speak. Nothing came out. He ground his teeth and laid his hand on his sword. Ready to slay the entire crew. He took a step forward. The crew around him stood back, giving him space, and placing a hand on their own weapons. Avery took a step back and raised his hand.

"Spencer! Quarters! Now!"

Spencer saw red. He sheathed his sword and headed to his quarters. Shouldering men out of his way. The crew stood dumbfounded. Spencer was one of the most even-tempered people, it was one of the reasons he was held in such high regard. He was fair and thought through his advice. To see him ready to challenge the captain, brought the crew to a standstill. The beatings of the tribesmen momentarily stopped while they watched the scene unfold.

Avery shouted, "Weigh anchor."

The crew scrambled to oblige and left the harbor, leaving the tribe's escorts chasing the ship down the shoreline as they watched their chieftain and brothers taken into slavery. Their wails faded into a tragic memory as the *Fancy* continued south.

CHAPTER TWENTY

Spencer slammed his shoulder into his cabin door, throwing it open. He wanted to hit something or someone. Of all the horrific things he had seen or been a part of, being tricked into taking those men into slavery was more than he could handle. He pulled his bandolier over his head and hung it one hook next to his door. He pulled his jacket off and threw it across the room. The fire inside him grew into an inferno. He pulled his knife off his belt and threw it against the door–the tip wedged into the wood. He worked the knife out and threw it again. A roar escaped him as he threw it again. One more time. He hoped it would pierce through the door and find its way through the hearts of everyone who was involved with the enslavement of the tribe.

He was involved. His shoulders sank. His heart fell into the pit of his stomach. He convinced the chieftain to come. Staring out the small window over his bed, he mocked his earlier words to the chieftain, "My word as a gentleman." He held the knife in his hand wanting to jam the blade into his stomach to dig out his heart, which he was certain was turning black and wicked. "I'm a shit gentleman."

He spun around and threw the knife at the door with all his might. The door flung open, Avery stood in the opened door frame, as the knife wedged into the door only inches from his face. Spencer sucked the air out of the room.

Avery's eyes cut to the knife, then back to Spencer. With a growl, Avery pried the knife out and closed the door behind him.

"Henry," Avery began, his voice held a hint of anger, though he wasn't yelling. "You seem to have misplaced your understanding of your position on this ship. I'm the captain."

"I haven't misplaced anything. I'm the quartermaster and that means that the men listen to me. You seem to forget that I was bringing them here to trade." Spencer sat on his bed, propped his elbows on his knees, and covered his face with his hands for a moment. He dragged his hands down his face, trying to wipe away his anger, and proceeded with his disapproval of the day's events. "We can do this without taking slaves."

"You're too soft, Henry." Avery played with the knife he pulled out of the door, moving it around testing the weight and the sharpness of the tip. "Those men look to us for guidance. They'll quickly stop looking at us if we're divided." He handed the knife back to Spencer.

"Slavery? There's got to be a better way to make our fortune." Spencer studied the knife. "Slavery is a despicable business, and I don't want any part of it."

"Pirating is a despicable business. Yet here we are." Avery stretched his arms out. He pulled the chair out from the small desk at his right, scraping it along the floor, and placing it in the center of the room. He lowered himself in the chair, coming eye-to-eye with Spencer. "Before all this, I was employed by Governor Richier in Bermuda to transport slaves from here to America."

"Is that why you picked that spot to trade? You planned on taking them as slaves and you set me up." Spencer contemplated using the knife in his hand to gut Avery. What Spencer thought was a target of opportunity was a calculated ambush. "Just as you don't want to attack English ships to keep them from targeting us, I don't want my conscience to target me. We're pirates, not slavers."

Avery stroked his beard, taking time before he answered. "You're fine with killing someone, but not taking them as slaves?"

"Kill or be killed, I'll do what it takes." Spencer leaned towards Avery, pointing a finger in his direction. "But, if you take slaves again, you won't be using me to do it."

ON AN OVERCAST DAY nearing the end of July, the *Fancy* came upon an island jutting out of the ocean twenty miles off the coast of Guinea. "We need to careen the ship away from the Portuguese and their slave ports." Avery pointed to the map on the western side of the tall-peaked island. "They have ports here and here."

Avery's knowledge of the slave trade ports came into good use. As far as Spencer was concerned, keeping the crew safe was the only good part of it. "What about local inhabitants?"

"The Bubi moved deep into the jungle."

"Good. We don't need to be attacked while we're vulnerable," Spencer stood up from his leaned over position above the map.

"'Tis not only the people you need to fear." Avery straightened his back and looked Spencer in the eye. "'Tis the White Man's Death."

Spencer gulped down. *What in the world is White Man's Death?* "Illness or curse?"

"Both." A slight twitch to a corner of Avery's mouth left Spencer worried about what they would encounter.

The *Fancy* rounded the island, careful to avoid the Portuguese ports. Dark blue waters surrounded the volcanic and mountainous land. Men ran to the rail to take in the sights and sounds. Thick rainforest hid the inhabitants: man and creature. Birds circled and flew around the lush green landscape. Barks, howls, and screeches from primates pierced the canopy.

Young Jonesy ran over to Spencer, who stood on the quarterdeck next to Avery, ready to bark out orders. "Mister Spencer, have you seen anything like this?"

Jonesy had sailed under Captain Murray on the merchant ship, the *Good Fortune*. They would sail from

THE TIME WRITER AND THE ESCAPE

Scotland, England, France, head to the Caribbean, and up through America. They would pick up and deliver goods. Though none would admit, they found their way to illegal privateering under the flag of the *Wicked Winnie*. It lasted until the English caught wind of the pirating, and the men disbanded before being caught. Captain Murray claimed he lost the *Good Fortune* to shipworms, but his men believe he is hiding until it's safe for the return to piracy. Throughout Young Jonesy's travels, the jungle of Africa was nothing he'd seen before.

"Nay, lad." Spencer's eyes transfixed on the jungle. "Take heed, it's as deadly as it is beautiful."

Readying the ship to careen it took a good part of the day. Every removable item that could be taken ashore, was removed, and secured. A few men made shelters and gathered wood for the bonfires that would smoke out the insects and keep the wild animals away. For the rest of the crew, one more night aboard the *Fancy* before the laborious task of pulling the ship ashore to scrape the hull free of barnacles and shipworms.

The following morning, any remaining items were removed, and ropes were tied around the bottom part of the masts and additional anchor points on the ship and pulled to shore. With ropes attached to tackles on the masts, the ship was tilted on its side, exposing the keel above the waterline. The loose ends of the ropes were pulled and secured around trees. Spencer guided the crew to place timber outriggers to help prop the ship in position. The angle allowed the crew to access the underside of the hull to clean it. "Heave her down, men. A clean ship is a fast ship," shouted Avery. "I want the fastest ship to sail the seas."

The enslaved tribesmen were put to work with the rest of the crew, scraping and removing the creatures holding tight to the ship and eating away the wood. The men would scrape and pry the crustaceans and mollusks, until their hands bled.

The sounds of the jungle called to them day and night. Large lizards nearly a foot long, brightly colored with gold, red, and black, scurried across the rocks. Screams and barks from primates hiding in the trees threatened the men to stay away. Fog hung heavy over the mountainous terrain. When it wasn't heavy with fog, it rained and rained. There might have been some more days filled with rain.

Up a river, working their way through the mangroves, the men found fresh water to refill their supplies, and an idyllic waterfall that beckoned them to stay awhile. The water was gentle enough to swim and bathe, but the concern of what lurked below the surface in the unknown waters kept them on task.

When they finished the first side, they released the ship, took her out far enough to turn her around, and tackle the other side. It took weeks to complete the job of cleaning and repairing, all the while the men stayed on dry land. That is except when the waves splashed on their legs while they were in the water accessing the hull and when the rain poured down on them.

"She'll be faster now." Avery inspected the hull, a satisfied grin spread across his bearded face.

"Henry," Spencer said as he stood next to Avery. "A clean hull does make her faster. The East India Trading Company's ships are still a threat. Aye? Mayhap, we need to make her lighter, faster."

"Aye, what do you have in mind?"

"Razing her. Let's gut as much as we can. We can pile any goods we confiscate at the bottom." They walked around the ship, continuing to inspect the work. Pointing out issues and additional repairs. "Let's remove some of the below decks, structure, whatever we can. Run her light. If we don't need it, we leave it behind."

"And if we do need it, I'm sure there'll be a prize more than happy to donate to the cause."

"We can also lose that cargo." Spencer looked towards the group of enslaved men. "We won't need them after we're finished here. They'll just be more mouths to feed and men to watch them. We're pirates, not slavers."

Avery stared at the group of men. "Aye, when we're finished."

Spencer let out a deep breath. He knew that could've gone a few different ways, one of them with the accusation of insubordination. As the quartermaster, he was responsible for the men and operations, almost an equal to the captain. The men voted for him to lead them. Surely, they would take his side in the matter. Not necessarily. The crew was divided on their thoughts about slavery and most considered the tribesmen as a prize to be used or sold as they pleased. He might not change their mind, but he hoped to lead by example and treated the enslaved men like one of the crew and with respect.

The razing of the ship's guts took weeks. They removed posts which held up flooring Extra tables, chairs, books, planks, and whatever else they could spare was left in an unceremonious pile on the beach.

Nearing the end of September there was nothing more for them to strip and repair. Groups of men boarded the ship; Spencer was one of the last on shore. He turned to the group of tribesmen awaiting their return to the ship.

"This is the best I can do." He began removing the shackles from their ankles.

Young Jonesy, Gunn, and Locke ran over to help. Whether they did it as the right thing to do, or if they wanted to hurry up and get on their way, Spencer didn't care. He wanted to see the men freed.

Before the last shackle hit the sand, the men sprinted to the jungle.

"They didn't say thank you." Young Jonesy stood with his hands on his hips, lips pursed.

"You want them to show us gratitude for what?" Spencer turned sharp to Young Jonesy. "For taking them from their home without their consent? Or for shackling them like animals? Or for forcing them to provide us labor? Or for leaving them on this god forsaken island with no way to get back home? Which part should they be grateful for?"

"We could have taken their stuff and killed them. Mayhap, they should be thankful for that. Isn't it better to be a slave rather than left for dead?"

"Mayhap, Young Jonesy, we shouldn't have to make

that decision." The shackles clanked as Spencer picked them up, knocking off bits of sand. "Let's go find us a prize. I've got to pay for their freedom."

CHAPTER TWENTY-ONE

"*H*oist the colors!" shouted Spencer.

"Show them our broadside!" shouted Avery.

Stock shifted the tiller to bring the *Fancy* around.

Men scurried to the gun decks, manning their cannons.

"Send them a warning signal. On my mark."

Bells rang. Men yelled.

"Danish flags," called out Avery, handing the spyglass to Spencer.

Spencer peered through the glass and saw the two ships ran flags with white crosses on a red field up their ensign. "Ah, 'tis a good day for a prize." Spencer confirmed Avery's assessment of the flags. Henry called out to the gunman to prepare to fire the swivel cannon, "Warning shot on the captain's mark."

With full square sails and a light load, the *Fancy* flew to the ships of the coast of the island of Principe. The Spanish Expedition flagship was built by the Houblons to be sleek and fast, despite the hefty weight of forty-six cannons–it was! The stripped-down version was about to be put to its first test of speed against other ships.

On the *Fancy*'s gun decks, twenty-three cannons divided between two decks pointed out the gun ports on the port side, and twenty-three cannons on the starboard side. Two men were assigned to each cannon, requiring half the crew. The other half of the crew stood on the top deck, ready with pistols, knives, and boarding axes in hand. A few readied with ropes and poles with grappling hooks held firmly in their hands, ready to throw to pull their prize into their clutches. Nervous energy overflowed the *Fancy*'s decks and worked its way through the men

Attached to the rails, on either side of the quarterdeck were swivels–small cannons, a little over three feet long, mounted upon swivels, and currently attached to points on the rail near the aft. The swivels could be loaded quickly. The charges were preloaded, wrapped in linen, and stored in a bucket. The projectile was smaller than a lime. They had no intention of hitting the Danish trade ships with the small cannon, but it could be used to defend the *Fancy* from a boarding party.

Locke manned the swivel on the starboard side, Ollie on the port side. When Stock brought the ship around with the starboard side on full display to the two Danish ships, Ollie joined Locke to help charge the swivel. Their crew was too small to man both sides of the ship. Besides, they would show their force with one side of the ship, and if the Danes were smart, they would relent and lower their sails.

On the captain's mark, they loaded the swivel, poured gunpowder down the small touch hole at the breech of the gun, and lit it using the linstock. Ollie shoved the matchstick into a bucket of sand. The pointed end went into the sand, and the forked top–which had a slow burning cord wrapped around it–was ready to light the cannon again. They cleaned the barrel, and awaited orders from the captain.

The *Fancy* moved in closer to the two ships. Anticipation rose. Spencer began to pace.

"They'll lower their sails," Avery said, his voice flat and confident.

"Aye," Spencer said. "The men are ready either way." The last part was spoken more to himself than to Avery. They discussed and trained what they would do. If the other ships lower their sails, they will do the same as they did at Moia. They wouldn't need to fire their cannons. No loss of life. Loot what they needed. If the ships didn't lower their sails, that would be a clear indication they wouldn't surrender. The cannons were ready, awaiting signal. Men were ready to board the ship by force when they got within range. "They're not going to lower."

Avery clasped Spencer on the shoulder and pointed towards the front ship. "Look."

The first ship's sails began to lower.

"Huzzah!" called out the crew of the *Fancy*.

Then the second ship's sails came down.

Another, "Huzzah!"

"You're correct," Spencer said to Avery. "I despise it when you're correct."

Avery laughed and said, "That's why I'm the captain," as he walked away. "Stand down the men and prepare the boarding party."

Spencer called out to the crew, "Stand down cannons."

Shouts from the gun decks confirmed they were standing down the cannons. Orders were repeated back as confirmation that they heard the orders and heard them correctly.

"Prepare the boarding party!"

Even though the ships surrendered, it didn't mean things couldn't get violent. Clearly, the *Fancy* outgunned the Danish ships. Even if the ships tried to run, the *Fancy* would easily catch them, and would bring down the fury of the kraken on them.

Stock brought the *Fancy* in close to the two ships. Henry led a group of fourteen men, to include: Gunn, Young Jonesy, One-ear-Bern, Smythe, and Peterson, to the second ship in two of the longboats they towed behind the *Fancy*. Armed with cutlasses, pistols, axes, and knives, they would secure the second ship while Avery began negotiations with the lead ship.

Gunn and Smythe climbed the shrouds to board the ship to secure it for Spencer's arrival. The Danish crew offered no resistance. Spencer stood next to the captain, giving him directions to repeat to the crew. All crew were to toss their weapons and sit in the middle of the deck. Young Jonesy brought Spencer the ship's log. Spencer ran his finger from line to line, taking note of supplies, cargo, and ports they had visited. A couple of items caught his eye: ivory and gold from Africa. His share would easily cover the cost of freedom from the enslaved tribesmen he set free.

He tapped his finger further down the neatly written list and found rice, wine, rum, and freshwater were recently added to their stores. As he was turning the page, a commotion between Gunn and one of the members of the Danish crew caught his attention.

Spencer leaned over to Young Jonesy, who was standing off to the side, "Go over and ask Gunn what seems to be the problem. Tensions can flair and we're trying to keep this peaceful."

"Aye, Mister Spencer," Jonesy said as he sprinted over to the men.

Loud voices and animated arms continued as the men stood toe-to-toe. "Enough!" yelled Spencer. "Captain, tell your man to stand down before I allow my men to make him stand down. It will not be gentle and it's a line, I pray, we don't have to cross."

"Aye," the Danish captain said. He called out the orders to his men.

Spencer looked towards the *Fancy* and the other ship. Cargo was being moved over to the *Fancy*. Spencer sent four of his men to lead a group of ten Danish crew to bring up the cargo of ivory, gold, and food supplies. They would leave just enough so the crew wouldn't starve. But Spencer claimed the rest for his crew.

Tusks piled and counted. Gold counted. Barrels and crates all stacked in the middle of the deck.

At last, the *Fancy* made its way to side up against the ship, as it groaned from the hulls rubbing against each other. A gangway connected the two ships, allowing for easy removal of the cargo. As each item was carried onto the *Fancy* by the Danish crew, Newman recorded it into *Fancy*'s log. When they would sell the cargo, the crew would each get a share, one and a half shares to Spencer, and two shares to Avery.

The man Gunn argued with earlier, started up again. Gunn nodded and the man sat down. Leaving his position, he approached the area where Spencer stood watching the removal. "Mister Spencer, a word?" Gunn approached at Spencer's nod.

"Gunn, what is going on with you and that Dane?"

"He is my cousin."

Spencer's eyebrows knitted, ready to tear into Gunn and his cousin. "Then keep your cousin in line. If you hadn't noticed, it is causing tension amongst the crew. I will have him flogged if..."

Gunn interrupted, "He wants to join our crew."

"Does he now?" Spencer's back straightened.

"That's why we were arguing. I told him he would be like me, unable to go home. He insisted."

Spencer took a moment to think it through. With an extra man, no one would notice a lighter purse when they sell the goods, but they could use the extra hands.

"I'll inform the captain. Carry on."

Gunn went back to guard the crew members. Following a tusk being moved over the gangway, Spencer found Avery on the quarterdeck, with a glass of wine in his hand and a satisfied grin on his face. The prize would keep the men happy and him in his position as captain.

"Captain," Spencer approached Avery. "Gunn's cousin is on that ship. Wants to join our crew. I thought we could use an extra set of hands."

Avery nodded and raised his glass to Spencer. Apparently, he'd begun his celebration a few glasses ago. As quartermaster, Spencer oversaw the crew. It wasn't that he was necessarily asking permission from the captain, more along the lines of informing Avery. They worked together well.

Spencer headed back to the other ship to collect his crew, as the last pieces of cargo were loaded onto the *Fancy*. Gunn, his cousin, and nine other crew members walked over to Spencer. "He asks if they could join us."

Spencer crossed his arms and sized up the group. He looked around the men sitting on the deck, "Any others want to join our crew?"

A few men looked at each other. Some gave nods. Others shook their heads. In total, fourteen Danes joined the crew of the *Fancy*.

∼

A FEW DAYS LATER, they stopped off the coast of Gabon to trade some of their wool and rice for barrels of honey.

Sweet, sticky, delicious honey. A rare treat for the men used to diets filled with stale breads where they would have to smack the weevils out, dried meats, and water they would have to consume before it went bad along with the food.

The men might have gone a little overboard gorging on the honey. More men than they could spare, spent time hurling over the rail from their obscene consumption of the liquid gold.

While continuing down the coast of Africa, they spotted smoke from a large fire on the beach. Men on the island waved towards Avery's crew. "Let's see if they have anything to add to our cargo hold."

The *Fancy* anchored off the coast of the small island, and a small crew, led by Spencer, rowed two longboats to the shore. About two hours later, Spencer and crew were headed back to the *Fancy* with the French crew who had been abandoned on the island.

The *Fancy*'s crew had swollen to over one hundred men. Men who were hungry for fortune. Avery needed to find bigger prizes than the goods they'd looted. Silks, wool, rice, and grain helped support the crew, but what they needed was gold, jewels, and lots of it.

As they were rounding the Cape of Good Hope, they spotted a ship in the distance. Another prize to add to the small collection. The chase was on!

"Full sails!"

Men heaved the thick rope, pulling up the sails. The sails caught the good wind, and the *Fancy* was upon the ship. Locke raised the black flag up the ensign. Ollie lit the warning shot from the swivel. The other ship raised its Union Jack. It was an English ship and Avery had every intention of taking it. The men were restless and demanded more loot. When they left A Coruña, they were promised that they would find their fortune. All they've found by that point was honey overload and a small bounty of ivory and gold. Not the fortune they were promised.

The ship resisted and fired back at the *Fancy*. Stock shifted *Fancy's* trajectory for an interception. When they got close, he shifted direction, showing the English ship the *Fancy's* broadside. Cannons readied; Avery gave the command. The English ship, with its six cannons on its port side, was no match to the *Fancy's* twenty-three on its starboard side. The ship relented.

As the *Fancy* pulled alongside the ship, Avery noticed a familiar face of the captain. He had sailed with him when he worked on a slave ship.

The crew of the *Fancy* stripped what they could from the *Charlotte*, including one of their longboats, hitching it up to be towed. "Avery, you know you won't get away with this," said Captain Middleton.

"Burn it," Avery gave the command to Spencer in a whisper as they were finishing up. "Leave no survivors."

Spencer felt the blood drain from his face. Looting was one thing; however, murdering an entire crew was not what he expected to happen when they attacked the ship.

Reluctantly, Spencer gave the order to Smythe to set a fire in the hold and the crew deck, while the entire crew sat in the middle of the quarterdeck. He ordered another group of men to hack down the main mast, leaving it to crack and crash into the ocean. The *Fancy* pulled away to leave the crew of the *Charlotte* to burn or drown somewhere between where the South Atlantic and Indian Oceans meet.

CHAPTER TWENTY-TWO

"We can't go around killing Englishmen, Henry," Spencer fumed. "Unless you've forgotten, we don't need the wrath of England nor the East India Trading Company coming down on us." He slammed the logbook shut and threw the quill on the desk.

Avery sat in the chair across from Spencer, with his feet propped up on the desk. He used the tip of a small knife with an ivory handle to clean the filth from under his fingernails. "Middleton was a worm and wouldn't hesitate to run straight to the king to unleash the entirety of his majesty's navy upon us."

"Do you know that lad, Philip? The one that's all arms, and a bit quiet?"

"Aye," Avery replied, not looking up from his task of giving himself a manicure.

"His last name is Middleton." Spencer stood up and walked to the cabinet and pulled out a bottle of wine. He opened it and began filling two glasses. "The captain was his uncle. We killed his kin while he stood there and watched." He swallowed his glass in one gulp and poured another.

"Do you think he'll run?"

"I'll have a chat with him." He took a sip from his second glass. "He's too wrapped up in what we're doing. Hoping to make his fortune and get out of this alive." Spencer topped off his glass before settling back into his chair. "We've got to do something to keep the navy off our backs."

Avery sat back in his chair one hand over his stomach, the other held his glass of dark red wine. "I'll write them a letter."

"And say what?" Spencer raised an eyebrow.

"Grab your quill.

Spencer pulled out a clean sheet of paper and his quill.

"Say that the *Fancy* has never harmed any English vessels." Avery thrummed his fingers on his stomach. "Or Dutch vessels. Ensure both English and Dutch, I don't want either one coming after us." He took a sip of his wine. "That as long as I'm commander, never shall we attack. An Englishman's friend... and I'll sign my name to it."

"This is the biggest load of cow shit that I've ever seen spewed upon a sheet of paper," Spencer said as he looked over the page.

"Do you think it'll work?" Avery abruptly sat up in his chair, dropping his feet to the floor with a loud thud. "We'll leave it in Madagascar and have someone there send it on."

"We know it's an obvious fabrication. However, the English don't." He shook his head in disbelief. "It's so ridiculous that it just might work. God help us."

A week passed and the Fancy captured their ninth vessel, tenth if one was to count the *Charlotte*.

"Your hold is bare," Avery kicked a small barrel on the ship they had boarded. "Where are you headed?"

"Haven't you heard?" asked Captain Wilcox, a privateer from Rhode Island. "There's a large fleet sailing from Mocha to the Red Sea on their way to Surat, India. The Grand Moghul's treasure ships are to be part of the convoy."

Avery considered the information he was told. "Why would you tell me this? Why wouldn't you keep the information to yourself?"

"We cannot attack it on our own."

The sloop was armed, but if the fleet was as great as he was leading Avery to believe, even the Fancy would need support.

"We'll port in Comoros and overhaul the ship. I invite you to join us."

Spencer looked at Avery during the evening's supper. He thought about the journey ahead. What that kind of prize would mean to the crew, to Spencer.

"If we capture this prize, we will become legends."

"Rich legends."

"Aye." Spencer nodded his head and swirled his wine in his glass. "On to Mocha to capture our prize."

CHAPTER TWENTY-THREE

"*I*'m going to be sick." I threw my hand over my mouth and bolted into a seated position. Where was I? "Henry."

Why was the ground moving? Light crept in through a small window behind me. The room was small, about ten feet wide on the side with the door, was my guess, it could have been wider. I'm good with people's height, not room sizes. I'm complicated like that. The room narrowed down to about five feet wide, where the small window letting in the light was placed.

There was a bed, to the left of the door, if one could call it a bed. It was more along the size of a cot. However, there was a thin mattress, blanket, and pillow, on a long box. Opposite the bed were two doors that looked as though they went to closets. The walls and boxes were painted white, trimmed in a black paint. Unless one of those closets contained a toilet, I was going to make a mess. I scurried to my feet and flung open the first closet, it was filled with men's clothes. That wouldn't do me any good. The second closet was my next hope. I grasped the small, round, black knob and gave it a turn. Women's clothes. My stomach wasn't going to hold off opening doors only to find more clothes. I climbed up the narrow storage box at the narrow end of the room, unlatched the window, swung it open, and stuck my head out. The fresh air helped, but I dry heaved anyway. There wasn't any yogurt and berries left for me to offer. *How long ago was breakfast?* As nauseated as I was, a pang of hunger crept to the forefront of my mind.

Where was I? When was I? I remembered being on the *Susan Constant*, the larger ship at the Jamestown Settlement in Virginia. However, this wasn't what I remembered of the room. This room was smaller, painted white, and sailing in the open ocean instead of being harbored. *Cheese and rice. What was going on?*

I checked my pocket. The flattened penny with the imprint of Jamestown was missing. How was I supposed to know a flattened penny would allow me to time travel? I never carried coins around with me anymore because of that possibility. How was I going to explain how I ended up on a ship in the middle of the ocean to whomever was crewing the ship. I hoped they would offer me a life vest or floaties before they tossed me overboard. My stomach did another flip-flop. Nerves or seasickness, I couldn't tell. But I needed to think clearly to talk my way out of becoming shark bait.

I fell asleep and somehow ended up on a ship. Who knows how long they've been at sea? That wouldn't work.

Rode on the back of a whale? Sea turtle? Seems probable. Ugh. Probably not. Mermaid? Siren? I was screwed. Maybe I could hide in the room until we made it to land. Surely, we couldn't be that far out. I was at the docks only... Well, I didn't know how long that had happened. Or what year I ended up in. Although primitive by 21st century standards, the ship was in good shape and seemed modern enough. The clothes! I ran over to the woman's clothes closet first and sifted through the clothes. None of it made sense. There were women's clothes–from an ancient looking toga that I would expect Aristotle to wear, to mantua of different styles, to a flapper dress of the 1920s. If there were 20th century clothes, then I couldn't have slipped through time. Maybe I just ended up hitting my head and then went on a cruise? *Oh, come on, Amelia. Do you really think that happened?* It didn't make sense, but I knew I wouldn't be able to stay in the cabin forever. My stomach was going to make sure that I left at some point.

I padded over to the door leading out of the cabin and grabbed hold of the black painted doorknob. Deep breath. Cleansing breath. Even if we are in the 20th century, they still might toss me overboard or have me walk the plank. Stranger things have happened to them. Right? Stowaway Amelia Spencer, reporting for duty.

Slowly, I opened the door. A few inches at first, peeking out through the crack. No one was walking by. I was below the main deck. There was a table in the middle of the room. On each side there were four crew cubicles. A bed on a storage box, like the one in the room I was in, curtains for privacy, and storage above. At the far end was a wood burning stove and little kitchen area. Was it safe to have a fire on a wooden ship? I supposed that was the only way for them to cook or if it was cold. Where there is a kitchen, there's food, and time travel can make a girl hungry. Careful as to not make too much noise, I slipped out of the cabin and made my way past the crew beds and into the kitchen space.

There were cabinets to the left and right of the central oven. I opened the first one to my left, pots, pans, dishes. No food. I swear I could smell bread nearby. I scurried over to the other side and opened a cabinet to find apples, oranges, bananas, a loaf of freshly baked bread, butter in a crock, in another crock was a light brown paste. I took a whiff; it was peanut butter. I stopped there. Bread, peanut butter, and a banana sounded like a perfect time traveling meal. If I was going to walk the plank in a few minutes, I might as well die with a full belly. It'll give the sharks more to eat.

I could comfortably stand up in the room, minus the slight movement of the waves that I could swear I felt. At my height, I could stand comfortably in most spaces. Heck, even Henry could stand there too. After my last meal and swim with sharks, I would need to find my way back to my time and to Henry. How I was going to do that while on a ship was a complete mystery.

To my right sunlight shone down like a beacon on the ladder leading up. Might as well face my demise like a woman instead of letting someone find me cowering in the corner like a scared kitten. Standing at the base of the ladder, I looked up into the clear blue skies above. I could hear the occasional footsteps across the wooden deck above. A man's voice here and there. Another man's voice. Laughter. A squawk from a bird. "Ready or not." I said out loud. "Definitely not."

I climbed up the dark wooden ladder. A slow, cautious, ascent. I climbed out of the square port to the open air and sprinted across the deck to the rail. I grasped it with all my might and heaved out the lunch I had just enjoyed. Well, there goes extra Amelia for the sharks to dine on.

Through the sounds of my heaving, I heard footsteps running towards me. Louder and louder. There was more than one. Would they just toss me over and be done with it? I was about to find out. I spun around ready to fight and kick my way out of the situation. A man with a neatly trimmed gray beard took me by the shoulders. He stood about five-foot ten, broad shoulders, and dressed... normal? Is that the correct term for a pair of khaki cargo shorts, boat shoes, a wide-brimmed canvas hat, and a t-shirt? Normal? He looked like he was going fishing or to a barbecue. "You're safe," he said with an Eastern European accent—it almost sounded Russian to me. His face, close to mine, almost nose to nose, to make sure I paid attention to what he was saying. I just upchucked my lunch, he probably shouldn't have got that close to me. Brave dude, I guess. All I could do was nod in response. I was completely confused. I thought I time traveled. How did I end up on a ship in the middle of the ocean? My stomach started to do a flip, and I spun around ready to dry heave. He placed his hand gently on my back as I gripped the rail for dear life. "Is this your first time-travel?"

Wait! What? I shook my head and turned around. There was Barbecue Guy. To my left was a clean shaved Korean man sitting near the front of the ship, petting a very large wild tan tabby-looking cat. Another man with a close beard which came to a point, dressed in black puffy breeches and a white flowy shirt stood next to Barbecue Guy. And to my right was a petite ninja with a parrot on her head at the tiller.

"No." My eyes darted around the ship, trying to figure out if I was hallucinating. "No. It's just that I usually walk through doors. It's never happened on a ship. And I tend to get seasick, so..." I spun back around to give myself a moment to watch the horizon and calm my stomach.

"Schooner," said Barbecue Guy. I looked at him and shook my head in confusion. Is his name Schooner or is he calling me Schooner? "Welcome aboard the schooner, *Gretchen*."

"Did someone slip me mushrooms? Peyote? Opium? LSD?"

"No. Were you looking for some? Your breath tells me you found the peanut butter and bananas." He turned to the ninja and said with a raised voice, "Jasmine. You didn't add anything the peanut butter, did you? Or do you think the bread is about to turn?"

"No, Rick," the ninja, who I identified as a ninja by the fact that she was dressed like one. Covered head-to-toe in a black outfit, with her face covered, except for a strip between her eyes. She wasn't wearing an abaya or burqa, so

I went with ninja. "The bread is fresh, the flour is good, and Chris ground the peanuts yesterday."

Rick, who I previously referred to as Barbecue Guy, turned back to me. "See, no one is trying to poison you here."

I dug my knuckles into my eyes. Besides trying to clear my thoughts, it was bright outside. "I'm so confused. I time traveled, but that's not the confusing part. What's confusing is what does a ninja with a beautiful parrot on her head, Barbecue Guy, a Korean guy wearing white pajamas with a giant cat, and this man who looks like he stepped off the *Niña*, *Pinta*, or *Santa María*, have to do with me?" I could feel my anger and frustration building from the pit of my stomach. "This is ridiculous. I'm not supposed to be here. Where's Henry? How did I get here anyway?"

And there we have it, folks. I completely lost my temper. I wanted to throw everything and everyone over the side of the rail. I hadn't felt that much out of control since that morning when I wanted to poke Cathy Stevenson in her stupid pointy nose.

Rick stood there, calmly watching my face turn twenty-shades of angry. No one seemed alarmed. They just stood there. My tears poured down my face, sloppy, snotty, wet. I wanted a reaction from them, something. They didn't react to my overreaction. Columbus's friend nudged Rick, handing him a tankard. Rick held the earthenware by the handle. I swear he looked as though he could've been standing there with a cup of coffee in one hand, chatting with his buddy as they grilled steaks or watched the kids play in the pool. Time traveler? They know about time travel. Okay, Amelia, stop the waterworks.

"Do you always get this angry?" There was that calm demeanor again.

I shook my head. I pulled the bottom of my sweater up to my face. I needed a good blow. The Spanish Conquistador handed me a small hand towel and backed away. My anger began to subside. "I didn't always. I thought it was because the first... no, not first. Second? Yeah, the second time I traveled, I was taken hostage and beat up. Then I ended up in a couple of battles. I just figured I was suffering from PTSD or something like that." I blew my nose in the white linen towel. "It's like all of my emotions are playing in a band in the background, but one of them is playing the loudest. My anger is yelling over the rest of the music. I mean, sometimes the other ones are louder, but it's easier for anger." I shook my head. I hadn't given much thought to my temper, other than I'd been angry all the time. My teeth always felt on edge, ready to bite anyone that crossed my path. "I don't get it. And I certainly don't like it. So, I guess, this is your warning to stay out of my way?"

"How many times have you time-traveled? Two? Is this your third?" The Korean cat whisperer, dressed in a white, airy, linen long sleeved shirt and matching pants that hung loose on him, and was barefoot. A light breeze sent ripples through the fabric as he walked over to us. Like the other two men, he towered over me.

"No. This is my... hold on, I need to count."

He held up his hand to stop me. "Time travel comes with a price."

"Yeah, tell me about it! Every time I travel, I pay a coin." I reached into my empty skirt pocket, I had to be sure the coin wasn't hiding in a crevice. Nope! No flattened coin.

"That's part of it," he continued with a knowing smile. "Do you think you could travel through time unscathed?"

"Oh! And I'm famished and tired." I said triumphantly. "That's not unscathed. I mean, no one likes to deal with a hungry and tired Amelia." I looked around the group for confirmation. "By the way, that's my name, Amelia Spencer."

"Have we met before?" Rick asked, eyebrows knitted. "You seem familiar."

"Not that I'm aware of. It was Murray before Spencer, and before that it was Lindsay. Any of that ring a bell?" No response. He continued to study my face. "I've only traveled back-and-forth in time in Virginia. Oh! And the one time in Scotland, but I sometimes feel like that was just a strange dream, less than a day. I met a couple of young women and a tavern full of pirates, although they said they were just sailors on a merchant ship. However, I don't remember meeting you in any of those timelines."

"I'm Richard," said the Korean man, placing his hand on his chest. "Time travel can... how can I put this gently?" He paused for a moment to gauge me. "Jumble your psyche. You need to learn to control the party of emotions inside before it consumes you."

"Joan," said Rick solemnly as he bowed his head for a

moment. The rest of the group took a moment of silence, for Joan. She must've been part of the crew.

"I don't understand. I'm not Joan. And how am I supposed to control my emotions? That seems so much easier said than done." I stood a moment, thinking about my emotions and how they've spiraled since I started traveling back-and-forth through time. "Does out of whack make sense? They're either all there wrestling for control, or they're absent and I feel nothing."

"Therapy could help, but a little unlikely in your situation." Richard's voice was even, calming. He reached down and stroked the large cat, which looked like a large tabby, a golden tan with dark rings near the tip. The big ball of fur followed him over to our group. "You need to find your inner peace and embrace it. It won't stop the jumble every time you travel, but it can slow the impact."

"Are you telling me that time travel is making me go crazy?"

"I'm saying time travel rewires you every time you cross through the rip. It will drive you mad if you continue to let it go unchecked." The long cat stretched its tan and black body out and walked back to its spot in the sun at the front of the schooner. "If you're unable to find your inner peace, you should stop traveling through time."

"I can't control my inner peace or time travel."

He nodded at me and stroked his chin. Was he contemplating tossing me overboard and taking me out of my angry misery? "We'll work on that until we get to your destination."

"Where are we headed?" I looked over to the ninja at

the tiller. She pulled a rope over to the tiller, one end had a loop, the other was attached to a pulley system. She slipped the looped end over the end of the black tiller and locked the pulley system in place. Then, she pulled over another rope with a looped end and did the same with that rope. With swiftness and ease, she was in front of me, with the parrot flying over to join us.

"Back to the circus," squawked the parrot. No kidding, parrot, this place felt like a circus.

"Sam, we're not headed there," said the ninja as the parrot landed on her head. "I'm Jasmine." She pulled her ninja hood off her head. Sam flew to the top of the main mast. Perched up high, she opened her wings letting the wind carry her up and then back down. A full head of curly dark brown hair popped out the ninja hood like fireworks.

"You're not Japanese," I exclaimed, staring at the woman with round dark brown eyes and light brown skin. She looked like a mix of Mediterranean and North African to me.

The crew of the *Gretchen* laughed. "No," she said. "I'm Egyptian. Well, my grandparents were from Egypt. I'm from Los Angeles."

"Hey! So am I! From Los Angeles, that is. Well, at one point in time. That's where I grew up. I'm not Egyptian and neither were my grandparents." I scrunched the sleeve of my sweater up to my elbow and looked down at my pale arm covered in freckles. "Let me get this straight. You're an Egyptian ninja, but you're really not from Egypt, you're from Los Angeles. Are you even a ninja?"

"On this ship, I'm whatever I want to be." Her smile was wide and radiant.

"Can you be a navigator and let me know where we're going, when we are, and how I can get home?" My shoulders dropped. I had a feeling I knew what the answer would be to the last part of my question.

"Rick can explain more of this to you, but none of us chose to be here. We have different reasons and ways we found ourselves on board this ship. We're a transport ship for time travelers. We don't choose who comes or where we go, we just get you to where you're supposed to be." She looked towards Rick, who handed me the tankard of... water. I could've used something stronger about that time. "As far as when, we don't know yet."

"What do you mean? You won't know?"

Rick leaned against the rail next to me. "Time isn't linear. Especially for us. We show up where we're needed. We take the time traveler where they're supposed to go. Then, we end up in another location and time, with another traveler. Time is wibbles and wobbles. Have you heard of the green flash?"

"I've heard that about time once or twice, about it wibbling and wobbling." I shook my head. "But I haven't heard of the green flash. Is that like a superhero or something?"

His face split in an amused smile. "No. It's when the sun is setting on the ocean's horizon, if conditions are precise, there will be a green flash as it sets. That flash is where there's a rip in time. Conditions need to be correct, and we are gone, or here, whichever the case may be, in that flash."

I leaned hard against the rail, the heat, time travel, and ocean took its toll on my body.

Jasmine walked over and placed a gentle hand on my shoulder. "You need to rest and there will be plenty of time to explain it all to you."

"If you don't know where we're going, then how do you know there'll be plenty of time?" My head spun and I squinted.

"If it was a short distance, you wouldn't need us." We walked towards the hatch that led down to the crew quarters. "We'll set you up in the cabin and talk after you have rested."

CHAPTER TWENTY-FOUR

"Secure the rigging!" A man's voice boomed from above.

I spilled onto the floor with a thud. Aw, crackers! That wasn't a weird dream. I wasn't hallucinating. I traveled to some unknown time, heading to some unknown destination, with the strangest crew I ever met, aboard the schooner, Gretchen. Life. Was. Weird.

I opened my eyes to find a very large tabby cat staring at me. "You're pretty big to be a regular ol' tabby," I said as I reached out to give... her? him?... a pet. Unless there were noticeable furry marbles hanging from the back end of the beast, I would only be guessing. "Male or female, you look like a Whitney. Would you give me a spin and let me know if you're a boy or girl?" Whitney looked at me as though she—or he—had stepped in something rotten. "I'm guessing that's a no." I'd have to ask Richard about his feline companion's name.

Speaking of something rotten, the first item on my

agenda was to find the head. I hoped the toilet didn't consist of me going to the head of the ship and sticking my bare butt over the edge. I could barely stand straight on a ship, every wave, gust of wind, rotation of the earth was felt. Walking was risky enough, let alone doing a balancing act over the rail. The ocean was rough. Unable to gain my balance, I slid down to the floor. Whitney laid in front of the door, preventing my escape. My bladder would have to wait. This was one of those times I needed to listen to the cat. We sat there, sliding a little with the waves, out of the way from the crew of the *Gretchen*. The ginger tea Jasmine made for me earlier to settle my stomach wore off with the tossing of the ship. I laid down next to Whitney. Running my hand over her soft fur was soothing to not only her— or him— but to me as well.

Shouting and heavy feet running from one end of the schooner to the other, continued to pour through the ceiling of the small cabin. It almost sounded like the waves would pour in as well. The cabin window was closed, the walls and ceiling sealed, and Whitney and I stayed dry.

"Should we try and help them?" I sat up, looked at the door and ceiling, and then back at Whitney. It laid its head back down. I took that as a 'no' and closed my eyes. Twirl, twirl, rub, and another rub, we pretended everything was fine. We were on a time traveler transport ship. What could possibly go wrong? If things didn't calm down soon, I would wet myself and possibly toss my cookies, all in one go. However, the gods of time travelers wouldn't let anything happen to the ship. I stretched out, removed Whitney's head from putting additional pressure on my bladder and tried to think of anything but crashing waves, waterfalls, rain, a faucet running, or a toilet.

Thirty minutes passed, the storm subsided, my stomach settled, and it was time to empty my bladder. A light rap at the door pulled me from my dazed cuddle session with Whitney.

"What are you doing down there?" Jasmine asked as she opened the door.

Whitney stood up, stretched, nudged past Jasmine, and wandered into the crew area. "It was safer down here." I looked over towards the bed, unmade from my earlier nap. "How do you use the toilet on this ship?"

"Sorry about that," she giggled out. "I should have shown that to you yesterday."

"Yesterday?" I exclaimed. It felt like a little nap. Sure, I was hungry. I was always hungry after time travel, that wasn't new.

"Don't worry, it's still the morning, you have a lot to learn about being part of the crew while you are with us," she said as she held the door open for me. "Now, let's get you to the toilet and we'll have breakfast in a few." Whitney climbed up the ladder to the top deck in no time flat. One paw after the other, until they pranced out onto the deck.

Along the outer wall there was a small closet. Unless one was looking for it, it easily was overlooked. I say that because I easily overlooked it. Behind the door was a small closet with a toilet. It reminded me of an outhouse or port-a-john. Instead of the hole leading to a reservoir filled with chemicals or a hole dug deep in the ground, it led to a small, piped port out of the ship. It was primitive, functional, private, and above all, safe. I wasn't sticking my rear end over the rail and throwing caution, and whatever else there was, into the wind.

In the middle of the crew cabin sat a table with four stools underneath it. Closet business taken care of, hands washed, and a grumbling tummy settled from motion sickness and ready for food. I helped Jasmine prepare French toast, eggs scrambled and over easy cooked in the leftover bacon grease. I sliced strawberries and placed them in a bowl in the center of the table. "This is my favorite breakfast and you just so happened to have the ingredients," I said as I marveled at the bounty. The kitchen area was small, split in half by the oven. It was easier for me to prep on one side or at the table, as she cooked at the stove.

"It's funny how that happened," she said with caution. I wasn't sure if she was being sarcastic or not. I cocked my head to the side like a curious kitten.

"How do you get food, especially these strawberries on the ship? I can barely get strawberries to last a few days in the refrigerator at home, let alone on a ship."

She stopped for a moment, flipped over a slice of bread, and then looked at me. "How many times did you say you traveled?"

"Well, each time I traveled to the past, I returned to my time. Somewhere around eight times, I guess."

"Wow!" Her eyebrows raised nearly to the top of her hairline. "Have you ever experienced an extraordinary event, besides traveling through time, where you couldn't explain how you got something? Maybe you somehow found a basket full of food. Or you never shot a gun before and you had perfect aim, and were able to hunt?"

I thought back to the many events, strange and not so strange, and it struck me. "Yes! There was this one time when we were running low on food and I was washing up in a stream, and there were these fish just swimming about. They were thick and I thought I could just reach in and grab one."

Using her spatula, Jasmine slid a perfectly browned piece of French toast onto the pile of toast. "And did you?" She added another slice of eggy bread to the pan.

"Well, it took me a couple of tries, but yeah, I did."

"Didn't you find that odd?"

"I felt like a great provider. Henry tried to do the same and came back to our little camp empty handed. I just thought I was better at catching fish."

"It's more likely that your god was providing for you."

I shook my head and scrunched my face. "I don't believe in a god."

"Well, one sure does believe in you." She shrugged her shoulders.

"I only went to church because I had to, not because I believed in the bible or anything like that."

"Listen, you travel through time."

"Rips in time as Rick mentioned yesterday. And I experienced it firsthand, so I know it exists."

"What about aliens? Extraterrestrials? Beings from another planet? Do you believe that there is life somewhere out there?" She pointed to the sky with her spatula.

"I think it's arrogant for us to think we're the only intelligent beings in all the universes. So, yeah, I think there is life out there."

"Have you seen a spaceship? Little green men?"

"Of course not! It's just..." The anger and frustration bubbled deep in my stomach.

"So, you can believe in something you haven't seen or can prove." She turned back to her pan. I was speechless and all I could do was stare at the back of her curly hair.

"Does that mean that I'll be taken care of when I time travel?" I stopped for an answer that didn't come. "So, whichever god is sending me through these rips in time will make sure I'm good?"

"No. Sometimes a prayer is answered, most of the time you're to figure it out on your own." She took another slice of bread from the pan and removed it from the heat. She had used all the slices of bread. "You can die in another time. Nothing is guaranteed, your safety, food, or returning home. Nothing." She choked a little on the last 'nothing'. I wondered if that had anything to do with the person named Joan that Rick had mentioned the day before. "Are you sure you don't believe in a god?"

"Maybe I've met one? I don't know. In my time, my friends Elizabeth and Hector Bennedet have two dogs named Apollo and Artemis. Then, I met Elizabeth Woods and Hector Bennet in seventeen fifty-four, and Hector had two dogs named Apollo and Artemis. Apollo was injured chasing wolves, and Artemis caught a deer on her own. We were running low on food, so that deer was needed by our entire group." Did I believe that the two dogs could have been the Greek gods, Apollo and Artemis? No. Of course not. How could they be? *Obviously*, it's just a coincidence that I met people in two different time periods that look the same, have the same first name, and have two dogs that look the same with the same names. Super strange coincidence, that's all."

Jasmine didn't say much. A tilt of her head and a soft hmm. "That *is* a remarkable coincidence." And she left it at that. Okay, so no answers from her on my grand posit.

If she wasn't going to fill in those blanks for me, then, perhaps, I could learn more about the *Gretchen*. "Okay, so you're an Egyptian ninja, that's not really a ninja, and you're really from Los Angeles."

"Strange how that happens," she said, the song in her voice was more inviting to my questions. Curiosity getting the best of me, I continued, "Why a ninja?"

She walked and set the last bit of the French toast on the plate and placed it on the table. "I wanted to learn self-defense, so when I get back to my place and my time, I could protect myself from my ex-husband."

Well, that left a huge door open to more questions! She walked over to the ladder leading to the top deck. "Oh? Is it possible for you to get back?"

"Sure, when I've finished my service to the gods, I will earn my way back to home and my time."

"How did you end up here?"

"I walked through a door. Well, I suppose ran for my life through a door would be the best explanation."

She climbed up to the top of the ladder towards the bright square of light shining down into the crew deck. A beacon to the world outside and off the ship. "Breakfast," she called out. She took a moment as she descended the stairs. "I don't like to talk about it too much, but it's rare that I have another woman aboard."

She hopped down, skipping the last step. "My ex was a manipulative ass. He tried to make everyone think I was an unstable madwoman. He stood at the end of my driveway, chatting up the neighbors like they were best friends. You know, he just wanted to be friendly to *my* neighbors. At least, that is what they all thought. So, when he would come around at night and jiggle my doors or stare into the windows, it was all my imagination. Until he realized I set up a camera at the front door. One night, I let my dog, Turtle—yeah, I know, a strange name for a dog—well, she had to do her last nighttime business. I let her out in the backyard, while I stood on the back porch. She wandered into the dark corner next to the fence." Her voice grew quiet as she stared into the beacon from the square port. She wiped a tear and gave a strong smile back towards me. "She yipped. I called. She didn't come, but Frank did, bloody knife in hand. I ran inside, he barreled in after me. I made it to the front door. I had to escape. I slammed it shut behind me and collapsed. That's how I ended up here."

Rick, Richard, and the Spaniard–I hadn't found out his name yet–chatted as they approached the port. I don't know what they were discussing, but the interruption annoyed me. Still hadn't found any inner peace, I guess.

"I should've died but ended up here instead," she said.

"So, you now must pay a debt to earn your life back? Is

it worth it? I mean, it seems safer here. Sharks may be a problem. Pirates? Seems like they would be more afraid of ferryman ship than you would be of them."

"My children," she choked on her emotions. "They were spending the week at camp when I ended up here. I must get back to them. I can't leave them with that monster," she said through gritted teeth and with fire in her eyes.

I was scared for her children. What if she couldn't get back to them? I worried about my daughter, Hannah. She was in college, worked at *The Salty Dog* in Williamsburg, Virginia, and could always turn to my friends Beth and Hector Bennedet. I knew she would be fine. But to never see her again? Or to hear the excitement in her voice when she told stories of her and Emily's trips to the Outer Banks of North Carolina, where they would go on treasure hunting explorations and dives? I didn't want to imagine a life without her, or without Henry. Wiping away the few tears I shed for both of us and our families, I finished setting the table for breakfast.

CHAPTER TWENTY-FIVE

*R*ick's boat shoes were the first to come down. Followed by a barefooted Richard, who landed softly on the deck. The Spaniard was last to join us. Sam, the parrot, and Whitney–the very large tan tabby-looking cat, but to be honest, I had never seen a cat that large in my life–remained on the deck. Were they sailing the ship? At that point, I would believe it.

There was a place setting at each of the four stools, and I had my plate and utensils off to the side. I could sit on the floor out of their way or head to my cabin if they didn't want me around.

"Señora, por favor," said the Spaniard offering me his stool next to Richard.

"Thank you, mister... you know, I never got your name."

"Sí, Cristobal Roberto de Gutierrez, at your service," he said with a flourished bow and a Spanish accent. Oh, thankfully I didn't need to dig deep and pull out my terrible Spanish. The last time I attempted to speak Spanish was during my Spanish final in 11th grade. It had been more years than I cared to count since that class, and I barely passed the class with a C. He sat on the bunk behind me, maybe we could find a box or something so we could all sit together. I wasn't sure how long I would be on the ship, but if I was going to be part of their crew, then by all means, we were a crew that would sit together.

"If you ferry time travelers, why is there only seats for the four of you? I mean, it's not like you're not expecting guests."

"Most are timid and hide out in the cabin. We have additional seating, but we'll have to move the flooring to get to it. Later, of course. Let's start before the food gets too cold," said Rick. Even though he spoke English quite clearly, he held onto his Eastern European accent, it sounded close to Russian to me.

I sat and watched, picking up clues on how they proceeded. I learned that little trick the first time I went back to 1754. While visiting Elizabeth Woods, with Henry, in Fredericksburg, we sat down for a formal dinner. Well, formal as far as I was concerned. Forks, spoons, knives, plates, saucers, a glass, another glass, for someone that tried to convince her eighteenth-century husband to go through a drive-thru for breakfast, all the accoutrement was a bit much. I remembered working my way from outside to in with the utensils, but it all felt foreign to me. There was nothing that complicated about our set-up on the *Gretchen*. However, I wasn't sure if there was supposed to be an order to who plated first. Or if they passed plates around the table. Then, the group bowed their heads in prayer. "Thank you, God, for providing us with this bounty," Rick began. He finished the prayer with an "amen," which was repeated by Jasmine. Richard mouthed his prayer quietly. I watched the group, and turned my head to see if Cristobal was participating with the rest of the crew. Cristobal made the sign of the cross. I sat there, quiet, and respectful to their beliefs, but unsure if they expected me to pray to their god or gods. Heads raised, I smiled at them, and we passed the plates around serving ourselves breakfast.

"That was quite a storm this morning," I looked across the table to Rick. "The cat was a great comfort. She? He?" I turned to Richard looking for the answer.

"Her name is Starboard," he said with a smile of a proud father.

"She's beautiful and possibly the largest cat I've ever seen. I'm pretty sure I've seen dogs smaller than her. What do you feed her? Small children?"

"She's a wildcat from Scotland," he laughed. "She joined our crew with... oh, what was that woman's name, Rick?"

Rick half-chewed his piece of French toast, shoving it into his cheek before answering. "Wasn't it Winnie or Winifred? She left Starboard with us on the third trip." He chewed and swallowed. "That was the last time she traveled with us. I wonder what happened to her."

"Don't you know what happens to the people you drop off?"

Richard placed his fork on his plate and leaned into his

elbow on the table to turn to me. "We can't possibly keep up with everyone. It's our responsibility to get them where the gods need them. That is all. No more, no less."

"How do you know where they're needed?" The questions I really wanted answered, I asked next. "How do we know where I'm needed or if I'm needed? What if I'm not supposed to be here?" I didn't know if they had the answers, but they seemed to be doing this long enough that they might. I had no one else to ask; they were it.

"We're headed towards France. We don't choose where we go, but when I checked the star charts last night, it showed we're headed towards France," Jasmine said as she put her mug of tea down next to her plate. She had a half-eaten slice of French toast teasing me. I love French toast. "We could make it there. We could be intercepted."

"Intercepted?" I interrupted. "By whom or what? Storm? Pirates?"

"Yes," she giggled. Apparently, my question was funny. Were there that many variables to traveling through time or getting where I'm supposed to go? Questions bombarded my thoughts. "The direction isn't as important as the destination."

I threw up my hands, dropping my fork next to my plate. "Now, that doesn't make any sense." My emotions flared deep. The rising frustration flushed my cheeks and burned my ears.

Richard placed a calming hand on my right hand. "The answers will come." His voice was calming and direct. "Release the frustration you have bottled up. Don't let it consume you."

"Easier said than done, Richard." I took a deep breath in. As it released, it stuttered and choked me. The frustration held tight in my chest. Another deep breath in. Don't cry, Amelia, don't cry. The frustration loosened its grip on my chest. Another deep breath. *You've got this.* That exhale was more controlled.

"That's a good first step, but there is more to learn." He turned back to his plate and picked up his fork and cut a piece of the eggy bread.

More to learn? Cheese and rice, can't anything be simple? I simply nodded.

"I don't want to be a burden to all of you. I can help." My breakfast companions continued to eat. Cristobal came over and grabbed another piece of bacon and French toast. "You know, I can do more than just help prepare breakfast and pet Starboard."

I glanced over to Starboard curled up on Richard's bunk, with the black ringed tip of her tail wrapped around her. She lifted her head and plopped it back down, unamused by my declaration of doing more than just petting her. I picked up my fork to finish my breakfast. The syrup saturated the slice of bread. I poked at the cold eggs, which looked unappetizing at that point.

"What can I do to help when there's rough weather or even if there isn't rough weather?"

I needed something to do to take my mind off the unknown of why I was headed to France. France of all places! I didn't have the best of luck with the last group of French soldiers I met in 1754 Virginia. Perhaps, this was a way for the French to make amends for the abuse I endured from Bouchard. Ha! My luck would have me running into a young Bouchard setting his course to want to beat the snot out of me later in life. "So, there's no way to learn the year before we land? I haven't exactly made friends with a certain group of French soldiers."

"We won't know until we get there," said Jasmine as she stacked her empty plate on top of Rick's empty plate. Richard handed Rick his almost empty plate. I wasn't going to finish the rest of the eggs. I took a couple of bites, but the morning's stormy waters still tickled in the corner of my stomach.

"Finished?" asked Richard.

"Yeah," my voice was quiet and trailed off. Thoughts of breakfast with Henry came rushing to the front of my mind. Where was he? Was he worried about me?

Jasmine came over and gave my shoulder a rub. "Still feeling a little queasy?"

"Kinda, not really. I'm okay. It's just..." don't cry, Amelia. "I'm worried about my husband, Henry. We were together when I slipped here, but he wasn't with me when I woke up."

Rick picked up the plates and carried them to the galley. "Not everyone can travel. He's probably still at home, wondering where you ran off."

"He's traveled with me a couple of times and I saw him enter the room before I passed out. I thought he would have traveled with me. Like before."

"Henry," Rick contemplated his name. "We've had at least a dozen Henrys on this ship. What does he look like?"

"He's six-feet tall. About a hundred eighty pounds. Broad shoulders." I held out my hands to mimic the width of his shoulders. "Brown hair, blue eyes, devilishly handsome. He was from England, originally, then sailed to America in a seventeen forty-six timeframe. I met him when I traveled to Virginia in seventeen fifty-four." I pointed to just below my right clavicle. "He has a scar below his right clavicle from a bullet wound. It didn't go deep, but I couldn't find it. Got gross and infected. He traveled with me for the first time after that. Then again, a few months later back to seventeen fifty-five Virginia. Then, we came back that December. So, yeah... he can travel through time."

Rick closed his eyes and crossed his arms over his chest. Was he taking a power nap in the middle of my description? Was I that boring? I looked around to everyone else. They were all quiet, deep in thought. "There was that one guy, I'm sure his name was Lord something something Spencer. I remember he said 'mayhap' quite a bit," Jasmine was the first to speak up. "Good looking guy, with that adorable quirk."

"Yes! Lord Henry James Spencer, that's him!" I jumped out off my stool, ready to race around the cabin. "Where did you take him? When?"

"Ah, yes. I remember him. Really good guy. He knew his way around a ship," Rick said. "We were headed towards London and came across a ship. He joined their crew."

"He just joined a crew? Why would he do that?"

"It was his destination," Rick said.

"Did he know them? Which ship? Where were they headed?"

"I don't think he knew anyone. What ship was it, Richard?"

Richard ran his hand across his freshly shaved chin. Starboard stretched and pounced out from the bed and came over to Richard for a rub before she climbed up the ladder to the deck. "Wasn't it the Charles the second or something like that?" he asked and looked towards me for the answer. I just shrugged. How would I know? "There have been so many ships in the thousand years I've been doing this."

Cristobal stood from his bunk and joined the group, standing within inches of me, as the area around the table was tight. "I remember where they were headed." Cristobal's head dropped slightly. "They were headed towards my home. I wanted to join the crew, but it wasn't my time."

"Well, what time was it? Now? One hundred years from now? When?"

Richard held up his hand, motioning me to stop. "We had a couple of travelers since that transport. We cannot recall all that have sailed the seas with us. It wasn't at this exact time, but it could have been before or after this week. You must have faith that the gods know when and where you are to be. If that is with your husband, you will find him. If it is not, well, we cannot change your destiny. Only the gods can."

Frustration bubbled in my gut. Or it could have been the eggs. Either way, I wanted to throw up and cry, scream, and yell. Everyone went about their business around me, cleaning the galley, straightening up their bunks. A tantrum would get me nowhere, but fresh air might help clear my head. I took a breath, patted Richard on the shoulder as I passed by him on my way to the ladder.

I emerged from below into the bright almost noonday sun. I knew it was close to noon because the sun was directly overhead. I looked out towards the horizon in the direction of the bow. Starboard was stretched out in the sun, warming her belly. Sam, the parrot perched on the figurehead, as if she was telling the ship where to sail. A deep cleansing breath helped. As did the gentle breeze that filled the sails. France was out there, somewhere. Why did I need to go to France and Henry towards Spain?

Working my way towards the front of the ship, avoiding ropes and the mast, I found myself close to Sam. Another deep cleansing breath, and I caught her attention. "Back to the circus," she called out.

"Ain't that the truth."

CHAPTER TWENTY-SIX

"*B*ack to the circus. Back to the circus," Sam called out, circling the schooner. "Back to the circus."

"Why does she keep saying that?" I held my hand across my brow, blocking the bright sun as I tried to see whatever it was that Sam was alerting to us.

Jasmine ran to the tiller, pulled the ropes off that were securing it from moving back-and-forth while she stretched and practiced her self-defense movements.

"Back to the circus."

"We need to raise the mizzen," Rick called out. "Amelia, grab hold of this rope." I grabbed the rope from Rick and Cristobal joined behind me. We began pulling, hand-over-hand. The rope was heavy and thick. My back and arms burned only a couple of minutes into the workout. I wanted to quit and just drop the rope. I bit down, grunted, and pulled through the pain.

"You're stronger than you realize. Yes?" Called out

Cristobal from behind me. "Come, we raise the sail for the queen."

"For the queen?" The space between my shoulder blades screamed at me to stop. I continued to ignore it.

"Sí. We fight for the queen." Cristobal grunted into the pull. I tried to match his speed and strength. He stood about eight inches taller than me, causing the rope to creep to my armpit. I struggled to keep from getting rope burn and held out my elbow like it was a chicken wing. The awkward position didn't help the cussing coming from my back muscles.

"Hold the line," Rick called out.

"Hold the line," Cristobal called out in response and stopped pulling. I followed suit. Over the couple of days on ship, I learned a lot about crewing the schooner. When we were given orders, we repeated the orders. At first, I found it odd. Couldn't they see that I stopped or was pulling the rope? I would repeat the order, almost under my breath. By the second day, I found my sea legs, voice, and my confidence. If my focus wasn't on finding Henry, I could've easily joined their crew.

"Back to the circus. Back to the circus."

"What does that mean?" I turned to Cristobal as he took the rope out of my hand and wound it up out of the way. He laughed at my expense. I didn't get the joke.

"Back to the circus." Sam circled overhead and landed on Jasmine's head, as she pulled the tiller to the right, keeping us moving straight ahead.

"It looks as though you're about to get your answer," Rick said looking through his spyglass. "We'll land in

France by the morning. Richard will lay your clothes out for you."

I looked down at the pale blue linen pullover long-sleeved shirt I wore with a pair of matching, flowy, linen pants. I ditched the skirt and boots after the second day at sea, and went for lightweight clothes, a large, brimmed straw hat, and barefoot most of the time. I really don't care to wear hats, but with the sun blazing down on me, I preferred to keep my skin from turning a lovely shade of lobster.

"If you don't know when I'm landing, how do you know what clothes I should wear?" I lifted an eyebrow. That's a lie. I can't lift a single eyebrow. When I try, both eyebrows come up, nearly reaching the top of my forehead. I look like a surprised monkey instead of a curious one.

"The morning of the storm, while you stayed secured in the cabin with Starboard, a crate was thrown onto the deck by a great wave," said Rick as he closed the spyglass and handed it to Cristobal. Richard climbed up the ladder from the crew deck and joined the rest of us standing near the rail, as we looked in the direction of France. I couldn't see anything, but I had to trust that Rick knew what he had seen.

"I would have helped, I just didn't know what to do," I said with a slight whine. That morning left me feeling useless and incapable. Especially after all that I had learned over the past week aboard the Gretchen.

"Starboard was sent in there to keep you calm and out of the way," Richard said, his voice as calming as Starboard was for me that day. Jasmine nodded in agreement.

"In the crate was the food we've been eating, and clothes for your journey," Rick concluded.

"Huh? I was wondering how you just so happened to have some of my favorite foods on board. I just thought it was some sort of strange coincidence." I gripped tight on the rail. "Well, it's a lot easier than the other times I traveled. I was pretty much on my own the first couple of times. This is too easy."

My knuckles were white from the death grip on the smooth lacquered wood. The thought of traveling through time being easy left a sense of panic to brew.

Starboard strutted over to us, rubbing around Richard's legs, begging for attention and probably an early dinner. "Yes, my dear, I'll get your food." He turned to me. "Please, come help."

I nodded and followed them down the ladder to the galley. Richard opened a cabinet, pulling out a can of cat food and Starboard's dish. "Sometimes the easier it is on our ship, the more difficult your journey. You've come a long way with your breathing and centering, but I'm afraid you will find struggles ahead." He spooned out the food into the dish.

"Why do you feed her canned cat food when there's an entire ocean full of fish for her to eat?"

He looked at the label on the can, "This one is chicken dinner. There aren't any chickens swimming around out there."

Starboard fussed at Richard. She didn't necessarily meow, it was more like she was talking to another cat instead of a human. He placed the dish on the floor. "You will need to concentrate and work on seeking tranquility if you are to survive. I know you can achieve it."

"I'm glad you have the confidence. There really hasn't been much to trigger me here. Who knows what I'm going to encounter. What happens if I travel through time again and I end up acting like a two-year-old that had her juice box taken away instead of an insolent teenager?"

"You know what to do. Stay away from the spotlight and survive to travel home. Deep breaths." Within three steps, he crossed the small galley and stood in front of me. He placed a hand on each of my shoulders and looked directly into my eyes. "And don't worry, I'm not going to continue to tell you prayer may help, so continue the meditation."

"Cleansing breaths and meditation. Got it." I gave him a salute. "Anything else?"

"Try not to get yourself in trouble," he said with a slight smirk. He ran a hand over Starboard's back and headed to the ladder.

I let out a chortle. "Apparently, you don't know me at all."

With his hands on the rails of the ladder and one foot ready to climb, he stopped and looked at me. The look stopped me in my tracks before I entered my small cabin. "Winifred, the one who brought us Starboard, she traveled a few times. Back-and-forth to the sixteen eighties, she mentioned on her last voyage with us. She had met a sailor for the English. She was pregnant with his child when we took her to Scotland. Too many times she traveled, and she couldn't master finding her center and peace. I'd like to think she's living happily ever after with her sailor and their child. The past is not gentle to women, please try to..."

I held up my hand to stop him. "I understand. It's not easy, but I've listened to your instructions and have taken it to heart." I placed a gentle hand over my heart. "Truly, thank you for trying to save my sanity, and everything else."

In the cabin laid out a shift, stays, a dark blue and light blue striped underskirt, and I stopped before I looked at the rest. They were delivering me at least two hundred, if not three hundred years to the past, and to France! An English to French dictionary or a translator would've been helpful. Couldn't they have fit that in the crate? Ugh! Going to the past was one thing. Going to the past and to a country where I don't speak the language, not even passably? Well, the time travel gods better know what they're doing, because I hadn't a clue what was in store for me.

Later that afternoon, the clouds tumbled in, drowning our ship in darkness. The wood deck was like water under my feet—unsteady and unforgiving. The ship rolled back-and-forth and side-to-side. The choppy water sent the crew to work, and I was ready to help. My stomach might not have been ready, but I was going to throw myself into the middle of the melee regardless. Heavy ropes moved through my hands, pulling, and tugging to release the knots and bring the sails down. The wind picked up, and we didn't have time to spare. Loose sails would pull and rip under the force of the sharp wind. Secure the rigging.

Secure the sails. Secure the equipment. Secure ourselves. Even though the ship was on a mission from gods, aliens, or time itself—I hadn't decided which I was to believe— that didn't mean we were entirely safe.

Rick barked orders to the crew. Although he had every reason to have panic, his deep, commanding voice was smooth and calm. He stood near the helm with Jasmine, as she hauled a rope from the port side of the ship, attached through the pulley system, and slipped it over the end of the black painted tiller. A section about a foot down from the tip was worn from hands and ropes. Rick stepped back as she scurried in front to grab the rope on the starboard side. The pulley system would allow her to hold the tiller in place, locking it in, if necessary. Sam drew my attention away from Jasmine's efforts at the tiller, as she flew two laps around the ship. Her call of going back to the circus was drowned out by the sound of crashing waves against the hull. I expected a third lap, instead she flew down the port in front of the poop deck where Jasmine and Rick stood, then down to the crew deck with Starboard just moments behind. Two less passengers to worry about. We scuttled around the deck, releasing sails and binding them to the arms of the masts.

First one drop smacked me on the cheek. Then another poked me a little too close to my left eye for comfort. The rain began to pelt down on us, becoming a deluge as the ship was tossed about the waves. Time wasn't on our side, we had to secure the ship without protective clothing. Although I questioned the efficiency of the dryness a raincoat offered with the flood that spilled across the deck with every wave, I stopped myself from darting to my cabin to grab one.

The deck slick from rain and ocean water, I slid towards the rail from the swell of a wave rolling thunderously under the ship. A rope offered me hope as I slid down the deck towards the wooden rail. I reached out to grab it, only to find the rope just out of reach. I clawed for anything to stop my descent. The angry ocean reached up to snatch me. I clenched my eyes tight and took a deep breath. I was startled out of my acceptance of plunging into the frigid waters when Richard grabbed my left forearm with his left hand. With a renewed hope that I could live through that ordeal, I grabbed his left forearm with both desperate hands before I tumbled over the side to be lost at sea before stepping foot in France. Maybe that was the ocean knowing I needed to get to Spain and find Henry. Perhaps, I would bob along until a ship on route to Spain would pluck me out of the shark infested waters and reunite me with him.

"You need to get below," Richard growled, digging his heels into the deck, and readjusting his grip on my forearm. His white linen, nearly transparent from the water, offered no protection from the cold and storm.

My light blue linen clothes, although not nearly as transparent, clung cold to my skin. My teeth chattered out, "But you need my help."

"Now is not the time for heroics," he grunted through his teeth, his grip tightened on my slipping arm. His muscles began to shake from the cold and strain. The vein in his neck bulged and throbbed under the pressure.

Neither one of us could hold on to each other for much longer, and if I continued to be stubborn, I would send us both over the rail. "Keep Starboard safe."

I nodded, slipped once more with another harsh swell of the ocean, banging my knee on the deck. Before the next swell could hit, I was shimmying down the ladder to the crew deck, with a slippery grip and slick footing under my bare feet.

Starboard, Sam, and I scuttled into my cabin to weather the storm. My clothes soaked from rain and salty ocean water, took effort to peel off my body. My stupid foot kept hanging up on the leg of the pants, and with the help of another rogue wave, they sent me flying backwards onto the bunk I tried to keep dry. Landing on my rear end, I braced myself with my elbows. I looked over to my left to find a wet Starboard slipping under the blanket. Sam called out, "Back to the circus," before joining Starboard under the blanket. Well, there went a dry bed. Sheets stuck to my wet skin as I slid naked under the blankets. I thought my teeth would crack from the chattering. Where was Henry?

The tossing, turning, rocking, and rolling, lasted a good hour. Conversation crept under my cabin door, alerting me, Starboard, and Sam, that everyone had secured themselves on the crew deck. I threw back the quilt, flopped my legs over the side of the bunk, and willed my body to find dry clothes. With my usual linen outfit heaped in a wet mound on the floor, I dug out a shift and a robe from the closet. They would have to make do until I could rinse the salt water out of my clothes and get them dried.

Starboard popped her head from underneath the quilt, exposing Sam loafed up against her. The three of us were fairly dry, albeit still cold. Starboard reached her paws out in front of her, lifted her rear into the air, and opened her mouth in a stretched yawn. Leaning over, I offered my left forearm to Sam. After the abuse I experienced from Bouchard and the wound from a bullet grazing me—or was it part of wagon shrapnel, I will never know—during the battle on the Monongahela, the small bruises from Richard's fingers were nothing to worry about. "Back to the circus," she squawked, as she hopped on my arm.

"Yup, back to the circus, Sam."

CHAPTER TWENTY-SEVEN

"*S*tarboard off the starboard bow!" Jasmine called out. I whipped my head around towards the splash.

"Cheese and rice," I responded with matching excitement. I slid to the side of our little wooden dinghy. "I can't see her. It's too dark." I began to panic. Over the past week I spent many hours with Starboard. She followed me around the schooner with her tail up and her movements sleek. The thought of not petting her soft fur as we soaked in the sun, brought an ache to my heart. Finally, a cloud moved just enough from in front of the moon that I could see her head bobbing as she swam towards us. I pulled my sleeves up, ready to scoop her out of the water the moment she was close enough. Cristobal held our boat as still as he could with the waves rocking us back and forth. She was close! Close enough, I could reach out and scoop her into the boat. "I got her!"

Soaked to the core, she was heavier than usual. She

easily weighed in over her normal ten pounds. Water poured off her body, heavy and loud, and drenched my arms to my elbows. She was on the larger size for a female Scottish Wildcat, but lean and muscular, with the water soaked deep into her fur, it felt as though she doubled in weight.

Starboard stretched out her paws onto my lap, ready to curl up. "You can't go with me, sweet girl." I sloughed a puddle of salty ocean water off her head and down her back. Shaking my hand when I reached the tip of her tail. Of all the things I packed in my satchel, a towel was not one of them.

"She has made her choice, señora," Cristobal positioned the boat to start our journey towards the French beach. He estimated it would take us an hour to get there, and he would be back at the *Gretchen* before the sun would give away their location.

"I'm barely responsible for myself, let alone a cat."

"You will find a way. No?"

I let out a defeated sigh and ran my hand over her head, attempting to remove more water from her thick fur. She was wet and now cold. I scooped her up and wrapped her with the bottom of my shift. The rest of my clothing was tucked away in the satchel I brought. My shift wouldn't be dry by the time we made it to shore, but it could be covered with my skirts. Starboard was worth the little discomfort. Closing my eyes, I made a mental request to the universe that I would be able to keep her safe. I wasn't willing to call it a prayer, but it was a request. "What about Richard? Won't he miss her?"

"They looked after each other, she didn't belong to him. Symbiosis. If it is meant for her to come back, she will." He dug the oars into the water—stroke after deep stroke. "Now, it is your turn to care for her, and she will take care of you. Sym..."

"Symbiosis. Got it." I ran my shift over her to remove more of the water. "It's just, I was supposed to settle down with Henry and get a cat, and Henry isn't here, but the cat is, and..."

Tears welled up in my eyes, bubbling over and down my cheeks. I had begun to rely on him as a partner in the mayhem I continued to find myself in. As I sat in a little dinghy, with a wet cat, and a Spaniard from 1475 rowing me towards a country where I didn't know anyone or speak even passable French, I knotted my dark green wool cloak in my hand. We moved further from the *Gretchen* under a cloudy cover in the hours leading to dawn. Ships in the distance patrolled the shore, to prevent smuggling and attack. I wondered what the fine would be for a twenty-first-century woman smuggling a Scottish wildcat into France... well, I didn't know exactly what year or century I was slinking into France. I hoped their English was better than my French.

Moonlight flashed across Cristobal's contorted face. He struggled with the waves as we got closer to shore. "Ah, I know this shore all too well."

"Oh?" I scooted closer in my seat, ready for juicy gossip or an exciting story.

Shadows from the moonlight accentuated his solemn face. Joan was all he said. Nothing more. Joan who?

Okay, change of subject then. "Why doesn't Rick talk about his past?"

"He's from your future and worried that if you went back you would try to change things."

"My future? Like I will meet him in my future?" My neck and jaw tingled as the blood drained from my face. I was in a panic. "And what do you mean if I go back?"

"No. He is from Ukraine; he was a businessman before Russia attacked his country. Men and women picked up arms. He put his wife and children on a train to Poland and stayed behind."

The foggy mist was thick and chilly. I pulled my cloak tight around me, covering the curled-up Starboard in the process.

"A building he was in was bombed and he slipped through a rip in time, through a door, before it came crashing down." His voice wavered. "He didn't want to burden you with the knowledge."

"When I get back, I have to find a way to warn him." I didn't know how I was going to do it. I couldn't stop a war in colonial Virginia, could I stop a war between Russia and Ukraine?

"No, señora," replied Cristobal. "That is why he chose not to tell you. No sympathy. No changes. We all have our paths. Sí?"

"Sí." My heart sank. Why couldn't I keep my curiosity to myself?

Rocks crunched as the bow of the boat scraped upon the shore. My satchel, basket, and hat were the first items I hauled out of the boat. I carried Starboard to my pile plonking her on top.

"Can you give it a push?" Cristobal asked in a whisper, trying to keep our excursion unknown. "I cannot touch the land."

I placed my hands on the bow, shoved my weight into each grunted step, digging into the smooth rocks, and pushed the small boat off the shore. Cold waves lapped at my bare feet and onto my ankles.

"Gracias por todo, amigo," I said, placing my hand over my heart and gave a nod to Cristobal.

He stopped at a couple of strokes of his oars and asked, "When did you learn español?"

A small giggle danced its way out from between my ear-to-ear grin. "I took Spanish in high school. I don't remember much, but for some reason, that came back."

"Sí. You may survive this little adventure of yours after all," he replied. I shook my head. Did he just say that in Spanish? No. My imagination and lack of sleep was running away with me. "I'm in France, not Spain. My French is so terrible, I'm sure they'll be talking about it for centuries to come."

"Mira," he held something the size of a baseball in his hand. It was difficult to see clearly what it was with the moon playing hide and seek with the clouds. "You'll need this." I stumbled to catch the small pouch he threw to me. I held it up, victoriously. "Bueno. Adios, Amelia."

"Adios, Cristobal." Metal clanked together as I tossed the pouch in my hand, judging the weight and contents. Starboard stood near my bare feet and let out a noise that was half purr, half meow. "I might have understood Cristobal speaking Spanish, but I didn't study cat." I tossed the pouch again. "Cristobal wasn't about to let you go hungry."

Smooth rocks shifted under every step as we walked away from the water. My bags heavy with clothes, shoes, and a few supplies only suffered a little wetness from the occasional splash from a wave, a slipped oar, and the water that escaped Starboard's fur. The cool breeze whipped around me fluttering my shift and cloak. Out of reach of the tide, the bags slid from my shoulders with a thud.

The sun was still at least an hour away from gracing the green land, and blue waters of France. I would need to be dressed by sunrise, and without attracting the attention of the locals. "Sorry, girl, no fire this morning." I looked down at Starboard, who gave me a disapproving *meow* in response. "I'm cold too, but we don't need anyone questioning why a woman and her cat are camping out on the beach."

Petticoat, pockets, mantua, stomacher, stockings, shoes, and a hat were stacked unceremoniously in a pile as I began to layer one on top of the other as much as I could while wearing my cloak. Goosebumps exploded out of my skin like the Alps, pushing me to move quickly to dress. I tied the pockets around my waist and pulled my skirt on. "I love a good set of pockets," I declared to my curled-up companion.

And they were a great set of pockets! If so inclined, I was sure I could stick a bottle of wine, a book, the bag of coins, and the cell phone I left on the *Gretchen* in each. I gave my coin purse a pat, safe in the depths of my pockets. Sewn into the lining of my pocket was my debit card. A cell phone wouldn't be able to hide very easily.

I remember trying to hide my phone the first time I traveled through time. When I was captured by the French, I snuck it in a hole near the base of a tree. I wonder if anyone found a two hundred-sixty-year-old cell phone? A debit card was easier to hide, and possibly would be easier to explain. Fully dressed, with my mantua open in the front, fully displaying the front of the skirt, and it pulled towards the back with drapes and ruffles going down the end. A large bow on either side helped accentuate the back, giving the appearance of a larger bottom and hips than already sported. I finished dressing down to my black leather shoes with a delicate buckle. I pulled my cloak over my shoulders, wrapping it tight around me. I sat on my blanket to await the dawn with a sleepy cat curled up on my lap.

Light peeked over the land behind me, bringing a soft golden hue to the misty morning. Large formation of rocks attached to cliffs stood in the ocean. Arches cut through the thick rocks from millennia of the ocean beating and pounding the cliffs, and wind gusting through the arches. The shoreline reminded me of a trip I took to Brighton, the beach was much the same. Tall white cliffs stood guard in the distance. Smooth stones lined the shore. It was said that if you found a stone with a hole through the middle, you would return one day. Was that the same wife's tale about the beach I was abandoned under the cover of darkness?

I picked a light brown stone; it was smooth from the water rolling around it over the years. No hole. I flicked a couple out of my way. A dark brown, white, light gray, another light brown rock—all solid. I tossed a few more towards the water. Ha! I wouldn't be pitching in the majors anytime soon. The stone thunked and tumbled probably thirty feet in front of me if I'm being generous. I leaned back, my hands on the cold stones behind me. Starboard lifted her head, giving me the look of "did you really disrupt my sleep to play with rocks?" I ran a hand across her head, dried and warm from her nighttime swim. As I slid my hand back down, the tip of my pinkie slipped into a tight hole. I turned to look at my hand. A tan rock with dark brown stripes running through it, crowned my pinkie. I picked up the small rock and held it in the palm of my hand. A little divot near the top looked creased, giving it a shape resembling a heart. I held the stone up and looked through the middle of the heart-shaped stone to the crashing waves on the other side. Starboard looked up at me again. "A hole in this heart, like the gapping one I have without Henry. We've got to find him, Starboard." I slid the stone in my pocket, wiped the stray tear from my cheek, and slung the heavy satchel across my chest.

A few boats dotted the shore, awaiting the fisherman who were making their way down to the shore. They were dressed in long loose breeches. Hard and dirty work showed on the light-colored breeches, stained or on another day's wear before they were laundered. I'm certain the dark brown and black ones offered the same level of cleanliness, just less noticeable. The men laughed and joked, carrying baskets, nets, and other supplies for a hard day of work on the water.

"We should get a move on," I said as I crouched next to Starboard, as I finished tying a red ribbon around her neck. It was the best I could do for a makeshift collar. Flinging my satchel over my body and securing my blanket through the loop, I picked up my basket and looked back at where The *Gretchen* once anchored. It was long gone, and I was on my own with Starboard. "Bonjour," I said as we passed the men. I regretted speaking up the moment the word left my mouth. I crossed my fingers hoping they wouldn't try to engage in a conversation. Bonjour was the furthest I could get in conversational French. A few dropped jaws, and a couple of silent nods from others. "I suppose they don't see many ladies with pet cats coming from the beach this early in the morning," I said to Starboard. "Stay close, my sweet girl."

She strode past the men. Her tail held tall and straight, until it hit that little curve to the right near the tip, which she flicked left to right, with sass. They mentioned something about that cat. *Chat*, I knew that word. Whatever they said before or after was lost on me. They continued towards the ocean, and I let out the breath I held.

CHAPTER TWENTY-EIGHT

"*Y*ou're not going to fit in the basket with the food." Star plopped down on the dirt road in front of me. She was tired of walking, and I couldn't blame her. A few hours had passed, and we headed in the direction of Paris on foot. The coins secured in my pocket needed to stretch as far as Spain, and walking would afford me to only spend when absolutely necessary. When I traveled to 1754 Virginia, Henry paid for my every need. Little did I know at the time, his generosity was supplied from the discovery of Blackbeard's treasure. The remnants of the treasure secured in our basement in Fredericksburg, in the 21st century. Fat good it did me in France. I didn't even know what year it was. I couldn't rely on my luck of finding another stranger to pay my way.

I was in search of my husband. I walked up, down, and across the state of Virginia, while pushing carts, boobs deep in mud. So, what if France was five times the size? I could walk it as well if that was required to reunite with

Henry. A stroll through the beautiful country of France, with my attack cat at my side, no problem.

The grass on the side of the road was brown and still damp from the early morning mist. I shrugged my satchel to the ground, placed my basket next to it. I pulled out the blanket and folded my cloak into a makeshift pillow to sit on. On my knees, I rearranged food and clothes from basket to overstuffed satchel. An extra kerchief made for a picnic blanket and an extra pouch to carry food. To be fair, I needed a break as well. I rotated my shoulders back and forth, brought them up to my ears, rotated forward, and back again. The bright sun burned overhead. My wide-brimmed straw hat hung by the ribbon from my satchel, giving me easy access to plop it on my head to protect my eyes and face. My kerchief would keep my fair-skinned chest from getting too sunburned.

By my guesstimate, it would take us five days to walk to Paris, where I could stock up on supplies, rest a couple of days, and try to earn some money for the next leg of our journey which was to find a boat to take us down the Rhone. Just a hop, skip, and jump on over to Spain. I was making this stuff up as I went along. There was no rhyme or reason to my journey, other than, "Spain is over there... somewhere... in that direction... over yonder." What was I doing?

I didn't want to pull out the coins Cristobal had given me, while we traveled on the roads. It was bad enough I was dressed like a lady in my blue striped ensemble, but if someone knew there was a pouch in my pocket, we certainly would be robbed. "How much of an attack cat are you?" Star didn't answer, as she stuck her nose in the basket looking for cheese. "Could you hold your own in a fight?" A tan and black paw swiped around the basket sitting next to me. "Here," I said, pulling out a piece of salted fish from a cloth. "I'm not sure the salt is all that good for your kidneys, but you left abruptly, and Richard didn't pack your food."

The fish was between her teeth, and she high tailed it to the crunchy grass, barely taller than her head, and a few feet away, before I could blink or fuss at her to chew slowly. My Campfire Guides First Aid badge I earned in fifth grade didn't include kitty Heimlich. "Don't choke!" I called out into the field. The man with a cart walked by as I yelled into the field. He tried to avert his eyes from the crazy woman shouting into an empty field.

On the third day of travel Star ran off into the nearby field as the crackle of wheels on the path grew louder from behind our small encampment. A gray-haired man, with years of hard work written over his face and his slightly hunched shoulders, rode in the seat of a wagon pulled by a chestnut horse, which was only slightly younger than her owner.

"Bonjour," I called out with a wave.

He responded with a tip of his black felted brimmed hat, and more words beyond a salutation than I could understand.

"English?" My face doesn't have an inside voice to keep my confusion hidden. Nope, my face contorted, partially from the confusion, the other part from the rising sun. There was less gray in the skies that morning, giving me hope that we would feel the sun's warmth by noon. The temperature remained chilly most of the day. My cloak and five billion layers of clothes kept me warm enough during the day. At night, I would gather whatever wood and grass I could find and keep a little fire burning throughout the night. I hardly slept. Too cold and too concerned about my surroundings. I should've stopped at a public house that we passed, but I didn't think I could sneak Starboard inside. Also, there was my brilliant idea of conserving money, and that didn't include staying in a room when I could freeze my ass off outside.

The man shook his head, and replied, "non."

"Español?" Again, my quest for communication in a language I could understand was met with a negative. Sugar snaps!

He pointed at me, said something I couldn't understand, then pointed down the road ahead of us. "Paris?" I asked.

He again pointed down the road. I thought he was asking me where I was headed. He must've thought I was asking for directions. With a wave of his hand, he pointed to the back of his cart, filled with sacks of grains, dried and ready to take to market. "Rouen," he said. Did he say get in? Why didn't I take French in high school instead of Spanish? Growing up in Los Angeles, it seemed reasonable to learn Spanish. We were within a couple hours' drive from Mexico, and the neighborhood had a large Latino population. Other than the short conversation I had with Cristobal, that was the extent of my usage of Spanish since high school. I've had to know more French in the past few years than I could have ever imagined. If I made it back to my time, I would get one of those language apps for my phone. My poor phone, unceremoniously left behind on the *Gretchen*. It wasn't going to work anyway. No electricity. No cell phone service. No Internet. It was best —safer, smarter—to keep modern technology out of the past.

Perhaps, I was closer to Paris than I thought. I hadn't made this trip before, especially by foot.

"Oui," I answered. "Merci."

Unable to hide my enthusiasm for a ride, I hopped up off my makeshift pallet that I sat on while picking at bits of food from my pack. A shove here, a stuff there, and I was packed up within moments. "Star," I called out to the field. "Let's go!"

I hopped in the back of the cart and called again. "Starboard, we're leaving."

The man said something I didn't understand, but he seemed confused and slightly frustrated with me. We exchanged stressed smiles. Tall stalks of brown grass swished and swayed. Starboard ran out of the field, a field mouse dangled limp from her mouth. Within four graceful leaps, she was sitting next to me enjoying her morning meal. The only word I understood from the man was "chat". There was, perhaps, a ridiculous reason why I even knew the word. There was a vintage poster I had seen for a cabaret in Paris. On the yellow poster was a black cat, its tail curled down as it sat on a red block. Was it a wall or a table? I can't remember, but I remembered it sat on something red. To its right were the words "Tournee du

Chat Noir," *black cat tour*. The poster was iconic and the only reason I knew *chat* translated to *cat*.

"Oui, my chat." Starboard's fur was soft and warm from the morning sun, as I ran my hand over her head and down her back. Her red ribbon lost the day before was replaced with a blue ribbon. If she kept that up, I would need to spend our travel money on replacement ribbons. She continued to munch on her meal. I found it gross and couldn't watch, but she was fed. She left the butt and the head for me to unceremoniously, and not very gracefully, flick off the back of the cart with my foot. Dust from the wagon covered the wet lump as we continued down the road. She licked the back of her paw and gave herself a morning bath. With a full tummy and an easy ride, she found a spot to curl up and nap. I continued to watch the dusty lump until it was out of sight.

The ride was uneventful. Chilly, but uneventful. I pulled my cloak tighter around me. A man dressed in brown breeches and coat, with a black felt hat, riding on the back of a black horse gave me a nod as he rode past. Middle class? Perhaps. I imagined he was a merchant, on his way to do merchant things. Or he could have been a doctor, on his way to bleed another patient and do absolutely no good. A carriage with giggling women came from the opposite direction. It was nothing too fancy, but the curtains were drawn for privacy, and to keep out the dust and sun. A young boy, no more than twelve or thirteen, with a head full of dark brown hair, a dingy white shirt, black pants that went just below his knees, and shoes that looked too small for his feet. Perhaps he was in that awkward teenage growth spurt where they look like puppies, with big goofy paws. Their feet grow faster than the rest of their bodies. I could never keep up with Hannah's shoes during her spurt. One minute I'm buying a new pair; the next minute, her toes are bursting out the ends. The puppy held a stick in his hand as he guided a brown and white cow down the path.

Foot traffic continued to increase. I recognized the pattern. I twisted my body to look ahead. Oh, my! A tall Catholic cathedral was being repaired. Men moved large bricks with pulleys and ropes. To our right was a river, bustling with boat traffic. The crowded streets, lined with buildings two and three stories high, slowed our pace. Starboard raised her head to take in the scene. I slid my hand under her front legs and brought her to my lap. She was ready to pounce and run away from the chaos. On board a time traveling ship was much quieter than the streets of... I turned and looked around. I wouldn't recognize historical Paris compared to any other city. However, I knew that cathedral was not Notre-dame in Paris. "Where are we?" I asked, hoping he would understand my English.

"Rouen," he replied over his shoulder, keeping a steady eye on the children running up and down the streets. There was that word again. It must be the name of the city. It was larger and busier than I had expected. I had it in my head that the only big city in France was Paris, and that is why I had set my eyes on using it as my starting point.

Women carried baskets of laundry, vegetables, and breads. People talked, negotiated, bartered, and argued. A young girl, of around seven, with blond hair, barefoot, and wearing an ankle length brown tunic over a shift, carried a wiggly baby, no more than a year old wearing what looked like a shift, on her hip. Her blue eyes focused on our cart as we clopped past. Where are her parents? She should be playing or going to school, anything but... no, Amelia, you can't throw 21st century ideals on... I still didn't know what year I was tossed into. The clothes of the common people didn't tell me anything, other than late 17th or early 18th century. Even then, I could be wrong.

The cart driver pulled up next to a warehouse, stopping the cart with a small jerk. Two large wooden doors opened to a large room stacked with barrels, bags, jars, bottles, and bundles. A middle-aged man, with a medium build, dressed in a brown suit with breeches and waistcoat over his tan shirt. White stockings covered his lower legs. He was dressed well enough to pass off as someone with some standing in the community. His shoes told a different story. They were clean with a plain buckle, and very worn around the bottom. His dark brown eyebrows knitted, and his face contorted when he saw me in the back of the wagon, gathering up my belongings and cat.

The two men discussed, negotiated, and poked around the packages while I chased down Starboard to get her in the basket. The old man grabbed a bag from the cart and walked inside. He came back for another.

"Are you taking all of the bags inside?" I asked, gesturing with my hand in a circle around the cart and then pointed to the warehouse.

"Oui, madam," he grunted out while picking up another bag.

I looked at Starboard and said, "Stay in here while I help." I pulled a few bags to the edge of the cart, using my body weight to get them moved. With a deep squat, I was able to get down enough to work it on my shoulder. "Use your legs, not your back." Good grief! Did he have lead in the bag?

The bag knocked my straw hat a little to the side, exposing the wild locks of my auburn hair. I followed the man in the warehouse to the corner and added my bag to the pile. He turned and began to fuss at me in French. By his animated speech and hand gestures as he walked back to the wagon, I'm sure he was telling me a lady shouldn't lift the bags. Good thing I didn't understand him and continued to help. He mumbled something under his breath as I picked up the next bag. With a shake of his head, he conceded. I hopped back in the wagon, pulled more bags to the edge, and he would tote them inside. We had a decent little operation going on. Starboard poked around the bags while she waited for me to finish. His pace slowed as he carried the final bag into the warehouse. In total, we moved about forty bags. His horse will appreciate the lighter weight, and I'm sure he appreciated the reduced time to unload.

"Let's go, Starboard," I said, pulling the cover back on the basket. She poked her nose inside and pulled her head back out. "Get in there," I growled and snapped my fingers at her. *Remember what Richard said, deep cleansing breath. Pet the kitty. Calm your anger.* "Please, Starboard. We need to leave. I promise we will find you something to eat soon."

She walked over and allowed me to place her in the basket. Satchel on, hat squared away, and we were off to find a boat to Paris.

We walked down the busy street and found a quiet pass through towards the river. We emerged near the docks and went looking to hire a boat. Walking towards the docks, I thought I heard a familiar voice. I turned around, "It's you!"

CHAPTER TWENTY-NINE

"*E*lizabeth," I called out to the woman standing in front of me, her eyes grew five times in size. "And Anna. I thought I would never see you two again."

"Amelia?" Elizabeth's face scrunched at the sight of me. "What happened to you?"

"What do you mean, what happened to me?" I returned the confused scrunched face back.

Anna reached in and gave my face a small poke. "How did you get so old?"

"Pardon?" I squeaked, picking my jaw off the ground. Old! I wouldn't call forty-two old. They didn't look a day older since I last saw them ten years ago. Cheese and rice! "How long ago was it since we last saw each other?"

"One year has passed," Anna said slowly. Each hesitant word hung on her tongue with confusion.

"Wow. A year? I thought you were getting on a ship with Captain Murray and his crew of merchants.

"Aye," Anna answered. Her eyes remained steadfast on

me, as if she was trying to figure out my angle. She still didn't trust me.

Elizabeth pulled Anna by the elbow as a man carrying a large bundle twisted and angled to get behind her. "As you may remember, they were merchants and had a few stops along the way. Then the ship ran into a few issues delaying our voyage." She spoke with her hands more than I had remembered, more relaxed and animated. When I first met her, I thought she gave off confidence, prim, and proper, like a lady that was to marry an old earl.

"But a year?" I had to ask, "I've been traveling quite a bit and lost track of time. Do you happen to know today's date?"

"February second, in the year of our lord sixteen ninety," offered Elizabeth.

"Cheese and rice. Sixteen ninety." The fingers on my right hand began to tingle. I shifted my basket with a sleeping cat to my left arm and flexed my right hand to bring back circulation.

"As I said, there were a few detours," said Elizabeth. Her face couldn't hide the deceit. Maybe it had to do with her escape from her father, the old duke, and Lord Hector.

"I'm headed to Paris," I blurted out. "Then on to Spain. I need to find my husband."

"Have you lost him again?" scoffed Anna. "You were lost and looking for him a year ago. You're still looking for him. Are you sure he wants to be found?"

"I... what? Oh!" I had forgotten about that. Ugh. "Actually, that was my first husband, and I had found him. I'm now going to meet with my current husband." Do I

THE TIME WRITER AND THE ESCAPE

dare use his title? It's not like he was alive in 1690. Ah, why not. Maybe Anna will stop trying to scrape me off the bottom of her shoe. "Lord Henry Spencer, second son of... oh, it doesn't matter now. Does it?" I looked towards the Seine, sparkling from the warm afternoon sun. "I'm going to find a boat to take me there. Where are you headed?"

"We're headed to Paris as well. My cousin Margaret lives there." Concern hung on Elizabeth's words. "I'm hoping to stay with her for a while."

"Hiding out in Paris sounds dreamy." At least, I hope it did. I wasn't sure what 17th century Paris had to offer, but I was excited to find out. "Are you going by boat?" I motioned towards the river. Elizabeth turned her head to look behind her.

"I... I mean... We... it's been a difficult year."

Oh. Right. "Let's find a captain, or whatever they're called, and see if we can scrounge up enough money to get us there together." It was the least I could do for them. Elizabeth looked identical to my friend Beth Bennedet from the 21st century, and oddly, identical to Lady Elizabeth Woods from 1755. I felt compelled to help her and Anna. There must be some sort of connection to the three women. Maybe this Elizabeth is the ancestor to Elizabeth Woods, who is the ancestor to Elizabeth Bennedet. Not to mention, this Elizabeth gave me the coin I used to get back to the 21st century when I had slipped through a door and a rip in time while in Scotland. Thank the time traveling gods for that! When Silas and his brother had me thrown in jail, I was sure to have been put on trial as a witch.

The weight in my basket shifted around. Starboard was awake and ready to get going. "Let's go before Starboard gets cranky."

We turned to walk down the path towards the Seine. "Starboard?" asked Elizabeth.

"My cat."

Anna's nose snarled, "Why do you have a cat in your basket?"

"Because the satchel is too full for her to lay in it." I knew what she was implying, but I chose to blissfully ignore her attitude. I had to if I wanted to keep the wires in my brain from shorting out.

Along the busy river, boats were tied up to docks and bridges. Large boats carrying cargo. Small row boats piled with fish and goods. There had to be someone willing to transport three women and a cat to Paris. A forest of masts welcomed us to the Seine. A young boy of seven helped a man in his twenties, maybe early thirties, tie up his boat. The boy scuttled around with a rope in his hands. Swiftly, he dragged and wrapped the rope around a pylon, while the man gathered items in the boat. "Excuse me," I held my hand up and waved at the man and boy. "Do you know where we can find transportation?"

The man stared at me, blank and unwavering. "Pardon?"

I turned to Elizabeth and Anna, "Do either one of you speak French?"

"You don't?"

"My French is terrible. I recently mentioned to my friend that I'm sure people will talk about how terrible my

French is for years to come. Spanish, I can do. French? Nope."

"What were you expecting to do? Just come down here and make hand and arm signals?" Anna bit at me.

"Seriously, I have dumb luck." I had to shift Starboard's weight back to my right hand. "I just thought I would figure it out when I got here. However, if either one of you can fake enough French to help negotiate, I will do what I can to pay for our transportation."

After some discussion and me hoping that I had enough coins in the pouch, we were scheduled to set sail in the morning. Next item on the agenda, food. It's always food. And a place to stay.

The hills surrounding the town were pocked with homes. I wondered what it looked like during the 21st century. I'm not sure I would ever find out. Henry couldn't leave the United States without a passport. He couldn't get a passport because he was undocumented in every way possible. Being married to an 18th century time traveler was proving to be a little more complicated than I expected.

CHAPTER THIRTY

*T*raveling to Paris wasn't ideal. A small boat with three women, a cat, and a young boy and his father traveled up the Seine–cramped and determined to make good time. However, after two extremely long days–and more stops than I would've liked–we pulled up to the shore and were on our way to visit Lady Elizabeth's cousin. With a little extra pay for the work they missed hauling us to Paris, the father and son dropped us off at a dock and they were on their way back to Rouen.

I exhaled a long breath and gave a worried smile to Elizabeth and Anna. My coin bag was lighter. Traveling was becoming expensive, and I was only halfway to Spain. I just needed enough money to find Henry and pay the time travel gods to get back home.

"I'm certain my cousin will repay your kindness," Elizabeth said, as she straightened her satchel across her body and pulled the hood of her cloak on top of her head.

I'd been to Paris a few times when Todd, my first

husband, was stationed with the State Department in Poland. *My* Paris was busy with modern buildings mixed with classic buildings. Metro stops. Noise from cars. Asphalt and concrete everywhere. There was no Eiffel Tower announcing our arrival, not for another 200 years. No cars racing through the streets as if lanes are a mere suggestion. No tourists with cameras hanging around their necks.

"Oh! I recognize that building!" I exclaimed as I pointed to the building to our left in the distance. It was more than a mere building–more of a complex. There was a large domed cathedral building, surrounded by more buildings. "Les Invalides. There's a military museum. Oh! And Napoleon is buried there."

"Who? Les Invalides means the invalids, you know, old and sick. That's not a museum," said Elizabeth, sharing a confused look with Anna. "Who is Napoleon?"

"He's..." In my excitement of seeing a familiar building, I forgot my company and that I was in France in 1690, not 2020. And definitely not with people who knew I was a time traveler. "Cheese and rice. I forgot." *Find an excuse. Find an excuse.* "I saw a painting of the mu... uh... building. I might have confused it with another purpose, or another building, or I'm losing my mind, or something like that. How much further until we get to your cousin's house?"

With a dissatisfied look on her face, Elizabeth said, "We'll be there no later than supper."

We walked through the busy streets. Tall buildings three and four stories high flanked us. From children running on the streets, to men and women passing by in carriages and wagons, the life of Paris breathed and swirled around us, swallowing me whole.

It. Was. Exhilarating.

The slight temptation to stay in Paris, learn French, and settle down tickled the back of my mind. Maybe, after I find Henry, we could move to Paris. The universe's law on cat distribution brought me Starboard. All I needed was Henry.

Could a cat time travel? I know she was aboard the *Gretchen*, the time traveling schooner. What would happen if we walked through a door and into a rip in time? Was it possible? Did she need a coin? Oh! Perhaps, her payment is one of her furry, little, dead gifts she would bring me. Apparently, I don't know how to feed or take care of myself, and she feels obligated to ensure I don't starve. I suppose I haven't been that hungry as to cook up one of the field mice.

That's not to say that I hadn't trapped small rodents like squirrels and rabbits to feed me, Henry, and some of the men he commanded. It was emotionally difficult to deal with the slaughter and skinning of the animals. I try to act like I'm tough, but when it was time to do that... I... I failed. Panic in the rabbit's eyes as I went to the trap, tore through me. A heavy anvil was tied to my heart and dragged it down to the pit of my stomach. I asked one of the soldiers to do the slaughter in exchange for a cooked meal.

Heck, every time Starboard brought me a little present, I cringed. It impacted me more than the death of Casper. I mean, his actions came back and bit him in the ass. I'm not going to say he deserved to die, but I'm not going to say I was sad about it either.

"You've been abnormally quiet," Anna said, pulling me out of my thoughts of seeing Casper lying at the bottom of the stairs, bleeding out from the knife jammed into his side. The knife he killed Noah with, and the same one he intended to kill me with. Jerk.

My head shook as I looked towards Anna's confused blue eyes. "Hm?" The pool of blood lingered in my thoughts. "Oh! Yeah. I was just thinking about eating."

I looked around for Starboard. I was being neglectful thinking about my time in 1755 Virginia, instead of my present situation. She insisted on walking next to us. Although cozy, my basket didn't offer enough room for her to stretch out. When I put her on the ground, she did a long stretch with one leg back, took a step, and stretched the other leg. A yawn was thrown in for good measure. We had lost the blue ribbon I had on her days ago. A new ribbon would be on my supply list. Between the flowing brown and green capes worn by Elizabeth and Anna, Starboard's little nose popped out in front. Panic subsided.

"Aye, we're nearly there." Elizabeth pointed down the road, to the left side. There stood a neat row house. Yellow stone facade, white trim, and three stories tall. Heavy red curtains hung in the windows, split in the middle to allow the afternoon light to slice through the tall windows.

I slowed my pace to a stop and looked down at Starboard. She looked up and meowed at me. "You need to get in the basket and lay low." Squatting, I sat the basket on the ground and pulled back the flax-colored linen cloth which covered it. My satchel slid from behind my back to my left side, throwing me slightly off-balance. She made no effort to climb inside. Instead, she long-stretched one rear leg, then the other, sat down, and began licking her front right paw and rubbed it on her face. "How nice of you to clean up before meeting Elizabeth's cousin, but you still need to get inside the basket."

Starboard continued to ignore me. I scooped her up and was met with a disapproving hiss, but she relented and allowed me to set her inside and cover her with the cloth.

"Shall we?" Elizabeth asked with a smile.

I nodded, straightened my oversized satchel to my back, and picked up my Starboard-laden basket. "I think we'll need to start baby wrapping you to my chest," I laughed out. Really, that sounded like a much better idea than carrying ten pounds off my forearm.

Elizabeth pushed back her hood and ran her hands over her hair. Her auburn hair was pulled back in a braid trailing down her back. The flyaway strands of hair remained untamed. She took a stuttered breath and knocked on the large black painted door. A moment later, a young man in his mid-teens, dressed in blue breeches, red stockings, and a tan waistcoat answered the door. He wore a light blue coat, trimmed with a silver piping, matching his breeches, and contrasting the dark tan of his skin and brown eyes, and a pair of white cotton gloves. His shoes were simple black leather with a silver-colored buckle.

Before the teen could open his mouth, Elizabeth

nervously blurted out, "Lady Elizabeth Lindsay. I'm here to visit my cousin, Lady Margaret."

Did she say her last name is Lindsay? That was my maiden name. I wonder if we're somehow related, and that's why I keep running into her.

Why on earth would she be so nervous? When I first met her on the streets of Edinburgh, she seemed so confident. While traveling here from Rouen, she didn't display this much diffidence. My eyes shifted to Anna looking for any acknowledgement that she sensed what I was sensing. She stared at Elizabeth, with worry in her eyes. I'm guessing Margaret didn't know the three of us were going to show up on her doorstep.

The young man's eyes looked at our worn and tired group. Our appearances did not look as if we were ladies of anything, perhaps ladies of the night. Our hair out of place, clothes worn beyond acceptable for a Lady, and dirt lined the bottom couple of inches of our skirts and cloaks, we were quite a sight. There was no way I was going to take a sniff of my armpit. I knew I was beyond ripe. If Elizabeth and Anna were as well, I couldn't smell them over my pungent aroma.

February afternoons in Paris were cold. Standing on the street, with the cold beginning to seep in, staring at the young man who appeared to not believe the timid Elizabeth, caused me to lose whatever patience I had stored. *Take a deep breath, Amelia. Find your center. Ah! Screw my center.* I was cold, hungry, and tired of carrying Starboard. "Is Lady Margaret in residence?" I blurted out. There might have been a tinge of annoyance in my voice.

The young man's eyes widened to and gave a slight nod at my brusque question. I shifted my basket to my left arm, moved next to Elizabeth, and grabbed her hand. I nudged past the young man, still standing there in confusion. "Tell your mistress, her cousins have called upon her." I stepped through the threshold, pulling Elizabeth with me. The smell of food being prepared hit me like a ton of bricks. I drew in a long sniff through my nose. Beef and bread dominated the air. My stomach growled loud enough to catch looks from everyone. I shrugged my shoulders. "And tell the cook to prepare enough food for us. We'll wait in there," I said, pointing to the parlor to the left.

We walked into the parlor, delicate and pristine. Two chairs flanked either side of the fireplace, which filled the room with the warmth I desperately needed. Two matching sofas, fitting three people, easily, faced each other across the center of the room. The light blue silky fabric with delicate cream and darker blue flowers was the same fabric which covered the cushions on the wooden chairs near the fireplace. A service table sat to our right and close to the wall. To our left, two tall windows faced the street. The heavy red drapes were pulled to the side to let in the afternoon sun. When the sun would dip beyond the horizon, they would close the drapes to keep out the cold Parisian night. I didn't find the red drapes matched the room, but the heaviness of the fabric would keep the cold from creeping in at night. I had to find a flaw in this showcased room. It helped remind me that Elizabeth's cousin was like any other person, even if we were desperate for her help.

I sat Starboard, still lying patiently in the basket, near the chairs next to the fireplace, and warmed my frigid hands. Elizabeth and Anna joined me. "Elizabeth," I said, turning towards her, but keeping the palms of my hands facing flat towards the fire. "I'm not sure what's going on here, but I've never seen you cower like that to anyone–let alone, a servant."

"Aye, it's my cousin Margaret. She makes me feel so small." She shook her head. A tear bubbled in the corner of her eye. "We shouldn't have come here."

"Then why did you?" I asked.

"Yes, Elizabeth, why did you come here and bring these women with you?" A commanding voice boomed across the room. Our heads spun to see a woman standing in the doorway. She must be Margaret. She was a finely boned woman in her thirties. She looked like a cake topper, with a tall gray colored wig plopped on her head. She wore a blue skirt, with yellow flowers, a yellow matching bodice, her mantua matched her skirt with sleeves to her elbows, where laced sleeves flowed to mid forearm.

Elizabeth stood, staring at her cousin. I gave a slight pinch to the back of Elizabeth's arm to pull her out of her trance. With a slight tug at her elbow, she walked with me towards our unwitting host. I fell into a slight curtsy and gave a dignified nod to Margaret. Elizabeth and Anna followed suit. "I know who these two are," Margaret flicked her hand towards Elizabeth and Anna before continuing, "although I haven't seen them since they were nine years old."

Ah, that would explain their intimidation of their

cousin. It's been ten years and they were young children. "Yes, thank you for welcoming us to your lovely home. I'm Lady Amelia Spencer, wife of Lord Henry William James Spencer," I paused for a moment. I couldn't give his lineage. Technically, in 1690, he didn't exist anywhere on his family tree. *Keep it vague, Amelia.* "Son of the Duke of Marlborough. I'm accompanying Lady Elizabeth and Lady Anna on their journey."

Margaret straightened up and gave a disapproving clearing of her throat. *Find your center, Amelia.* "It would've been proper to have notified me of your arrival, Elizabeth." She spread out her arms. "Now, come to your favorite cousin."

She scrunched her nose as Elizabeth approached. I guess I wasn't the only one in need of a bath.

CHAPTER THIRTY-ONE

"Where did that cat come from?" Margaret squeaked out. Disgust oozed from the look on her face. We turned our heads towards the fireplace, only to find Starboard sitting in the middle of one of the sofas, staring at us. She let out a meow.

"That's my adorable cat, Starboard." I gave a sly smile and hurried over to sit next to her on the sofa. I leaned close to Starboard, and said softly, "I told you to stay in the basket for good reason."

"Cats have fleas and don't belong in my house."

"She doesn't have fleas and she is well behaved." I stroked Starboard's back. I knew I was going to lose this battle. It wasn't my house, and I brought the cat inside without asking permission. That was a huge reason I wanted Starboard to stay in the basket until we got settled in. "I'll take her out when she needs to do her business, but it's too cold to keep her out at night."

Margaret opened her mouth to admonish me, while I

lifted my hand to stop her. "It's just for the night. I really must get on my way to Spain. I'm going to meet with my husband."

"The cat..."

"Starboard," I interrupted.

Margaret scowled. "Starboard must remain in the room with you. I will not have it slinking through the house at night ready to kill us in our sleep."

"Cheese and rice. She's a cat." I picked her up and placed her on my lap. "Not a serial killer." Well, unless you're a field mouse or a little bird minding its own business. Admittedly, she was probably on the Mouse B.I.'s most wanted list.

"We'll get you cleaned up before we discuss what brought you here." Margaret turned her nose up at Starboard as I walked by holding her in my arms.

This was going to be a fun visit.

We followed Margaret up two flights of stairs. Elizabeth made small talk with her along the way. Anna and I followed close behind. On the third floor, we were welcomed with a dimly lit hall with two sets of doors on either side. The window at the end of the hall let in the only light. The fading late afternoon light wouldn't offer much within the next couple of hours. Another flight of stairs led up another story, where I assumed the servants were housed.

"The children's rooms are across from you," Margaret said, opening the second door on the right.

"Are we to share this room?" Elizabeth asked, stepping

inside the small room with an even smaller bed. It would be a tight fit, but we would manage.

"Lady Spencer stated she and her cat were not staying long." I do believe she picked up a slight French accent when she was belittling me. Perhaps, she thought it gave her an air of importance. How could I tell her that I really didn't care what she thought of me? I only wanted to make sure she would take good care of Elizabeth and Anna. "There will be plenty of room for just the two of you."

I sat my basket near the door and let Starboard jump out of my arms to start her inspection of the room. "Thank you, Lady Dando. I'm sure Starboard appreciates your generosity and will ensure any little mouse she finds will be probably disposed of. That is, of course, if they are not your children's playthings."

She huffed in disgust at me and was ready to tear me a new one. *Sugar snaps! Find your center. Don't be a brat.* "I meant no offense, madam. I merely thought that is why you had concern for this well-behaved cat to be in your home. It would break my heart if she had the children's pet for dinner." Starboard jumped on the bed and sniffed around the blanket. I turned and gave a cheeky smile to Margaret. "Oh, very good. I will ensure she dispatches any varmint she finds in your home. She will earn her keep while we are your most humble guests." I placed my hand over my heart and tilted my head in a modest bow.

"Yes, well," she began, as she grabbed the door handle to pull it close, before she continued, "I'll have Ellie bring up water for you to wash. You do have clean frocks to wear to dinner?"

Elizabeth and Anna stared at each other. "Lady Cousin, we have not much more than the costumes we wear." I've got to admit, Elizabeth is much better at sucking up than me. However, I'm sure Elizabeth didn't have the wild hormones of time travel invade her blood like a cancer. I had another mantua in my bag, nicer than the one I wore. It matched my petticoat; however, my skirts were filthy and could use a good cleaning. If Margaret allowed us to wear her frocks, I wasn't going to argue. Maybe, she wasn't as stuck up as I thought.

Ellie brought us clothes to change out of filthy road-worn clothes, and into, clearly, hand-me-down clothes that Margaret no longer wore, but appreciated hand-me-downs, nonetheless. I was given a linen suit of clothes and a clean shift. The petticoat was a dark blue linen with red and yellow flowers printed on it. Green leaves and vines swirled around the flowers. The mantua was the same color blue as the skirt, but without the flowers. The sleeves went down to my elbows and a white linen, flowy sleeves popped out the end, going down to my mid forearm. The mantua pulled to the back with a big poof, accentuating my rear end. The stomacher matched the skirt.

Elizabeth and Anna's clothing were of similar fashion. Elizabeth was given a dark green suit, highlighting her eyes and hair. It made her fair skin appear even more so. A few bows went down the front of her mantua and tied across her stomacher. Anna's suit was a pale yellow. It was a little too pale for winter dress but would be wonderful during the spring and summer. However, the fine lace detail along the trim was exquisite.

Ellie took our filthy clothes to launder them the next morning. We washed the layers of body odor with a heavenly lavender scented soap. On our travels with the man and his son, we lacked the opportunity to wash, since privacy was nearly non-existent.

Smacks of children's feet running up and down the hall interrupted our dazed washing of our bodies. We were so tired; they could run throughout the middle of the night and it probably wouldn't wake us. I wasn't sure if Margaret really had children or if she was saying that to keep us in one room. She proved me wrong... again.

After dressing for dinner, I gathered Starboard and carried her. down the two flights of stairs to the back garden. Streaks of light from inside the homes pierced through the darkening evening. The night temperatures were dropping quickly with the sun no longer warming the city. If I was thinking properly, I would've grabbed my cloak. I didn't know I had to stand out in the cold, watching Starboard make a stupid concentration-face—eyes squinted and a grin. Who knew cats could grin while they pooped?

In the middle of the tall buildings, the homes had small, nicely manicured gardens. They would have been lush, if it wasn't for the fact that we were at the beginning of February, still during winter. The kitchen garden was bare. Ornamental bushes had long lost their leaves. The trees stood naked. She found a strip of dirt to do her business near the back corner. I would have to remember to pick it up in the morning, when the lighting was better. She turned to me and meowed out her satisfaction with me.

"Are you coming in? It's cold out here." I ran my hands over my biceps, trying to start a fire with the friction with my hands and the linen fabric. Cheese and rice! It was cold outside. Pulling my hair back in a chignon and without a cape, my ears were being bitten by Jack Frost. Starboard took off in a little sprint, ignoring my pleas to go inside. "Be back when I'm finished with dinner." I turned to go inside, before adding, "and don't let anything eat you."

As I walked inside the house, which felt only slightly warmer than outside, I found myself nearly knocked over by Elizabeth and Anna bounding down the stairs. "Splendid. You've returned."

"I was just in the back with Starboard," I said, pointing to the backdoor.

Anna looked at the closed door, then down at my feet, and then to my hands. "Did you forget the furball?" Her eyebrows knitted in confusion. Perhaps, she thought I had frozen my brain out there.

"No," I chuckled. "She decided to go exploring while we eat our dinner."

"You realize, cats cannot speak." Anna continued to have a quizzical look spread across her face. *Definitely* a frozen brain.

"Of course, she doesn't say actual words, that would be ridiculous." We started to walk towards the parlor at the end of the hall on our right. We were meeting Lord and

Lady Dando for pre-dinner drinks. All I wanted to do was stuff my face and go to sleep. However, proper etiquette kept me from grabbing a plate and heading to my room. Not to mention, my curiosity of meeting the lord of the manor house. "We have a unique way of communicating. I'm certain she is fluent in English but can only answer in meows. She's quite intelligent... for a cat... that is." Yup! My brain was frozen.

We strolled in the room, and sitting next to the fireplace, sipping on a glass of white wine, was my late husband Todd? What in the world was going on? I shook my head. The room spun, either from the lack of food, me shaking all the blood from my head, or the complete shock of seeing my dead husband sipping wine in 1690 Paris. "Todd?" I muttered out. One heavy lead foot after the other, I made my way across the room.

The man stood from his chair and placed his glass on the mantle. I couldn't see anything else around me. The only two people that existed in the room were me and him. As I approached, he gave a slight bow to his head. "Lord Charles Dando, at your service, madam."

I blinked repeatedly and tried to catch my breath. "I... uh... pardon?" That had to be a joke. Right? Lord Charles Dando? Not Todd Murray?

"My Lord Husband, it seems as though your good looks and charm have overwhelmed Lady Spencer," Margaret said, as she joined Lord Dando. I looked towards the woman standing next to her husband, her eyebrows nearly touching in the center.

Slowly, I curtsied. "Lady Amelia Spencer." I stood up.

"I humbly apologize for my outburst. You reminded me of a long-lost friend." I turned and looked over my shoulder towards Elizabeth and Anna. They were close behind me. Good. I needed moral support. "I can see now that I was mistaken with my excitement."

He tilted his head and gave a slight smile.

"Not to say that I'm not excited to meet you. It's just..."

"Been a difficult journey." Elizabeth stood next to me and curtsied. "Lord Cousin, how wonderful to see you. It's been quite a while."

"I'm pleased to see you in good health. We have much to discuss over dinner." He looked over her shoulder towards the sound of the opening door. "Which appears to be served." He looked at the group of four women standing around him and said, "Shall we, ladies?"

We moved across the hall to the exquisite dining room. I might have used that word once or twice to describe their home. It truly was... exquisite, that is. It gave me the feeling that I could easily settle down with Henry in Paris. We found our seats, and for once, I wasn't a totally bumbling fool at a formal dinner. I learned enough over the course of my time in 1750s Virginia, that I could handle a fork and knife, but I continued to watch my hosts to ensure I was using the proper utensil, goblet, and plate.

"We had a visitor a few days ago," Charles said, clearing his throat. His mannerisms were different, but he truly reminded me of Todd. The same look in his eyes. His strong jawline that could cut a person in half.

"Visitors would be correct," added Margaret.

Ah, small talk. I couldn't imagine what their visitor had to do with us.

Elizabeth, Anna, and I looked at him with bated breath. With all the drama surrounding the announcement, it better be good. Like the king or something like that.

"Yes, you're correct." He looked towards Elizabeth. "Lord Hector Black, son of the Duke of Ormonde, showed up on our doorstep. Along with his ward, a little redheaded child, and two scruffy looking puppies."

The blood dropped out of Elizabeth's face. Her already pale skin became twelve shades lighter. I didn't think it was possible for someone to completely lose all the color from their skin.

My mouth went dry. My shaky hand reached for the glass of red wine in front of me. Normally, I could barely sip red wine. I found it bitter. However, I gulped that glass down faster than I could take a breath. Refill! I needed a refill. *Where's the bottle?* "Cheese and rice," I said slowly. "Is he still looking for you?"

"You are acquainted with Lord Hector?" Charles asked. Everyone turned to look at me. Panic invaded Elizabeth's eyes.

"Well, yeah, sort of," I stammered out. "I briefly met with him and a couple of his goons." I looked at Elizabeth and Anna sitting across from me at the table. "You remember, Silas, and the other guy. Anyway, after I left you at the tavern..."

"You left my cousin in a tavern?" Margaret said with disgust and disappointment.

"That's hardly the point I'm making." *Focus, Amelia.* "I went to find my husband..."

"You seem to lose him quite a bit. Aren't you looking for him now?"

She had no idea how many times I've gone searching for a husband. Well, they've been my husbands, not just a random man off a time traveled street to call my husband. Where was I going with that? Right! My story about Hector. "Please, Lady Margaret, let me finish."

Margaret picked her jaw off the table. The more she interrupted, the longer the story would take to tell.

"After I left the tavern, I was on my way back through Edinburgh, and I saw the goons. Next thing I knew, this dashing young lord rode over to us. He questioned me about where the two of you and how to find you."

"You didn't tell him," Elizabeth interrupted. "Did you?"

"Good gravy, no. Of course not." A servant refilled my empty glass. As they were walking away, I snagged the bottle out of their hands. This story was going to need a couple of glasses to get through it. "Well, Hector went looking for you in the direction from whence I came, and Silas and friend snatched me up and threw me in Tolbooth."

"The gaol?" Anna looked legitimately shocked. Honestly, I didn't think that was possible. Even more impossible than when Elizabeth turned whiter than white.

"Yup!" Another glass downed. "No worries, I got out... obviously," I said matter-of-factly, waving my glass of wine around. Whoa! That wine was starting to hit all the

THE TIME WRITER AND THE ESCAPE

right notes. "He seemed nice. He told the Tweedles not to harm me, just to keep me out of the way so they could search for you, and I couldn't thwart their plans." Snort... *thwart. Did I really use the word 'thwart' in conversation?*

"He didn't have a little girl with him when I saw him. Or dogs. Well..." I started to ramble. Nervous energy? Excitement? Another glass of wine? "I suppose if they were puppies a couple days ago, they wouldn't have been there with him. However, I know there wasn't a little girl. Does he have a daughter? No, that's not right." No, that's not right because... oh sugar snaps! No. I couldn't think about the thought which crept into my mind. It was my turn to turn whiter than white. He couldn't have a daughter if he was supposed to be with Elizabeth. Maybe he was already married? I gulped down another glass. Hangover be damned! I needed to get through this conversation without keeling over. "I need to get my cat."

I STOOD UP, pushing my chair back as I used the table to steady myself. I grabbed my glass, the remaining bottle of wine, and a small plate with a piece of beef and what was left of a cooked carrot, a small chunk of bread–*mmmmm... bread*–and a bit of butter. "My lord, my ladies, thank you for a lovely evening." I did a quick and dirty curtsey. "I shall take my leave with this wine and this meal for Starboard." I made it to the door and turned around. "Again, lovely evening. I'll depart for Spain the day after next."

I balanced the bottle in the crook of my elbow, and the

plate on top of the glass. Looking back on the situation, that was a terrible idea. It seemed like a good one at the time. Charles rushed over and opened the door and steadied the plate before it tipped over.

I looked up and met his concerned brown eyes. "I miss you," I whispered. It was the kind of whisper that held onto a secret I hid away, deep into the hidden recesses of my heart. Only for it to return on the breath I held since Todd died. The years I spent raising our daughter alone. Excitement over a new book or restaurant. Fussing about Hannah's "C" in Algebra, knowing he was much better at math than I ever wanted to be. I couldn't share any of that with him. I grabbed my phone so many times to send him a text. He was supposed to be there with us. Experiencing life with me.

I. Missed. Him.

"Pardon?"

I closed my eyes tight, a tickle crept at my nose, and a small tear escaped the corner of my eye. *He's not Todd*. "I'll miss your hospitality and your lovely home. Thank you both." I turned to Margaret and gave a sad smile. I wasn't wishing for Charles to be Todd, or for Todd to come back. I truly did miss him. My love? That was with Henry. As strange as it seemed to say those words to a man that looked like Todd, I had to say them. However, for me, it was the closure I needed. I needed Todd to know he was missed. "Your generosity has been appreciated."

CHAPTER THIRTY-TWO

I'm terrible with directions. Give me a GPS, and I will still get lost. When the voice says, "Turn right in one hundred meters." By the time I've figured out how far one hundred meters is, I've missed my turn. Then I'll make the next right, only to find myself on a one-way street headed against the flow of traffic.

Throw me in a country when I don't speak the language? I'm screwed.

Add in traveling back hundreds of years in time? Stick a fork in me, I'm done.

Fortunately, I didn't travel alone. Elizabeth and Anna decided to join me on my trip to Spain. They really didn't know where they wanted to go, only to leave Paris before Lord Hector found them and dragged Elizabeth back to Scotland, or worse, Ireland. Honestly, I have no idea how it happened. Between boats down the river, connecting to another river, walking a distance, connecting to another river, two weeks later we were on the shores of the Mediterranean.

"Let's go Starboard," I said to my furry companion, as I lifted her into the basket and grabbed the low-sided box she used as a litter box. I dumped the used sand over the side of the boat, noting to refill it after we found a place to stay for the night. "Welcome to Marseille!" We followed Elizabeth and Anna off the boat, and none of us had a clue where we were headed.

Starboard looked up at me, meowed, and settled into the basket. She didn't care where we landed, but I did! A few more days and I would be in Spain and reuniting with Henry. Or at least hoping to reunite with Henry. I was counting on my dumb luck to lead me to him.

"Food, a place to crash for the night, and find passage to Spain," I said, as I quickened my steps to walk next to Elizabeth.

Goods moved up and down the river, we passed many boats along the way. Our boat shared not only a tiny space for passengers, but we had a load of a plant they called "pastel." I didn't know what it was. I know pastel meant light colors, such as the colors of spring and Easter. Light airy colors. Or when I took art class in high school, we used pastel sticks of chalk to draw. The plant looked like neither of those things. The leaves were dried and made into these balls of... I don't know what... dried plant material or a ball of dung? It looked as though someone had pulled it out of storage and should've been used to fertilize a garden. The pastel was offloaded at the port. I wanted to follow the delivery to discover its use, but priorities took over curiosity.

We walked down the docks, bustling with activity, and found an inn. The owner didn't put up too much of a fuss when Starboard jumped out of the basket and jumped on the bed, when we were shown to our shared room. Charles and Margaret gave Elizabeth a small purse of coins, but without knowing how to earn more, we stuck to a tight budget. It didn't make sense not to share a room.

"I need to get some sand for her box, a little something for her to eat and drink," I said, as I placed the litter box in the corner of the room. I pulled my heavy satchel off, placed it over the chair. My back was tired and sore from being a pack mule day-in and day-out. Rotating my shoulders and massaging my neck didn't help. I needed to stretch out in a proper bed. A massage and a hot bath would have to wait. *No rest for the wicked*. I pulled my cloak back on. It was nearly the end of February, and still chilly out.

"We passed a couple of taverns," said Anna. "Perhaps, we can find a meal and a captain?"

"Find us after you finish caring for Starboard," added Elizabeth.

"Sounds like a plan." I walked to the door. "I think I need to find a hat and a new ribbon for Starboard."

Starboard pried an eye open and looked at me as though I lost my mind. She closed her eyes and enjoyed the warmth of the sun coming through the window. I think she was purposely losing her ribbons.

I balanced my purse in my hand, trying to judge how

much money I had left. It was dwindling faster than I liked. I shoved it deep in my pocket, hidden under my dark green linen petticoat. I moved over to the corner, grabbed the litter box to fill with sand, and coaxed Starboard back into the basket.

"Come on, Toto, let's go find the wizard," I said, as I closed the door behind me.

At the bottom of the stairs, there was a small lobby area with a dining area to the right. I took a quick glance around the room. We needed to find transportation to Spain. In the past, we lucked out by finding ship captains in taverns instead of inns. And by the looks of the dining crowd, we weren't going to find one hiding in the group of diners.

Starboard's little nose twitched, as she raised her snout in the air and sniffed. My stomach agreed with her. We needed to hurry along so we could get food.

The innkeeper directed me to a milliner and offered to have a bowl of food tucked to the side for Starboard, upon our return from our errand.

Down the street to my left, heading away from the docks, and three streets over, I found a small factory building with a quaint storefront. Hanging from a rod above the door, was a sign with a hat carved in it. The name "Moreau" was carved above and "Le Chapelier" below the hat. There is a hat on the sign, that had to be the place. Ha! Who needed to speak French? Me. I needed to speak French. I hoped the vendor was ready for a game of Charades. I propped the litter box against the wall outside–no need to take that stinky thing inside a shop.

I walked inside, greeted with a little bell jingle from the door opening and warm air. I placed Starboard–who was still in her basket–on the counter. She really was an excellent cat.

The space was quaint and small. Wide brimmed hats in colors from tan, black, and dark blue. There were feathers on some, trim on others, and some had both feathers and corded trim. The brims on some were shaped with a cocked side, some had two cocked sides, and others without any cocking. They were displayed on shelves and stands around the shop.

The walls were painted a yellow ochre. Which might have explained the yellowish tint to the shopkeeper.

"Bonjour, madam," said the older man as he walked out from a room behind the counter. His steps were slow and measured. I should've brought a translator with me.

"Good afternoon," I blurted out. "That is, bonjour. Do you happen to speak English? My French is terrible and..."

He raised his hand to stop my rambling and shook his head. Okay, no English and I didn't speak French.

"Español?" I was hoping my high school Spanish was in handy in France.

His eyes lit up. Well, sort of. There was something about him that seemed off. Like he was sick. I know that it was rude to think about someone's health when you only met them. That could have been a healthy day for him, and I thought he looked yellow and sickly. It must've been the paint.

During one of our moves, I insisted Todd paint the

front restroom yellow. It was lovely and matched the painting I picked to display on the wall. However, every single time I stood at the sink to wash my hands, I stared at myself in the mirror and thought I had jaundice. My skin had a slight tinge of yellow. I looked closer to find the whites of my eyes seemed to have a tinge of yellow. Jaundice! No. It wasn't jaundice. The walls made me look a sickly shade of yellow. Certainly, that must be the case with the frail hatmaker who stood before me.

"You make lovely hats," I said, our conversation continued in Spanish. "I'm looking for a hat for me. I notice only men's hats. Do you make women's hats?"

"My apologies, señora. I'm le chapelier. You are looking for la modiste. They would specialize in the woman's hat."

My shoulders sank. A thin boy of no more than six or seven, came out from the back room. His brown hair was patchy and scraggly. His clothes hung on him, as if he had been given hand-me-downs from a much larger and older boy. In his hand he played with a crystal substance. My confused look brought the attention of Monsieur Moreau.

"Mercury nitrate," he said, answering my unasked question.

I looked closer and shouted, "Cuidado! That's mercury." my panicked eyes looked at the shopkeeper. Certainly, he wouldn't let this child play with mercury.

The man looked down towards the child's hands. "Sí. I use it to make hats. It's part of the process."

Oh, good grief! That would explain why they look so sick. They've been handling mercury with their bare hands giving themselves heavy metal poisoning. Did they know? Did they care? The method to their livelihood was killing them. By the looks of it, their organs were slowly shutting down.

"Would you like to see?"

"I would love to see how you make these hats." I forced a smile to hide my sadness at their impending and painful death.

He led me to the back, where he had a workshop with forms, vats with liquid dyes, wools, a colorful collection of feathers, and a large container filled with those dung balls... pastels. Why would he have garden fertilizer in his hat workshop?

I pointed to the container of brownish-green balls piled on one another. "Pastels?"

"Bien sûr... ah... of course. I like to grind my own."

"Grind it to make what?" My voice went up an octave or two. "Do you smoke it? Is it like a *wacky tobacky*?"

"I don't know what wacky tobacky is." He shook his head. "You don't smoke pastel, you make a blue dye of a dark color, like that hat out there."

"Oh," I said, drawing out the word to at least five syllables long. "What does mercury nitrate have to do with the process?"

"Ah, that is for stiffening the wool during the felting process." He picked up a cocked sided hat and pointed to the brim. "This would sag and flop if I didn't stiffen it. Men want to cover their head, not their face."

I nodded as I poked around his table, looking at his tools. "Do you have family here?" I was worried the man would pass away, leaving his dying son to follow close behind.

He shook his head. "The edict drove my family away. I was to follow, but my wife died and now, I'm too ill to travel."

My knees felt weak. A nearby wooden chair offered me a safe place to sit, instead of falling over from his heartbreaking story, or the lack of food.

"I'm sorry, I don't understand." I cocked my head to the side. "What edict?"

"The Edict of Fontainebleau."

"That means nothing to me. I don't understand."

Moreau pulled up a stool and rested his weary legs. His son stirred a pot of liquid, attempting to help his father work. He looked towards the empty shop and looked back towards me. "We're Huguenots. Protestants in a Catholic country. Five years ago, the king declared we were not allowed to practice our religion anymore. Most of my family and friends fled the country. My wife and I stayed and pretended to go to their silly church, but we kept strong in our faith." He held a finger up, pointing it to the heavens, making sure I knew where he could find his god. "She died two years ago. It's now me and Francois," he gave a caring look to his son before continuing, "we care for each other and make hats."

"Forgive me if this sounds crass," I began. My emotions bubbled. This time, it wasn't the anger that pushed its way to the surface, but sadness and disappointment. "Are you experiencing the same symptoms your wife did before she died?"

He slowly nodded. "It's killing us. This sickness." He looked away, not wanting me to see his eyes water.

"It's the mercury you're using in the hats. It's poisoning you."

"And if we stop using it?"

"You'll have limpy hats and will still die," I said with a slight laugh, as I tried to make light of the situation. I know it wasn't funny. There was no coming back from the heavy metal poisoning. I wiped a tear off my cheek with the back of my hand.

"You know, in Scotland they are facing some of the same problems. Except the opposite. The English wants to rid the country of Catholics. Elizabeth, my friend, was telling me about a local Protestant priest that liked to have women tried as witches." Moreau looked at me in shock. He thought he had a confidant, and there I was bashing the Protestant faith. "Oh, I'm not Catholic." His face lightened. "I'm not Protestant either. I really don't care what religion anyone practices, it's just not for me."

We shared a gentle smile. I'm not saying my stomach knows how to ruin a moment, but it definitely ruined the moment with a loud growl. "I'm supposed to meet my friends for dinner." I stood from the chair.

At that moment, the bell above the door jingled when someone entered. He looked out the doorway of the workshop into the store. "It's Señor Carabajal. He buys my hats to take to Spain, he swindles me every time."

Señor Carabajal was a middle-aged man, with a light brown wig that was full and flowed down his back. His eyes were deep and dark. His skin was tanned, as if he spent a lot of time outside. He wore a dark brown coat trimmed with a thick white silky fabric. His blue breeches matched his blue waistcoat. Dark red stockings covered the bottom half of his legs. On his feet, he wore black shoes with the shiniest buckles I had ever seen. A large sash draped over his shoulder and was tucked in around his sword belt. The way he arrogantly removed his gloves, told me that Moreau had probably been slapped with them once or twice.

"Why don't you refuse to sell to him?"

"He threatens me and my son with the local authorities if I don't sell him all my hats. I'm powerless against him." He looked out towards Carabajal who was making his way around the counter to where we were in the workshop. He stopped in the middle of the doorway.

With an unmistakably loud voice, I said in Spanish, "Thank you for the business deal. I will be back tomorrow to pick up all the hats after I secure my passage." I looked at Carabajal. "*My* hats. I'll be here to pick up all the hats that are now *mine*." Nervous ramble. *Smooth, Amelia.*

I gave a small curtsy to Carabajal, as I tried to nudge past him. He glowered at me with his black eyes, reluctant to let me pass. I picked up the basket with Starboard curled up inside. Sweet girl. I ran a hand over her head, and she popped open her eyes.

Carabajal snatched me by my biceps, his grip tight and his fingers dug into my flesh. "Your hats? You are mistaken, señora. Moreau knows those are my hats."

His grip tightened around my arm. I could feel the

bruises forming under his fingertips. "Unhand me." I yanked my arm. He didn't relent.

"No. I will not unhand you." He spun me around to look at him. His grip remained tight. "They are *my* hats. He and I made a deal."

"You got here too late. I made the deal first." I sensed my false arrogance was about to get me in trouble. Sometimes, I hate being correct.

He raised his free hand, back. He aimed for my face. My heart pounded through my ribs. I flinched and held up my free arm, his grip too tight on my left arm for me to move it.

And with that, Starboard sprung out of her basket with a hiss, and claws ready. I could've sworn the light reflected off her weapons of mass destruction as she lifted her murder mitten and brought the fury down on Carabajal's hand. He screamed out. I broke free from his clutches. Blood dripped from his hand. Starboard left quite the impression.

I grabbed Starboard–still growling at Carabajal, begging him to try something else–and spun on my heels to hightail it out of there.

"Do you know who I am?" He shouted at me.

"Frankly, señor, I don't give a damn." I flipped him the bird and rushed out the door.

CHAPTER THIRTY-THREE

"*F*inally!" I called out enthusiastically, as I entered the tavern, *Chaton Moustaches*. Kitten mustaches? Did I read that correctly? I wanted to run out and double check the name, but I was hungry and didn't want to bother. It was the fourth tavern I had entered during my search for Elizabeth and Anna, and by far, the rowdiest bunch. A few heads turned when I exploded in the room, but they quickly went back to their cards, food, booze, or harassing one of the young barmaids.

Near the edge of the room, at a small round table, sat Elizabeth and Anna. Plates of food, and tankards of ale in front of them. I pulled an empty chair from another table and joined them. "Hey," I said, as I slumped down in my chair.

No sooner than I sat down, an older woman in her fifties or sixties, holding a serving tray came over. She looked like a magical sprite amongst the rambunctious crowd. She was just about as tall as me, and about half my weight. She wore her hair pulled back under a white cap. The women in the tavern wore the same style of clothing. Long skirts of various colors, a bodice, covering their stays, no mantua or coats, the tops of their shifts and their sleeves exposed, and an apron.

Her expression on her face gave off a I'm-nice-until-I'm-not look. A drunk man in his thirties, barely sitting straight in his chair, grabbed her ass as she walked by. Ah! There is the until-I'm-not attitude on display. She turned around and gave him a smack, knocking him over onto the floor. His friends laughed at the fool trying to figure out how to untwist himself from the chair.

I looked up and met her hazel eyes, gave an approved smile, and said, "I'll have whatever food you're serving and a cider, if you have one." Dang it! I ordered in English. How do I order that in French? "Sil vous..." I began to stutter out.

She held up her free hand, and with a French accent, she said, "I speak English, Spanish, Italian, and évidemment, French. My German could use some practice. Do you speak German?"

I smiled and shook my head. "No. Really, only English. Eh. That's not entirely true. Recently, I've picked up a little Spanish."

"How do you forget that you recently started speaking another language?" Her laughter was interrupted by a sudden start of a song being loudly sung by the women and joined in by some of the men.

The barmaids sat trays on tables, or on the long

wooden bar in the back of the room. A couple of young women came running out from the back of the room. A young blond woman, with a button nose, called out, "Genevieve!"

Genevieve, sighed, looked at me, and handed me her tray. "Dinner will have to wait."

"What is going on?" I mouthed to Elizabeth and Anna.

The ruckus was loud, almost to the point of overbearing. A few of the women climbed on top of the long bar. A couple climbed atop some of the larger tables. Two women climbed between men and made their way through the plates and cups on a long wooden table, flanked by two equally long benches. Men moved their food and drinks out of the way, giving the women plenty of room to navigate.

That was like college all over again! Twenty-one years earlier, that would've been me climbing on the table to dance at a party. Except... I didn't do that! Oh, boy! Women grabbed the bottom of their skirts, hiking it up either over their cheeky bottoms, and some hiked it to just below the crease from ass to thigh. At a certain point in the song, their hands went to their knees, bare asses propped up in the air, they started bouncing their legs and backs.

"Are they twerking?" I searched the room to see if Genevieve had joined in the twerking ass display. Call it curiosity. Call it envy of being comfortable with age, body, and beauty. I couldn't find her in the middle of the revelry. I leaned over to Anna, "What are they singing about?"

"Kneading the bread," she said with a flat tone, as if this was an everyday occurrence.

Throughout my time traveling, I've learned that women and men tend to be the same no matter the year. When we read books about women being prim and proper, I've learned that isn't necessarily true. That's the story that people tell. I've heard the conversations of women on the march to battle. They were real, uncensored. Sure, just like during my time, modesty, subservience, and religion can have women ruled over by the men in their lives. That happens just as much as bare ass-twerking in a tavern in 1690 France or at a 1995 California college party.

"Kneading the bread?"

Anna put her hands up in a grabbing motion, as if she was kneading a loaf of bread. I looked up at a pair of pale ass cheeks on full bouncing display.

Oh. Sweet. Cheeses.

Those were two loaves of dough, taunting the men to knead them. "Like they want the men to knead their doughy cheeks?"

"Aye, and maybe the men want their baguettes kneaded by the women." She lifted a sly eyebrow.

"That's vulgar!"

Anna almost laughed herself out of her chair. I joined her. Wow!

Speaking of loaves of bread, I was beyond hungry. I considered raiding the abandoned plates of men preoccupied with the evening's entertainment.

The song ended to the disappointment of the men.

The women dropped their skirts, and walked around to the men, collecting coins and a few swats on their loaves. Some played off the swats, others tried to ignore it, but the coins kept flowing to the women.

In the corner, a patron decided to get too handsy with one of the women. In no time flat, Genevieve was in the middle of it, roughly escorting the man out the door. He swore and hurled insults as he tried to push his way back in. Genevieve wasn't having any of that disrespect. With a swift knee from Genevieve, the man doubled over. On his way down, her elbow landed in the side of his face. Everyone in the room could see the stars as he blacked out and tumbled over. Two men—who had been seated with him—scurried over and dragged him outside into the dark and cold night. The rest of the tavern roared in laughter and cheers.

The tavern began to thin out, leaving me to start looking at what they left behind. Scraps of bread? Oh! A chunk of beef! I started to stand up from my chair when Genevieve walked over with a tray of food and drinks.

"Apologies for the wait. The sooner we finish the song, the sooner we can get the men out of here."

I grabbed my spoon and dug into the beef stew. Sweet cheeses, it smelled wonderful. "Oh! So that is a nightly event?" I asked through a mouthful of beef.

She let out an infectious laugh. "Yes. It brings good money to the chatons."

"Kittens?" I asked.

"This is my *Chaton Moustaches*, and they are chatons."

"Mustaches?" I asked, laying my right index finger over my top lip.

"*Moustaches*," she replied, splaying three fingers, like a "W" and putting them next to her cheek.

My eyebrows knitted together. "Oh! Whiskers! Kitten Whiskers."

There was that laugh again. Elizabeth and Anna laughed along with her. It was wonderful to see everyone happy and having a good time. There had been struggle after struggle for our trip. Taking the time to forget about lords, forced marriage, and being on the run, was definitely needed. I swear Anna was so wound tight from the stress of leaving home and trying to keep Elizabeth safe, she probably needed the night more than anyone else.

Genevieve left us to finish our meal. I took a sip of the cider; it had a hint of apple to it. Perfect! "Did you find a ship for us?" I asked swallowing the cider. As much as I would've liked to enjoy the night without the talk of business, it had to be done.

"Yes, we met with Captain Julio Grondona," Elizabeth said, pointing to a man in the corner eating a meal with a group of men. I glanced over and saw a man wearing a dark jacket. Men huddled around him, deep in conversation and food.

"Did you find the hat you were looking for?" Anna asked.

"Sugar snaps!" I exclaimed, collecting the attention of the room. "Sorry." I lifted my hand to let everyone know I was good. "Yes and no. I went to the milliner, but I should've found the modiste, apparently. Well, while I was

283

there, this jerk of a guy, named Carabajal, came in to bamboozle Moreau, the sickly hat guy." They sat there watching my mouth move a hundred miles an hour. They learned to just sit back and let me finish rambling. "Well, one thing led to another, and I need to go back tomorrow to buy Moreau's entire stock of hats."

"What are you going to do with all those hats? You don't even like wearing ones when you must." Elizabeth had a point.

"Apparently, Spaniards really like French hats. And this guy makes incredibly beautiful hats. So, I thought I could take them to Spain and sell them for a profit. Easily three or four times what I'll pay for them. We need money, and unless you want to become a chaton..."

Elizabeth and Anna looked at each other and laughed.

"I'll take that as a no, and that you agree I made a great business deal." I took a couple of bites of food before continuing. "When do we leave?"

"Two days we sail," Elizabeth said, putting down her cup.

"I need to speak with the captain and make sure there's enough room for me to bring my hats."

We finished the meal and headed over to the corner where Grondona held court.

"Buenas noches, capitán," I figured with a name like Julio Grondona, I could use my newfound Spanish skills. He looked up, and I continued, "Thank you for allowing us to take passage on your ship. I have a large bundle I will need to transport as well."

"What is it?"

"Just some hats I'm picking up tomorrow."

"You have only one head. How many hats do you need?"

"I have enough that I could use help tomorrow collecting them."

Grondona looked to the man on his right, "This is Señor Muñoz. He'll meet you tomorrow."

I shoved my hand out to shake Muñoz's hand. "Amelia Spencer, nice to meet you."

He looked at the captain, then back at my extended hand. He took it in his hand and placed a kiss on my knuckles. Sugar snaps! I forgot my place. We don't shake hands like that. Ugh! Time travel rule number two, pretend to fit in. "Alferes Muñoz, at your service, Señora Spencer." I'm glad one of us knew how to bring that awkward moment under control.

I looked over to Grondona, "I'm not sure if my friend told you, but my cat will be joining us."

"A cat and hats?" He laughed in disbelief. The crew joined in.

I stood there with a smug look on my face. Keep control, Amelia. "Yes, a cat and hats, but the cat is not in the hat. And she has a temper just as feisty as mine."

"I believe it!"

Plans were arranged for Muñoz to meet me to collect the hats and travel arrangements the following day. There was nothing more for Elizabeth, Anna, and I to do than to head back to the inn, laughing and joking the entire way, to get some much-needed rest.

The next day at noon, Muñoz met me at Moreau's

millinery to pick up two very large bundles of hats. His brown eyes bugged out when he saw the bundles. "I could have brought another man to help."

I'd given Moreau all but a few coins. I needed just enough money to get to Spain. Selling the hats for top dollar would be easy, but I had to get to Valencia first. "I can carry a bundle," I insisted. It was heavier than I had anticipated, but the rope tied around it gave me something to hold on to. I could shift it from shoulder-to-shoulder, front-to-back, and take a break or two. I was determined to help.

We discussed his family along our walk to the ship. His wife and children were at home in a town outside of Valencia. The crew had spent the past few months traveling the Mediterranean trading goods and bringing back a few items home. Transporting us was just another way for the crew to earn money. A week–at most–and I would be in Spain. I told him of my plan to find Henry.

"You don't know where he sailed?"

"I was told he sailed on the *Charles II*."

"Sailing from England, they probably made port in A Coruña."

"Hm? Then that's where I'll go. A Coruña. Do you know where that's at?"

"Sí," he said, the word long and drawn out. "You know you are very far away from A Coruña."

"No?" Why would I know that? I knew I needed to get to Spain, finding Henry should've been simple. Just get to Spain. That was my plan.

We stopped to adjust the bundles. He held out his hands. "Damelos."

I put out my left hand, he took it in his. He ran a finger across my thumb. "Portugal. Sí?"

I nodded.

He touched the heel of my hand, across from Portugal. "Valencia. Sí?"

I nodded again.

He touched the top of my index finger. "A Coruña. Sí?"

The blood drained from my face. "No."

"Sí. I wouldn't lie to you, señora."

I was traveling the longest possible distance to reach Henry. It might have been faster for me to circumnavigate the entirety of the planet by snail and carrier pigeon, than the path I took. Maybe he moved on from there. We always find our way to each other. Why would this time be any different?

I closed my eyes and pinched the bridge of my nose to regain my composure and not break out into a full temper tantrum. *Calming thoughts. Find your center. All is not lost, even if you are.* "Well, then," I cleared the wad of emotions stuck in my throat. "I better make sure I get a good price for these hats."

As we approached the ship to load the hats, I groaned out loud when I saw Carabajal boarding a ship close by.

"Problem?"

"You see that guy over there?" I flicked my head towards Carabajal. "He's upset with me because I bought the hats." I looked at the heavy package I struggled to hold on to in front of me. "These hats."

Muñoz gave a laugh and headed up the gangway with the bundle.

Carabajal changed direction and practically pounced on me at the bottom of the gangway. "Back up! Or my cat will finish the job. It will be your jugular instead of your hand." Empty threat, I'm sure. Using her murder mittens on the back of his hand was one thing, slicing his throat was quite another.

He looked at the ship we were about to board, turned to me, and said, "You'll regret coming up against me."

"Doubt it." I turned on my heel and lugged the bundle of hats up the gangway. There was no way I would leave the ship until I was sure he was gone.

I'm feisty, not stupid.

CHAPTER THIRTY-FOUR

"*I* hate ships," I moaned to Elizabeth and Anna. "Maybe not ships, but I hate waves. Okay, I don't hate waves. But I hate ships and waves together."

We shared a small cabin on Grondona's ship, the *Jesus, Maria, y Joseph*. Repeatedly, during the first day, each time I felt the need to curse, I would say, "Sweet Jesus, Mary, and Joseph." No one found me amusing. I mean, it might have been because the ship was named after biblical people and using them as a curse word was highly inappropriate, but I still thought I was funny.

I happily chose to make a bed roll on the floor next to the wall. Starboard made biscuits on my blanket, then curled up next to me and fell asleep. We had made it through our first day on ship, and I survived with only a little bit of a queasy stomach.

"What are your plans after we get to Spain?" I asked Elizabeth and Anna. They were snuggled on the narrow bed–if you could call it a bed. It was a storage box long enough for them to lay on, just slightly narrower than two people could lay comfortably, with a bedroll laid on top. Henry and I stayed on one of those beds when we took the ship from Jamestown to Fredericksburg when we were moving Blackbeard's treasure.

"I don't know," said Elizabeth. "I feel like I've been running for so long, I just don't know where I'm going."

"Aye," said Anna. "We left Scotland almost a year ago. When we met you, Amelia."

"April," I said. It was now the end of February, almost a year later. These young women were still running. And I was looking for my husband. Not much had changed in regard to what they were doing the past year. Constantly looking over their shoulder, never staying in one place long enough to breathe, and then on the run again. "You've had quite a journey since then. Do you ever get tired of running?"

"Yes," Anna whispered.

"You could go back to your family," I suggested. The room was dark and chilly. Wearing only my shift, the blanket was not nearly warm enough. I crawled off the floor and pulled my cloak off the hook. Starboard was not happy with the disruption to her beauty rest. I threw the cloak on top of the blanket, and Starboard found her spot again.

"No. It's too late for that," Anna's voice was slightly above a whisper.

"You can always get a job at *Chaton Moustache*." That

brought a giggle dancing through the room. "Serve some drinks, do a little ass shaking. You'd be great! And you'd be making your own money. We laugh about it now, but those women were taking care of themselves. They were really the ones that were free. Not *us* chasing after something we can't find or running from something we don't want to find us."

"I thought you loved your husband. You talk about him all the time."

"Oh! I do. Somedays I feel like I will never find him. I'm tied to chasing after him, instead of just settling down. It isn't him that has me chained to this journey, it's..." I couldn't say the gods of time travel. They're the ones that continue to manipulate me. "I don't know. It's not like it was his choice either." I shifted on my bedroll. "You two have a choice. Really think about what you want and go after it. Don't let being a woman stop you from dreaming big. Hell, for all I care, you could steal a ship and become pirate queens. Take what you want and then disappear into the shadows to live a quiet life. If that's what you want. Or find a nice man or woman, or whoever, raise babies or don't, and knead bread. The actual fluffy loaf of bread. Not that ass shaking. Unless, of course, that's what you want."

I made it sound so easy. There was no easy choice for them. I rolled on my side and ran a hand over Starboard, tickling my fingers through her soft fur. A low purr helped drift me off to sleep.

∽

"WHY ARE THEY SHOOTING AT US?" I ran to the rail of the *Jesus, Maria, y Joseph*, and looked at the ship in the distance, with Spain's flag flying proudly from the ensign.

"That was a warning shot, Señora." Muñoz nudged past me and started pulling a rope to raise another sail. I grabbed the rope behind him and started pulling.

"Shouldn't we be lowering the sails instead of raising them?" I asked, as I continued to help raise the sail.

"You should get to your cabin. It's safer for you."

"But who is that?"

"That's the royal standard. It's the armada. Most likely want to check our cargo."

"So, we're going to run?"

"Yes! Now go somewhere safe."

Captain Grondona shouted orders from the quarterdeck. Cabral pushed the tiller to the left, to shift further from Spain's shoreline. We traveled close to the shore, we were headed to Valencia, there was no reason to sail deep into the Mediterranean. More shouts from Grondona, men ran around the deck. I was knocked over on my way to the cabin, where I found Elizabeth, Anna, and Starboard.

"We heard the shot fired." Anna rushed to me when I walked in the cabin.

Elizabeth was on her knees at the small porthole, trying to find where the action was coming from.

"Spanish Armada wants to board the ship." I slammed the door shut behind me and leaned against the wooden barrier. "Something has Grondona running. Muñoz said they would want to check our cargo."

"Why won't the captain let them check the cargo?" Elizabeth asked as she slipped down onto the bed. She couldn't see much out of the window.

"Good question! I'm not sure." I grabbed hold of the latch, the metal cold, ready to leave the room. Always running straight into danger. "I thought it was routine."

"You shouldn't go out there." Elizabeth's voice shook.

"You should know by now, I'm a fool that constantly does questionable things." I took a deep breath. "I can fire a pistol well enough. If the captain doesn't want these guys to board, it must be for good reason."

Anna grasped Elizabeth's hand and gave it an assured pat. Anna stood next to me with fire in her eyes. "I suppose I'm a fool as well."

Elizabeth bit her lip and slowly stood up. I threw my hand up. "You need to make decisions for yourself, not because you think this is what we want you to decide. Stay here. Stay safe. We won't think anything about it. Besides, who is going to look after Starboard for me?" I glanced down at Starboard, next to my heel. Elizabeth didn't move from her position on the bed. "You don't have opposable thumbs. Do you know how to fire a gun?" She meowed at me. She was right. "Only if you don't get yourself hurt."

Anna, Starboard, and I ran out the door, leaving Elizabeth to stay safe in the cabin. "We've come to help!" I shouted as we ran out on the deck.

"They're gaining!" Shouted Grondona. "Ready the guns!"

The Spanish ship was aimed straight towards us, gaining quickly. Our ship sat heavy in the water, we didn't have much in regard to cargo to weigh us down, but that ship was fast. Our crew ran from the lower decks, pistols in hand. Cutlasses and knives ready. They were prepared for battle. I looked around the deck for something to prepare myself for battle.

I needed a weapon. What could I find?

Pistol? No.

Cutlass? No.

Knife? No.

Cannon? No.

Cat? Yup! I had a cat.

Anna ran next to me. Pistol in hand.

"Where did you get that?" I squeaked out in awe.

She gave a sly smile. "The armory."

"They're merchants! Why do they have an armory?"

"Armory!" She pointed sharply at the stairs heading to the deck where I would find the armory.

Right. I spun on my heel and ran to the armory, my skirts flying around me. Starboard close to my heels. Men continued running back and forth, preparing for the imminent battle. The armory was raided clean. Except for a small ax left in a small crate. What was I going to do with an ax? It was better than nothing. I snatched the ax out of the crate, holding it by its wooden handle. The head of the ax was no more than four–maybe five–inches long. It felt a little top heavy, but with both hands, I might be able to do some damage. Damage to what? I have no clue. Hopefully, not to myself. "Let's do this!"

Starboard and I ran back to the deck. Elizabeth stood

next to Anna. She held a long pole with a hook on the end. Anna held her pistol ready.

Men yelled and grunted, taunting our opponents. My heart was going to burst straight through my ribs, land on the deck, flop around, before thumping and pounding its way into the Mediterranean, where it would be nibbled on by fish.

Just when I thought the most tragic thing was going to be my heart flopping around becoming fish food, the volley of bullets began to fly through the air. It was loud. Boom! Bang! Screams and taunts. More pistols. Men ran from one side of the deck to the other. More smoke. Men loaded more shots into their pistols. More screams.

I looked towards Cabral, standing strong at the tiller, still trying to outrun the ship.

"Señora, move!" shouted Muñoz. I spun to see what was happening when it happened. Alferes Muñoz collapsed. I ran over to him as he laid on the deck, blood poured out of his chest. This wasn't a little trickle of blood, where he may survive, only to die later of infection. No. My friend Alferes Muñoz died in my arms on the deck of the *Jesus, Maria, y Joseph*. And for why? Because the captain decided he didn't want to waste his time being boarded? There was no reason for us to care what they would've found on board.

With tears streaming down my cheeks, I looked up at Captain Grondona. His face dropped. Muñoz was dead. He ordered his men to stand down. The screech and groans from the wooded hull of the other ship rubbing against the wooden hull of the *Jesus, Maria, y Joseph*, tore at my ears like fingernails ripping down a chalkboard. Before the pistols could be lowered, the crew of the other ship was boarding our vessel. Grondona kneeled next to me and placed his hand on Muñoz, closed his eyes, and said a prayer.

"Why did it come to this? We don't have anything they want," I sobbed out.

"Drugs, señora. Drugs." He glanced over towards the men clamoring over the rails, and then back at me. "In some crates in storage near your hats, you will find the drugs. If you go now, they won't find you tossing them out the ports. If they catch you, don't panic, they won't harm a woman."

I nodded and wiped the tears from my eyes and snot from my nose. I ran down the stairs, Starboard followed behind. Down one flight of stairs, I flew through the crew deck and down the second flight of stairs. I opened port holes to let in the light. I searched for the bundles of the hats. In the corner, I found them. Next to the bundles were numerous crates. How was I supposed to know which one carried drugs?

Three issues arose while searching for the drugs. First thing: I was looking for drugs. I understood why Grondona tried to flee, but there I was trying to destroy the evidence. If, that is, I could find it. Cheese and rice. Drugs.

The second issue: How was I going to open the crates when I found them? I tried prying open one of the crates. The lids were nailed into the crate. My attempt at kicking in the side was met with a throbbing toe.

Third issue: Drugs! I might have mentioned that before. However, I'm not a drug runner. Of all the crazy things I've done in my life, being a drug mule wasn't one of them. Until that day. Hopefully, I wouldn't be sent to prison. I wouldn't do well in the slammer. I'm too delicate for prison.

My body went into full panic-mode. I needed to find those drugs and make it quick before I passed out from holding my breath. I dug my fingers into the tight space between the lid and the crate. I yanked and pulled. Dug in some more. The tips of my fingers burned and ached. I grunted as I pulled. Grunting always makes it work. Except this time. Once more, I ground my teeth together and pulled. Tears of frustration, anger, and disappointment poured down my face. There was probably some sweat mixed in with the tears. My sobs masked the footsteps behind me. A tight grip wrapped around my biceps and yanked me around. I caught my breath and blinked hard. My vision was messing with me. With my free hand, I wiped my tears and rubbed my eyes. A couple more blinks to be certain I saw who I thought stood before me: Carabajal.

He clamped down on my arm with one hand and grabbed a bundle of the hats with the other. Seriously? All of that and he was going to steal the hats from me. Starboard readied to attack, I waved her off. That wasn't the time or place for heroics.

He yanked me up the stairs, through the crew deck, up

the second flight of stairs to the quarterdeck, and threw me down at the feet of a man standing next to Grondona. My eyes trailed up to the face of a man I had never seen before.

"Captain, this is the witch," ground out Carabajal. "Here's one bundle of the hats. The other is down in the hold."

"Seize the ship," the captain said.

"I'm not a witch," I said. What else would you call a woman who travels through rips in time and is accompanied by a cat? Time traveler with a furry sidekick. But not a witch.

Carabajal laughed.

Grondona stepped forward, panic in his eyes, "Captain Figueres, please. It's just hats."

"Instead of declaring the French hats, you decided to flee and then fire upon my ship." Figueres looked down at me in a pile of pathetic mush. All I wanted to do was sell some hats and make some money. I didn't know it would lead to Muñoz being killed and Grondona's ship being confiscated.

Carabajal reached down, grabbed me by the arm, yanked me to my feet, all the while digging his fingers straight through to the bone. I screamed out. Starboard launched herself through the air and landed with her claws dug into his face.

He released me as he grabbed her with both hands. He pulled her off his face, but she kept her claws dug deep into his flesh. Blood ran from multiple lines from his ears to the tip of his nose. Holding her by the scruff, with a full arm extension to avoid being sliced in half, he raced towards the side of the ship. I was hot on his heels. He pulled his arm back to throw Starboard overboard. When his arm went back, it left his side fully exposed. I sucker punched him right in the kidney. He dropped Starboard on the deck.

I snatched her up as I tumbled into the rail. My breaths came in hard and heavy. I sat there for a moment, ready to move when he reached for her in my tight arms. I backed up a little more, holding her tight against my chest, when something hard and sharp pressed against my right leg. I reached underneath me and found my little battle ax.

Gripping the wooden handle, I pulled it out and held it up. Carabajal stepped back.

"Take the damn hats and take the damn ship. But if you touch my cat again, I will gut you like a fish and feed you to the sharks."

I turned to the shocked crowd of men and Elizabeth and Anna. "Captain Figueres, I can see this man has you in his pocket. What was his bribe to do this?" I raised my hand and shook off wanting to know the answer. It didn't matter. My ears burned in anger. "Whatever it was, it's not going to be enough to endure the wrath of me. I suggest you call him off before I wage a legal battle unlike any you've seen."

Figueres turned to Carabajal. "Leave the witch and her deranged cat." He turned to another man. "Lock her in her cabin."

The man led me to my cabin.

"We take the ship," Figueres declared, followed by an uproar of cheers from his crew.

If there ever was a time, I wanted to time travel in

order to escape, that was it. I had a few coins left from my purchase of the hats. Reaching into my pocket, I found one of the coins. The metal was warm from being kept close to my body. I white-knuckled the coin and hugged Starboard as he opened the door and shoved us inside.

CHAPTER THIRTY-FIVE

I landed hard on the floor of my cabin. The door slammed shut, the loud, sharp bang stung my ears. I pried my eyes open. No swirling lights. No frigid wind. No desire to fling myself into a light brighter than the sun. Nothing.

Nothing but the realization that I was stuck in the 1690s, probably going to a Spanish prison, and probably never seeing Henry again.

Starboard curled up into the corner, with a vicious look in her eyes. She wanted to kill me, taking one of her murder mittens to my throat while I slept.

"Nothing would have changed if I let you attack him in the storage hold."

She let out a growl.

"Seriously, don't be upset with me."

Another growl. I took a deep breath. "Thank you for saving me. You did quite a good job on tearing up his face." I scooted along the floor towards her safe spot in the corner, risking being torn to shreds to make amends. "You're my vicious velociraptor." I said to her as if she were a sweet baby.

She was not amused with my begging for forgiveness. I scooted back across the room. No need to anger the beast any more than I already had.

Noise of men walking with hard footsteps across the wooden decks had become background noise to me. I laid out my bedroll and fell asleep, giving up on trying to fight anymore. I was exhausted, defeated, and just wanted to go home.

Later–I'm not sure how much later; it was all a blur–I woke up to the sound of Elizabeth and Anna entering the room. "Hey," I said, sitting up on my bedroll. I sat with my legs crossed and my back against the wall. It was all I could do to stay upright. Starboard continued to glower at me from the corner.

"They're taking us to Spain," Elizabeth said, as they sat on the bed next to each other. Anna leaned against the wall. Elizabeth placed her elbows on her knees and her delicate face in her hands. She looked tired.

"I figured that much out." That might have been grumpier than I had planned. It wasn't their fault any of the day's events happened. Only if Grondona didn't run. Him and his stupid drugs. Ugh! Carabajal and the hats. Was the confiscation my fault? No. I couldn't blame it and Alfrese's death on myself. Not this time. "Sorry. You didn't deserve that. None of us did." I straightened up my skirts, and continued, "The plan was to go to Spain, and we're headed there. And with the hats confiscated I will need to figure out how to make money. Slight delay in plans, that's all."

"We will find ourselves in a Spanish prison," Anna said as she sat up. "Then what shall we do, Amelia?" She glanced at Elizabeth for the answer. "They will keep us there until they've contacted her father."

Elizabeth frantically shook her head. "I would rather stay in prison than to be taken to my father."

"No one is going to prison. I mean, we might be taken there, but none of us committed any crime. We paid for transport on a ship, it was the captain who was responsible for what transpired." A held up the bottom of my skirts and walked on my knees over to Elizabeth and Anna. I took a hand in each of mine. "Spain is only the beginning, for all of us. You can find passage onward. You may have to find jobs but look at all that you've done to get this far."

Elizabeth wiped an escaped tear.

"When I first met you, almost a year ago, I thought I had to protect you. You've proved that you are capable of anything." I sat back on my heels. "Starboard and I need to find Henry, and you need to discover where you want to go from there. When we get to Spain, we'll head our separate ways." I gave an encouraging nod.

Elizabeth nodded; she was silent, afraid she would burst into tears. She knew I was correct. Her plans continued to change, the further she got from home. She had Anna, they would be fine.

Two agonizing days later, we landed in Valencia. Grondona approached me as we walked down the docks, with whatever gear we could carry. Starboard in her basket, my satchel weighed down behind me, my coin purse with three coins left, and whatever pride I had left.

"You realize, it wasn't your fault," Grondona placed a hand on my shoulder. "Carabajal. Sombreros. Figueres. Drugas. Muñoz. It was an unfortunate circumstance."

"He was kind to me. I know you were friends longer than I was with him. I'm truly sorry for your loss." I straightened my back. "You seem quite calm for a man that had his ship confiscated."

"I'll take him to court and demand my ship back," he said with a shrug. "I have no choice. You need to find your husband."

"Yes, Muñoz suggested that I go to A Coruña to look for him."

"Before you run to A Coruña, I suggest you go speak with the authorities in Madrid. They may have heard of his ship." He dug into his bag and pulled out a couple of coins. "You'll need this."

"Gracias." I held onto the coins with a crushing grip. As much as I needed them, Elizabeth and Anna needed them more. I would find a way, I always did. "I can't take them... Elizabeth and Anna..." I held out my shaky hand to give the coins back to Grondona.

"Consider that money as your payment for trying to help me get rid of some cargo." He smiled. "I'll see to it that Lady Elizabeth and Lady Anna are taken care of."

He pointed behind me. "Madrid and A Coruña are in that direction."

With one of my notorious curtsies, I left Grondona on the docks in Valencia.

Ten excruciatingly long days later, I found myself in Madrid. Somewhere around day three, Starboard had finally forgiven me for not letting her take care of Carabajal. For a cat, she sure can hold onto a grudge.

I didn't know what to expect of Madrid in 1690, but it wasn't the thriving city I found myself in. Big, beautiful buildings filled with people. Streets filled with people. And like most places I found throughout history, the city lacked a proper sewage drainage system. The dirt smelled like urine. The cobblestones smelled like urine. To be fair, I probably smelled like urine.

I needed to conserve as much money as possible, I couldn't afford to stay in an inn along the way. Which meant, there was no way I was going to remove any clothing to clean more than I needed to. It was the beginning of March, and I'm not sure if any of the days got above fifty degrees.

Walking through the city, I was lost. All Grondona told me to do was come to Madrid. Why didn't I ask more questions? Who was I supposed to speak with? That would've been the smart thing to ask. Nope! What did I do? Say, "okay" and just started walking in the direction of Madrid.

Seriously! How have I made it traveling through time and through life without worse consequences? Dumb luck! That's how. Either that, or there's some other gods out there taking pity on me.

Where do I start? A church? No. I might be struck down as soon as I walk through the door. The palace? Surely, they wouldn't let some woman and her cat walk in off the street and ask to speak to the king. I didn't even know which king to ask for.

Plan C. Or was I on Plan G? Find a place to stay, ask the innkeeper who I should speak with, and then ask whoever for *Charles II*. That would also give me the opportunity to clean up. I pulled back the cloth covering the basket and looked at Starboard. She looked back up at me, with half-opened eyes, and yawned. "Let's get a place to stretch out."

I reached into my pocket and found the coins. Funds were looking grim. I would have enough for a couple of nights, food to stock up on, and then maybe enough to feed me and Starboard during our journey to A Coruña. Cheese and rice! My luck was starting to run out as quickly as my money.

After walking through the streets of Madrid, I found a comfortable inn for us for the night. A box to use for Starboard's litter was easy enough; however, finding sand was more difficult.

I found a park near the palace, where I could dig up some dirt. It wasn't as good as the sand, but it would have to do. There was no mistaking the large, squared building surrounded by a large, stoned wall, at the top of the hill, was definitely the palace. Our little inn wasn't too far, so maybe I could get in to see the king or queen. I rushed back to the inn to get us fed and plan for the following day.

The next morning after breaking our fast, I loaded Starboard into the basket, and we set off to find someone to speak with about a missing husband. The innkeeper, a man in his early fifties, a little thick in the middle, and a long, curly, black wig, that rivaled his long thin nose, was busy in the dining room. I found him laughing with a couple of men around one of the tables. His employees scurried about the room cleaning tables. Yes, I spent too much money on accommodations, but having clean water to wash in and a comfortable bed to stretch out in, was worth going hungry for a couple of days while we were on the road. Too bad I couldn't use my debit card I had sewn into my pocket when I was on the *Gretchen*. Starboard and I would make do; we always did.

I checked my clothes. They were clean-ish–I did my best to get them scrubbed and dried overnight. My hair pulled back, braided, and then I twisted the braid into a bun at the base of my neck–respectable enough. Shoulders back. Head held high. *You're Lady Amelia Spencer, you've got this*. I strutted over to the table, confidence oozing from me. So much oozing was going on, I was leaving a flaming trail behind me. Let's face it. The closer I got to the table, the more my stomach twisted in knots. I couldn't breathe. I straightened my cloak on my shoulders. Why should I be so nervous? Why? Because I had no clue what I was doing there, and I was so afraid of disappointment. I traveled from one end of France to the other, got in a battle over stupid hats–or drugs–and my friend died. Then, I walked from one end of Spain and was on my way to the other end. I was putting a lot of effort into finding Henry, and there was no guaranteed happy ending for us. At least I had Starboard. I shook off the negative thoughts.

"Good morning, señors," I said with my mouth full of

cotton. A small curtsy had the men standing to give me a slight bow. So far, so good. "My name is Lady Amelia Spencer. Might I have a moment of your time?"

One of the men offered me a chair, and I politely accepted. I sat between the innkeeper and a man in his late forties, with a large brown wig. My basket with Starboard quietly sleeping, rested on my lap. *I hope my hand is clean because I'm going to have them eating out of it.* It was too easy.

"I'm new in town, and I'm looking for my husband."

That raised a few eyebrows.

"I have a husband; I'm not looking for *a* husband. I'm looking for the one I have. My husband, Henry." Bring on the nervous rambling. Smooth. "I'm looking for the Charles the Second."

"Why are you looking for the king?" The older man sitting opposite me asked.

"I don't know why I would look for the king. I'm looking for the Charles the second. My husband was sailing from England to Spain with a crew. He was supposed to take care of or do something with the Charles the Second. A mission or something."

"Are you looking for a ship or are you looking for the king?"

I felt like I was dancing around the riddle trying to figure out who was on first. Or during the television show *Doctor Who*, someone would ask for the Doctor, and someone would ask, "Doctor, who?"

"My husband is or was on a ship from England to Spain. The Charles the Second is the name of the ship."

"Why would the English name a ship after the King? Are they trying to ridicule our sovereign?" I wasn't sure if the innkeeper was being serious about that.

"No. I don't think it's anything like that... they were on a mission."

"Are you trying to say they were going to assassinate the king?"

My jaw dropped quickly and hard to the floor. Perhaps I was using the wrong word in Spanish. Maybe my dialect was incorrect? "I didn't say that... Listen, I traveled through France trying to come here."

"I knew it!" The man to my left slammed his fist down on the table. "She is an English spy working for the French! She wants to kill our king!"

"That doesn't make any sense," I squeaked out. *What was happening?* How did the conversation get so complicated and twisted? "No. You don't understand..." I stood up and held onto the basket. I didn't need Starboard jumping out and raising ten kinds of hell while I was trying to defuse the situation. "My husband, Lord Henry Spencer, is on a ship and I need to find him. That's all. I don't have anything to do with your king or his assassination."

"You heard her," the man to my left said. "She said she wanted to assassinate the king."

"Cheese and rice!" I exclaimed in English. 'Queso y arroz,' doesn't have quite the same ring to it.

"And you're blaspheming our lord."

"No! I said *cheese and rice,* not *Jesus Christ*!" *It all had to be a joke. Right?* With one foot behind the other, I began backing out of the room. I didn't trust taking my eyes off the men, who had all stood and started walking towards me. How fast could I run? I was sure I could outrun the innkeeper and the older man that was sitting next to me. The one sitting across from me, he looked like he could catch me. *Sugar snaps!*

I needed to get out of there quickly. Outside? To my room? I didn't know where I was going, but it was going to be out the door instead of trapped in my room.

I flung open the door and ran outside and down the street to my right. The street curved to my right, and I continued running. I hate running. I shoved past a few people, the men yelling behind me. People's heads spun watching me fly by with a basket on my arm and my cloak drifting behind me. I'm sure they must have thought they were chasing a witch out of town.

At the intersection a few yards in front of me, I took a left. More people. More horses. More running. I could hear footsteps pounding on the cobblestone streets. Mine and whoever was still chasing me. I wasn't going to turn around and find out.

Another turn down another street, my pace was slowing. Carrying Starboard in her basket on my arm, adding some steep hills, I wanted to give up. If I struggled up the hill, those guys would as well. I could see a building under construction ahead of me. Perhaps I could hide in there? None of the construction workers had started for the day, leaving me alone to search for safety.

I ran inside, it appeared to be a church. Sanctuary! I could ask for sanctuary. That was a thing? Right? Like in the movies? The inside of the building was quite open. I ran to my right and found a door. I couldn't open it. I ran to the back and found another door to the side. *Please be unlocked*. I pushed it open and ran inside. Slamming the door shut behind me, I flung my body against the door, and searched for a latch to lock it. My chest heaved looking for air to fill my lungs. My lungs were on fire. I moved the latch over to lock the door and spun around to assess the room. That's when it hit me. The bright spinning lights. The smell of smokey oak and oranges filled the air. Swirls of frigid wind surrounded me. I reached deep into my pocket and pulled out two coins. I pulled back the cloth to the basket and found a terrified Starboard staring at me. She hissed in fear of what we'd been through, and I'm sure, what was about to happen.

"I won't let anything happen to you. The universe cat distribution system brought us together." I laughed at what I said to her. We were chased and we're about to travel through time, and I thought I would joke about the cat distribution system. "Come on, girl. We'll have to find Henry somewhere else."

I pulled her out of the basket and held on tight, clenching onto the coins in my hand. She struggled for just a moment. I took two steps forward. A deep cleansing breath. The oak and orange scents were intoxicating and brought a sense of peace. Another couple of steps. I pulled Starboard tighter into my chest. Her soft fur tickled my nose.

It all went black.

CHAPTER THIRTY-SIX

*T*here's a moment when you step through the rip in time when you feel weightless. Everything is at peace.

That moment is gone in a flash, and you have sandpaper being dragged across your face. Wait! That's not right! Hunger? It's there. Groggy? I didn't want to open my eyes. Sandpaper? Sharp barbs? That was new.

I pried my tired eyes open to find Starboard licking my face. Oh, thank goodness nothing happened to her. "Are you trying to wake me?" I ran a hand over her fur, she pushed into the rub with a purr. "Or were you tasting me to decide if you were going to eat me if I was dead?"

Propping up on my elbows, I looked around the room. Someone had left the light on. It appeared to be some sort of small storage space. Where was I? *Think, Amelia.* My head continued to spin. "A church! We ran into a church."

Starboard meowed in response.

"We've gotta get out of here before someone finds us."

I twisted to get on my hands and knees. One unsteady leg at a time, I used one of the boxes to help me stand up. "Let's get something to eat." I rubbed my hand along the inside of my pocket. My debit card was firmly secured in the lining. *Smart thinking, Amelia.* "I'm buying."

I picked up the basket, and a grumpy Starboard. "You'll feel better after we get some kibble in you. Now, please. Get in the basket."

I gave her a few extra scratches behind her tan ears tipped in black and slid her into the basket. The door out of the storage room had been replaced with a modern replica. It no longer had a sliding lock, but a knob with a lock. "Come on before they remember they forgot to turn off the light."

I covered the basket, turned the knob, and slid out the door. As I began to walk to where the sanctuary was, I heard a man speaking using a microphone. I stood at the entryway and saw a priest giving services. Of all the times to time travel into a church, during service was a terrible time. There was no sneaking out without being seen.

Just roll with it. I threw my hood over my head, settled the basket in the crook of my arm, and walked down the outside aisle. As I passed, the priest stopped speaking and all eyes focused on me. I tilted my head in a polite manner.

"Hello."

"How ya doing?"

"Lovely weather we're having."

"How's your mama?"

"Love your dress."

"Enjoying the service?"

"He's great, isn't he?"

Finally, I made it to the backdoor. Starboard popped her head out of the basket and gave a loud meow. "She said, have a blessed day," I said with a wave of my hand.

We high-tailed out of there. The clothing they were wearing was modern and the priest used a microphone. That was a good sign. We stepped outside, the sun was shining bright in the mid-morning. I turned to look at the front of the building. They'd done quite a bit of refurb over the years. *Our Lady of Montserrat* didn't have the facade completed when I saw it in 1690.

Cars drove up and down the steep hill leading to the church. A sidewalk was all that separated us from the scooters that zipped by and weaved in and out of traffic. It was loud and chaotic.

I shifted the basket to my left arm and reached into my pocket. I started picking at the seams which held my debit card in place. Pick. Pull. Pick. Pull. We continued to walk down the hill in search of a convenience store. We needed food and a burner phone. The growl from my stomach said food first.

Down the street we found a *Carrefour Express*. I covered the basket with the cloth. "You need to stay quiet if you want me to get us food. They don't allow cats in here."

The automatic door swished open, and I stepped inside. I missed the convenience of convenience stores. Cat food, a small disposable litter box with litter, premade sandwiches, drinks, fruit, toiletries, wine, everything I could possibly need. Except no burner phone. I carried my overfilled hand basket to the counter, threw in a couple cloth reusable bags, and checked out. I turned to the woman at the counter, and asked, "Where can I get a burner phone?"

She looked at me and said something in Spanish, which I didn't understand. How could I not understand Spanish? I was speaking it semi-fluently not a couple hours prior. I massaged my forehead. The rip through time must have screwed with the wiring in my brain again. *Find your center. Stay calm. Don't let the anger bubble to the top.* I squished up my nose. *I need to find a shorter mantra.*

I held up my card and said, "Buy." Then I made a telephone receiver using my pinky and thumb and held it up to my ear. "Telephono." My communication skills swirled down the toilet when I stepped through the rip in time.

However, she seemed to understand my request. She pulled a strip of receipt paper out of the machine and started scribbling on it. A rudimentary map with street names, and the name of the store. X marked the spot.

I bagged my groceries and paid. Thank goodness my card worked! Off to buy a phone and let Hannah and Beth know I was alive.

We walked down the street, following the map, when Starboard meowed from the basket. "I know. I know." I looked around. There had to be a hotel around here.

Down a small side street, I found a Hostal Residencia Flores. There were a couple of carved flowers on either side of the name. The building had to be at least twenty-stories tall, nothing fancy. It looked like it was recently painted a light tan.

At the counter, stood a young man, mid-twenties. His hair was dark brown with eyes to match. He wore a white button up, collared shirt, black slacks, and a brass name tag with the name Eduardo carved into it.

"Hi Eduardo, I don't have a reservation, but I'm hoping you have a room available for me." I thought it best to pretend that I wasn't going to sneak a cat into the hotel room.

His English was better than my Spanish, and he started clicking away on his computer. He began to take my information, typing it into the computer as I stood there silently pleading for Starboard to stay inside her basket.

And then it happened... he asked for my passport. I was lucky I had a debit card. How in the world would I get a passport? "I have to go to the embassy; my passport and all of my things were stolen."

"I cannot rent you a room without a passport. It's the law."

"Is there anything else I can do?"

"You can go to the embassy and get a new passport. Then I can rent you a room."

I was exhausted, hungry, and my temper was bubbling close to the surface. I took a deep breath and tried to remain calm. "Like I said, someone stole my passport.

Would you be willing to work with me until I get a new one?"

"I need a copy of your passport, señora." He stopped typing. I was losing this battle. "I cannot lose my job because you lost your passport."

"Right," I wracked my brain. "What if I can get my daughter to send you a copy and I provide you with a generous tip? Could you find a way to make that work?"

His eyes shifted and he bit his bottom lip. Good. He was considering my offer. During one of my research trips, I sent Hannah a picture of the identification page. I just needed to get her on the phone. A phone I didn't have yet.

I slogged to the electronics store, purchased the phone, sim card, and started setting up the online account. By the time I walked through the door of the hotel, I had signed into my ChatClick account to send Hannah a message.

ME

Hey! I'm alive

HANNAH

Where are you?

ME

Spain

HANNAH

!!!! WTH!

ME

Later. Send me a copy of my passport?

HANNAH

... ...

The photo popped up as soon as I got to the counter. I sent it to Eduardo's email, and he added it to my reservation.

Ten minutes later, I was freeing Starboard from the confines of the basket and setting up her disposable litter box, food, and water station. I used the restroom, washed my hands, grabbed my premade sandwich, and plopped on the small bed. The room was worn. The bedding was a drab floral print, with browns, dark greens, and mauve flowers. The furniture was a dark wood, which helped bring down the weight of the room. It wasn't my new home; it was just a temporary stop. I refused to complain about it. Starboard on the other hand... or paw, curled up in the window, I swear she was trying to avoid looking at the room.

I opened the ChatClick app and shoved another piece of sandwich in my mouth.

ME

Have you heard from Henry?

HANNAH

No. How? He doesn't have a phone.

ME

We didn't travel together

HANNAH

WDYM?

ME

I ended up being dumped on a beach in France.

HANNAH

You're in Spain now?

ME

Yeah, came here looking for Henry

HANNAH

How?

ME

Ugh! Long story short: time traveling transport schooner with an Egyptian ninja, a nine-hundred-year-old Korean man that doesn't look a day over forty-five, a Ukrainian fighter from our near future–he wouldn't tell me what happened, a Spanish Conquistador–wanting to fight for the queen, and a parrot who said, "back to the circus" and a large cat.

HANNAH

That seems like a story that shouldn't be short

ME

You'll have to read my next book then ((winky face emoji))

Will you search for a ship going to Spain called the Charles II and send me the results?

> My smartphone is not really smart. More of a smart-ish phone. And everything I search is in Spanish

> I'm going to jump in the shower. If I have to smell my pits any longer, I'm going to pass out. ((heart emoji))

I love hot showers. I want the water to be pumped straight from the water heater in hell. Flames could come out of the shower head, and I would still want it hotter. After I used the hot water for the entire hotel, I went to lay down in the bed. It was early evening, and I was done.

I picked up my phone and searched the screen for the yellow ChatClick icon. I tapped it open to check for a message from Hannah.

Hannah: This Charles II?

The link went to a wiki page of a ship called *Charles II* that went to A Coruña (Alferes was correct!). There was a mutiny, and the ship was renamed the *Fancy* when it became a pirate ship, captained by Henry Avery. What? Pirate ship? I scrolled through the page. The connection was slow, and the page kept refreshing. Every time the page refreshed, it would flash white, and then take a moment to reload. It must have been the terrible Wi-Fi... or my not-so-smart phone. Finally, I found the date: 1694.

It didn't matter how far I traveled. From one end of France to the other. Halfway through Spain. I was never going to find him when I was there three years too soon.

Starboard jumped from the windowsill and curled up next to me. Tickling my fingers through her hair was calming, for both me and her. Her purr was healing to my aching soul.

I opened ChatClick.

> **ME**
>
> This doesn't make sense.

HANNAH

> Tell me, mom... when did any of the times you traveled through time make sense?

> **ME**
>
> I need to find him. How could we've been there at different times?

HANNAH

> What?

> **ME**
>
> I was there in 1690. The wiki page said the Charles II was in Spain in 1694. 4 years!

HANNAH

> ... ...

> **ME**
>
> Exactly

> I'm going to find a way. Oh, and check this out

I opened the camera app and took a picture of Starboard snuggled up next to my side. I was under the blankets, naked, but she was on top of the blankets. No nudies being sent to my daughter. I would have to pick up modern clothes the next day. 1690s clothing draws a little more attention than I liked.

HANNAH

You got a cat! The cat from the time traveling schooner?

ME

Yup! So, does that mean I get to settle down now?

HANNAH

In Spain?

ME

No... I want to be home with you, Henry, Beth, Hector, and Starboard.

HANNAH

You named your cat Starboard?

Hannah and I chatted for some time. It felt good. Almost like everything was back to normal. I'd sent a few messages to Beth before I fell asleep with the phone in my hand.

That night I dreamt of Henry. We were back home, during modern times, it was peaceful. We walked along the Rappahannock River, across from George Washington's childhood home, Ferry Farm. We were reminiscing about our time spent with the young Washington. Out of nowhere a ship pulled up to the docks. Henry jumped on the ship and sailed away, the Jolly Roger flying proudly. He left me standing alone staring down the river.

I woke up with tears in my eyes. *Did he really leave me to join a pirate crew? Why would he leave me behind? How could he do that to me?*

My mind raced. Nope! Not on my watch. He wasn't going to get away that easy.

I opened ChatClick and sent a message to the group.

ME

Going to figure out how to go back

I wasn't expecting a response, it was 1 a.m. in Virginia, everyone was asleep.

BETH

u sure?

I woke them. Oops!

HANNAH

He might come back

BETH

you can wait for him

HANNAH

didn't u say u want to settle down?

ME

Did I? Where's the fun in that?

Beth, will you pull more info on the Fancy? Use those professor skills. I need deeper info than what's on the wiki page.

BETH

On it! I'll connect you with my friend at the university in Madrid.

ME

Hector, I know you have some sort of connection to people at the embassy. I need a new passport.

HECTOR

... ...

BETH

he fell back asleep in the middle of typing. He'll do it

ME

Hannah, I need for you to water my plants and do research on caring for a Scottish wildcat. Oh! Find out how to ship me some pirate coins

I had to get back to the 1690s, find Henry, and bring him home. First, a snack, some prayers to the gods of time travel, and a little more sleep.

The adventure continues with
The Time Writer and The Chase.

Thank you for joining me on this adventure. Join my
newsletter, *The Chrononaut*, to download the prequel,
The Time Writer and The Cloak
(ebook and audiobook available), and to keep up to date
with my shenanigans and new releases.
https://bit.ly/CloakB4

Reviews and ratings help readers discover books you
love. Please consider leaving a review or rating wherever
you purchased this book.

NOTE TO READERS

This wild ride through time has been brought to you by the letter "R" and my squirrelly imagination. As always, I remind you that this fictional story should not be confused with a history book.

I make stuff up!

The words and speech of our characters are remembered through a modern woman (and terrible historian!), and you will find anachronistic words through the dialog and story. This was not meant to be a history book, but a look at historical events and time travel through a feisty and outspoken Gen X woman.

Let's discuss a few fun stuff that occurred during the book:

The Dukes of Ormonde and Crawford existed during this timeframe, but EVERYTHING about their character is entirely made up by me. I needed a couple of names, and they were convenient.

Henry Avery

The events in the story that led him and the crew of the Fancy to mutiny is fairly accurate. The Houblons sent the crews to Spain to retrieve their letter of marque for the authorization to be privateers for Spain. Instead of receiving the letter, the fleet was, essentially, sold to Spain to serve for the remainder of their lives.

Many of the events portrayed in the book happened roughly the way I wrote them. Of course, I've added my own bit of flair.

Ooo la, la... the trouble with French hats

Didn't that part of the story sound absolutely bonkers? It was based on a real event. Captain Julio Grondona's vessel, the Jesus, Maria, y Joseph, resisted boarding by the Spanish authority, Captain Joseph Figueres. Figueres learned that Grondona's vessel may have contained contraband. The contraband in question was not the drugs on the ship, but French hats that were being brought into Spain without proper permissions. They took possession of the ship due to Grondona's resistance. Alferes Muñoz was an unfortunate victim in the battle.

Time Traveling Schooner

Why on earth did I bring a time traveling transport schooner to the party? Because it came about during a party... and I needed to transport our characters over the ocean. During my high school reunion, a few friends from high school approached me and asked me to make them characters in my book. Each one wanted these outlandish characters and I had to think of a way to bring them together and have it make sense. I'm not going to say there may have been some drinking involved with the creation of our ragtag time traveling schooner, but they're a fun group!

ACKNOWLEDGMENTS

The Time Writer and The Escape, A Historical Time Travel Adventure, couldn't have been possible without the assistance and support of my family, friends, and experts.

A special thanks goes to:

Roland DeLeon

Always amazing. Always supportive. Thanks for feeding me.

The Real OGs

Yo! Thanks!

My Dream Team (Stars and hearts in my eyes Dream Team)

Shellyrenee Sheehy, Vic Favia, and Donna Lee:

You are A-MAZ-ING! This has been the best writing experience EVER because of you. You kept me going, inspired, and told me when I got things right and when I didn't. You challenged me and kept me striving to be better. This book would have been a sad little pile of words if it wasn't for you. Thank you from the bottom of my piratey heart. I'm ready to do it again!

Lars Hedbor

I'm pretty sure it's obligatory to thank you in every book. So... um... thanks? I guess?

The Mighty Crew

Jasmine, Rick, Richard, Chris, and honorary member Sam. Thanks for inspiring the crew of the *Gretchen*. See what I did there?

ABOUT THE AUTHOR

Alex R Crawford is the author of *The Time Writer*, A Historical Time Travel Adventure series. Alex grew up in Southern California and traveled the world with her military husband and daughters. She has lived in California, Texas, Georgia, Missouri, Virginia, and over six years in Germany. Crawford now calls the history-rich Washington D.C. area home.

Alex obtained a Bachelor of Science in Marketing and International Business and was one class short of having a minor in History. She regrets not completing the history minor (she loves history!). She doesn't regret not completing the two master's degrees she started in International Relations and Human Relations.

Once upon a time, she worked for the United States Federal Government as a writer, copyeditor, social media manager, and webmaster. Prior to working in public affairs, Crawford worked for the U.S. Marine Corps and U.S. Army in managing various outreach programs supporting service members and their families. Now, she is a full-time novelist, avid reader, and dog and cat wrangler.

When her nose isn't in a book or fingers typing away,

she enjoys visiting historical points-of-interest and museums.

Stay in touch! Join Alex's monthly newsletter for updates on upcoming books, adventures in research, and more shenanigans. Your information is not shared, nor will you be spammed. If you like SPAM®, then Alex recommends her favorite SPAM® recipe, SPAM® fried rice.

Visit Alex's website to receive the prequel
The Time Writer and The Cloak
ebook for FREE:

https://bit.ly/CloakB4

Did you find a typo? I wouldn't be surprised. My proofreader hands me a perfectly proofread manuscript and I start changing things, because I can't leave well enough alone. Mistakes, typos, and whatnot happen. If you find an example of my disruptive behavior (typo, missing word, whatever...), please reach out to: editor@spilledredink.com and they will make updates to the book as necessary.

I stink at social media, but I'm getting better! Join me on: Facebook and Instagram @AlexRCrawfordAuthor

MORE ADVENTURES

The Time Writer Series:

Prequel: *The Time Writer and The Cloak* ebook and audiobook available for FREE download to newsletter subscribers https://bit.ly/CloakB4

Season 1 - 1750s Virginia - French and Indian War

Book 1: *The Time Writer and The Notebook*

Book 2: *The Time Writer and The March*

Book 3: *The Time Writer and The Hunt*

Season 2 - 1690s - The Golden Age of Piracy

Book 4: *The Time Writer and The Escape*

Book 5: *The Time Writer and The Chase*

(tentative release January 2024)

Book 6: *The Time Writer and The Surrender*

(tentative release May 2024)

Visit my website to purchase ebooks, audiobooks, signed paperbacks, special offers, early releases, and exclusive merchandise.

alexrcrawford.com

Printed in the USA
CPSIA information can be obtained
at www.ICGtesting.com
LVHW051224121123
763709LV00035B/688